For Lara
and to Eileen for always being there

First published in Great Britain in 1988 by
Century Hutchinson Ltd
Brookmount House, 62–65 Chandos Place
London WC2N 4NW

Century Hutchinson South Africa (Pty) Ltd
PO Box 337, Bergvlei, 2012 South Africa

Century Hutchinson Australia Pty Ltd
89-91 Albion Street, Surry Hills,
New South Wales 2010, Australia

Century Hutchinson New Zealand Ltd
PO Box 40–086, Glenfield, Auckland 10
New Zealand

ISBN 0 7126 2491 0
Printed in Great Britain by
Mackays of Chatham PLC, Chatham, Kent

PART ONE

1

The card from the university read '55, 3rd floor left'. Diane had seen number 41 a block further down the street, so it had to be somewhere close by. She was hurrying now, searching for the number plates on the doorways. If only the apartment had not already been taken! Rooms were so scarce, the competition so fierce, there was no time to waste.

It was just right, the street, the district, just as she had imagined it would be. Montparnasse, the famous 6th *arrondissement*, just a short walk through the Luxembourg Gardens to the university and right at the heart of everything. To be nineteen, in Paris, and living in Montparnasse seemed like the fulfilment of all her dreams.

Number 55 had to be one of these tall, narrow houses, six storeys from the street to their mansard windows set high under the eaves. The third floor would be just perfect, if only it were not too expensive, if only it had not already gone!

Ahead of her a tall young woman had paused at a doorway, drawing off a pair of little kid gloves and slipping them into her shoulder bag. Diane approached her tentatively, unable to see a number on the building.

'Excuse me, is this number 55?'

The young woman looked up sharply, appraising her with vivid grey-green eyes. She was a year or two older than Diane, her fine oval face framed by dark blonde hair which she wore caught back in a knot at the nape of her neck. The severity of her hairstyle and the plain black sweater dress was belied by a pair of garish red Chinese lacquer earrings which swung violently on either side of her face as she abruptly shook her head.

'No, it's there, at the end of the block.'

Diane followed the direction of her sternly pointing finger and attempted a smile.

'Thanks very much, Mademoiselle. Goodbye.' She stepped back into the sunshine and walked on swiftly down the Rue de Rennes.

Time was getting on and she just *had* to get something settled today. The thought of returning to the *hôtel-pension* spurred her on. The prospect of another week in the stifling embrace of the eminently respectable but agonizingly proper Mademoiselles Bonnet was alarming. Her mother had meant well, of course, but she really had no idea! Paris had changed a good deal since her time. Today, girls wanted more freedom and independence. Her mother would just have to understand.

There were, surprisingly, four more houses to the block. Diane came to the corner of the street and examined the ceramic plaque set into the wall. It read quite plainly, 'No. 61'. Between the traffic on the busy intersection she could make out the number of the next house in the row, number 63.

'Well, of all the –!'

Diane quickly retraced her steps, not a little angry as she came back to the house with high gables and green-shuttered windows in the middle of the row. But the other woman had vanished. She took a step further into the porch and saw there above the door of the concierge's *loge* the number '55' set into the painted woodwork.

'Very funny!' Diane cursed the practical joker who had sent her off on a wild-goose chase. She knocked on the concierge's door and waited impatiently, but there was no reply. For a moment she considered what she should do. This was certainly the right house, but if she went away now someone was almost certain to take the flat before she returned. She glanced into the small inner yard with curiosity. Perhaps there was someone else who could let her in and show her the apartment? Surely no one could object if she just went upstairs?

She crossed the yard and took the stairs eagerly, noticing they were neatly swept and the building well maintained. On each landing two doors led to apartments on either side of the open staircase. On the second floor some tenants had added an individual touch with a terracotta pot of flame-coloured geraniums outside their door. As Diane came to the third floor she had not met anyone she could ask about the flat, but the door to the left stood slightly ajar and the sound of female voices reached her out on the landing.

'Hello, Madame?' The door gave lightly to her touch as she took a step inside. 'Oh, excuse me –' She stopped on the threshold of the living room in stunned amazement at the sight of the two women in conversation there. The first, well beyond her half century, was extremely short, rake-thin, with an improbably brunette marcel wave, and was very obviously the concierge, whom the university notice had described as a certain Madame Laclos. The other, turning slowly towards the doorway with a vexed expression of exasperation on her face, was the blonde trickster from downstairs.

The apartment was just the thing, as Simone had known it would be. Two large rooms, bedroom and living room, light and not too badly furnished. She could add a few extras, perhaps from the Flea Market, and by the time she brought in her books, that watercolour Lucien had given her for her

5

birthday and the lamp they had bought together in Provence, it would really begin to look like home. There was a tiny kitchen with a gas cooker, and at the back, even a narrow bathroom little bigger than a closet lined in antiseptic white tiles.

It was a find, certainly, and there was no way she would have allowed the other girl to beat her to it, no way at all. Except for the slight matter of the rent. Madame Laclos was asking for key money and a deposit on top of a monthly sum that was already well above her limit.

As the concierge set the figure, folding her arms with intractable resolution, the two women silently sized each other up. Simone saw that her rival was younger, shorter, with a mass of unruly dark hair that curled on to her collar. Her face was strikingly attractive, long and narrow, alive with barely suppressed energy and vitality. Her wide mobile mouth twisted with disappointment and her fine hazel eyes flashed in Simone's direction. With relief, Simone realized that in spite of her expensive, deceptively casual clothes, it seemed that she too had money problems.

'The old bitch!' Simone commented bitterly, joining the other girl on the staircase outside. 'With the shortage of rooms she knows she can hold out for any price she likes and someone will be desperate enough to pay it.'

'And you were desperate enough to send me off to the wrong address,' Diane exploded.

'I knew why you were here the moment I saw the university card in your hand. Well,' she sighed glumly, 'it hasn't done either of us any good.'

'It would have been perfect.'

'Ideal.'

'But what she is asking is almost twice what I can pay, and I've looked everywhere else.'

'It's probably the last apartment left in Paris.'

'A pity there was only one bedroom –'

'Although there was a divan in the living room.'

'Yes, I noticed that, too.'

'I wonder –' Simone stopped on the first-floor landing and stared at her with shrewd cat's eyes.

'Are you thinking what I think you're thinking? You must be crazy!'

'It would need organizing –'

'Let's just say it's *not* what I had in mind.'

'Nor I, but it might not be such a bad idea. Turn and turn about, of course.'

'If you think I'd share a flat with you after the dirty trick you pulled –'

'Oh come on, just think about it! Two rooms, in this area. I don't know about you, but I'm sick of looking. If we don't take it, someone else will.'

'Yes, but –'

Above them they heard Madame Laclos' solid footsteps on the stairs.

'Come on, let's do it. Let's give the old girl a deposit now. What do you say?'

Diane looked from Simone to the staircase and back again. She hesitated no longer. 'All right. Why not?'

Simone gave a rich deep laugh and put out a strong unadorned hand. 'Simone Blanchard.'

'Diane Clements.' She grinned, infected by her new partner's good humour. She grasped her hand and sealed their bargain.

There was a *café-tabac* which Simone knew close at hand. Now the proud tenants of the third-floor left apartment, they sat over *café-filtres* and cognacs in the Café Bonaparte feeling very pleased with themselves.

'To us.' Simone raised her thimble glass.

'And the future.'

7

Simone sat back, examining her new flatmate with open curiosity. 'Diane Clément,' she rolled the name around on her tongue. 'You know, your accent isn't bad at all, but you're not French, are you?'

'Clements. We pronounce the "s". No, I'm only half-French,' Diane admitted somewhat defensively, 'half-English.' She had always prided herself on her accent, hoping it was good enough to pass. She shrugged good-naturedly. 'My mother is from Paris. She met my father over here during the war. They married and went to live in London.'

'So what are you doing at the Sorbonne?'

'Fine Arts. Just for a year. I thought it would give me a chance to see something of the city. I was here as a child, for holidays, that kind of thing, but I wanted to try it on my own, you know?'

Simone was amused by her unaffected optimism. 'Oh yes, I know.'

'You do?' She had begun to look at her companion in a new light. 'And what about your studies?'

'Third year, Faculté de Médecine.'

'Oh, really? That must be exciting.'

'Exhausting.'

'No, I mean, at least you know what you're doing with your life. You have a vocation.'

'I hate to disillusion you, *petite*, but I'm not in it for any grand humanitarian reasons. There aren't many professions which offer women a chance of real security. I'm afraid that's the sordid truth.' She looked round at the barman. 'Georges, two more cognacs.' She was suddenly businesslike, as if embarrassed by her revelation. 'Now, about the apartment. What do you say to a three months turn and turn about arrangement? For three months you get the bedroom, then we change around.'

'Sounds fair to me.'

8

'Except, of course, when either of us have an overnight guest.'

'A guest?'

Simone flashed a sudden dazzling smile. 'You *know*.' She touched her glass against Diane's.

'Oh yes, of course.' Diane hid her surprise in the bottom of the brandy glass. This was Paris, after all.

Diane refused to allow Simone to help her fetch her things from the *hôtel-pension*. For one thing, she had scarcely enough luggage to warrant assistance, and for another, she was deeply ashamed of the staid propriety of the Bonnet establishment and did not want Simone to think it in any way reflected her own style. The Bonnet sisters seemed genuinely distressed to be losing her. They fretted about her destination and discussed the suitability of a young girl taking an apartment on her own with such concern as though they were directly responsible to her mother for her good behaviour.

Having once escaped, Diane felt deliciously liberated and light-hearted. She was about to embark on a great adventure. If she could only stay in Paris for one year, then she was determined to make the most of every minute of her time.

She deposited her single suitcase with Madame Laclos in her *loge* and after an exchange of pleasantries, so different from the interrogation she had just left behind, she set out in ample time to meet Simone in the Luxembourg Gardens.

The hot summer sun made the gardens a popular excursion for many Parisians now returning from their annual holidays. There were several mothers with babies in prams or on reins toddling along the well-kept gravel paths between the statues. A group of older children raced wildly around under the rich canopy of the chestnut trees in pursuit of a girl about five years of age, her blonde plaits flying as she fled,

9

running directly into Simone's and Diane's way. The little girl tripped and Diane caught her firmly under the arms before she could fall.

'Are you all right?'

The child gave a tentative smile but she was hovering on the verge of tears. At that moment her boisterous companions came running up and a stern-faced boy of about seven or eight reclaimed her. 'Come *on*, Marie,' he commanded, putting an arm around her and giving Diane a suspicious look as though the accident was her fault.

'You should be more careful,' Simone rebuked the little group as they led their captive away. *Ces gosses!* They're always under your feet.'

'Don't you like children? I gather you're not going into paediatrics.'

'That's for sure! Besides,' she added brightly, 'there's no money in it!'

When she saw the students' hostel in the maze of back streets behind the Panthéon where Simone had been staying, Diane looked upon her time at the Bonnets' with a more appreciative frame of mind. The little back room was cluttered with clothes, medical textbooks, magazines and so much assorted bric-a-brac that there was scarcely room enough to shut the door.

'My, you certainly have a collection.'

'A lifetime's work,' Simone boasted cheerfully. 'I think we'll need a taxi, don't you?'

'Or two. Perhaps we could hire a truck?'

'Lucien would have helped us but his father is ill and he had to go home until terms begins.'

Lucien, Diane had learnt, was Simone's special friend, a political philosophy major in his graduate year and, as far as Diane could tell, the most likely candidate to become an overnight 'guest' at the Rue de Rennes. He sounded alarmingly serious, but

10

Simone had assured her flippantly that none of her friends took their work at all seriously enough and were all likely to *coller* their examinations.

'But you will see for yourself,' she promised slyly, 'when I show you off to them all, *ma petite Anglaise*.'

That August of 1938 passed in a blurr of activity as the Rue de Rennes began to take shape and character from its new occupants. They haunted the little second-hand shops on the quais of their Left Bank *quartier*, and made forays as far as Saint-Ouen to hunt down bargains in the *marché aux puces*. They went window shopping on the Faubourg St Honoré, were scandalized by the prices, and then treated themselves to a double feature of Jean Gabin at a cinema on the Rue de Rivoli.

They set a pattern of eating most evenings at home, enjoying the novelty of their very own kitchen, and eating off plates on their laps for lack of a proper dining table. The district proved rich in markets. Among the stalls of the Carrefour de Buci on the Rue de Seine they grew expert at haggling with the raucous, sarcastic women nursing their pyramids of shining fruit and fresh green vegetables.

But if they ate at home, they went out to drink. It was not long before Diane became familiar with the bars and café-restaurants of the *quartier*, now re-opening after their *fermeture annuelle*, from Chéramy's on the Rue Jacob to the Méphisto on the corner of Seine and St Germain where, in the cellar, they listened to the records of Louis Armstrong, Charlie Kunz and Charles Trenet. It was in the Méphisto, too, where Diane first made the acquaintance of Simone's inner circle.

Lucien Caristan proved far from the intimidating figure Diane had imagined. He was an amiable giant who made even Simone appear short. He was twenty-four years old, with a shock of dark hair that fell over his eyes. He was sadly addicted to Gitanes and an ancient leather jacket which he believed lent him an air of proletarian worthiness, although his family were solid bourgeois soundly based in Neuilly. His broad tanned face was pleasantly set into almost habitual good humour, the long full mouth naturally curving into a cat's smile, the chin strong but not pugnacious. Only his brown eyes, ardent, inquisitive and constantly alert, proved the lie to the first surface impression of ambling indolence.

By contrast, his room-mate Gervais Rousseau with his books and ink-stained fingers was every inch the perpetual student. His washed-out blue eyes blinked donnishly from under a mop of curling sandy hair between whorls of cigarette smoke. Until Diane's appearance Gervais had been the odd one out, the gooseberry between the two established couples in the group.

But Christian Fournier and Suzanne Drouot had gone one step further than Lucien and Simone; they were actually living together. Diane eyed the daring couple with interest. They sat entwined on the far side of their tiny table drinking cloudy yellow *pastis*, Suzanne leaning on her lover's shoulder, a Giaconda smile on her carmine lips. She was a carelessly beautiful woman with glossy dark hair styled in two soft wings which emphasized her perfect bone structure. She really did not need the amount of make-up she was wearing, she was stunning enough. According to Simone, she was several years older than Christian and rather too afraid of losing him. Perhaps that was why she clung so possessively to him all through the evening, eyeing Diane with a cautious blend of self-conscious challenge.

She need not have worried. Christian Fournier, for all his dark good looks and sulky presence, was

12

not Diane's type, in as far as she had any preference in these matters. She found Christian's flippant irreverence and acerbic jokes unsettling and increasingly galling long before the evening was over and he and Suzanne moved off to their love-nest on the Boul' Mich.

'Oh, you take him too seriously. He just likes his fun,' Simone admonished her.

'Well, he seemed pretty jaundiced if you ask me.'

'But Lucien, you liked Lucien?' Simone demanded eagerly.

'He's a lovely man. You're very lucky. There's only one thing that puzzles me –'

'Yes?'

' – and that's how he puts up with someone like you!'

'*Imbécile!*' Simone pushed her up the stairs ahead of her and their laughter echoed through the building until they remembered the lateness of the hour.

That night, as she prepared for bed in the bedroom that was hers exclusively until December, Diane stood at the window above the Rue de Rennes and looked over Paris. The moon was just beginning to rise above the grey rooftops of Montparnasse. The lights of the city sparkled against the grape-dark sky. Diane thought she had never seen anything so beautiful, so completely perfect. For the first time in her life she felt independent and able to do whatever she wanted, free of all interference and able to plan her own future.

How was she to know that within the month one chance encounter was to change her whole life for ever?

2

The carefree mood of that summer of 1938 was abruptly cut short in September, not by the advent of the new academic year, but by an international crisis no one in France seemed at all prepared for. The German Chancellor's demands for the annexation of Czech lands brought Europe overnight to the brink of war.

Diane, who had never paid enough interest to politics, became alarmed by the French reaction. They seemed to have taken leave of their senses. Not only had Premier Daladier flown to London to consult his British counterpart Chamberlain on possible action, but he had not delayed in issuing a general mobilization order for every able-bodied Frenchman under sixty; two and a half million men ready to take up arms.

On the streets posters began to appear, *Avis à la Population*, detailing blackout regulations in the event of air raids. It seemed too absurd to be true. Diane walked to the Sorbonne each morning through the Luxembourg Gardens as if in a dream. Men were busy outside the National Assembly filling sandbags. In the Boul' Mich a family drove past in a car that was laden with trunks, suitcases and every conceivable item of household goods it was possible to cram aboard. It was not the first such vehicle she had seen fleeing Paris as though the enemy were already at the gates.

Even the Sorbonne, normally a bustling hive of eager activity, had turned overnight into an echoing, strangely deserted shell of its former self. On the door of the main lecture hall hung a sign announcing all classes were temporarily suspended 'in view of the national crisis'.

Diane retreated and found herself in competition with other alarmed Parisiens clamouring for an early edition of *Paris-Soir* straight off the presses. Daladier and Chamberlain were flying to Munich to meet Adolf Hitler to try and find a compromise solution to the Czech question, but no one was holding out great hopes for a settlement. War still seemed the most likely outcome.

For ten days Europe had teetered on the brink of the unthinkable. To Diane's age group, war was the nightmare they had been brought up on as children, the cataclysm that had engulfed and destroyed their parents' generation. Diane's father had never really recovered from his own experiences of war gained at first hand in the trenches. She learnt that Simone's father had been held as a German prisoner for two years and 'it was nothing like Gabin in *La Grande Illusion*, that's for sure,' Simone recited bitterly. And now Lucien had received his call-up papers and was just waiting for word to drop everything and leave for the Front – wherever that would be. Was it any wonder that Diane voluntarily gave up rights to her room to allow the anxious lovers one night together, perhaps their last?

As the plane trees turned from gold to brown and the Indian summer waned, the crisis was suddenly over almost as soon as it had begun. Daladier's return with an agreement signed by 'Herr Hitler' was the signal for national rejoicing. Emotional crowds mobbed the victorious politician at Le Bourget aerodrome and around radios in every street-corner café friends and strangers alike embraced and wept with relief at the news. Simone, Diane and Suzanne treated the men to dinner at Chéramy's to celebrate their timely reprieve as the whole country breathed an audible sigh of relief. All over Paris parties went on through the night and into the early hours of a new morning that everyone seemed to appreciate all the more for their narrow escape.

The students flocked back to their studies with renewed vigour. Simone, nursing a hangover, envied Diane's unassailable optimism and good humour. As she rolled her white lab coat up under her arm, she wished she could take life so lightly, but she was facing a week of Pathology. Diane had better luck: she was taking the morning off to hunt down some missing titles from her reading list. She began with her favourite bookstore, Shakespeare and Company, which was something of a mecca for foreign students in Paris.

She was searching the tall stacks of shelves for an errant copy of Proust in translation when the orange spine of Ernest Hemingway's *A Farewell to Arms* caught her eye. As her hand stretched out to take it down, another hand approached from the left and seized upon it.

'Oh, I'm so sorry!'

The Hemingway fell to the floor and Diane was suddenly face to face with a tall, fair-haired man blocking the narrow passageway between the ranks of books.

'I apologize,' he repeated in his strongly accented French, stooping down to retrieve the novel and handing it to her.

'No, you saw it first.'

'No, please,' he insisted, 'it is yours.'

'Well, it's not as if I haven't already read it.'

'I also.'

'Oh really? Well, I shouldn't anyway. I mean, I ought to be reading something more serious, something French.'

'You are not French? Belgian, perhaps?'

'No, no, just half-French,' she found herself explaining although she was not sure why.

'Ah, yes, half-French, I understand. And what is the other half?'

'I'm not sure it's any of your business.'

He stared at her and immediately drew back.

'Of course, excuse me, please. I was impertinent. It is none of my business, as you say.'

She studied his pale affronted face and the veiled blue eyes and felt a moment of instant compunction.

'Look, I didn't mean –'

But he cut her short. 'No, you do not have to tell me anything!' He clasped the Hemingway to his chest and added, 'So now I will buy this book for you. Yes, I insist, to make amends.'

Diane watched helplessly as he produced the price of the novel and had it wrapped for her by a bemused assistant. They emerged on to the street together and he solemnly presented his gift with a little nod of his head.

'English, I'm half-English,' she volunteered, amused by his seriousness. 'And what about you?'

For a moment he seemed to hesitate as he examined her face.

'Swiss, I am Swiss,' he revealed, 'but now I am living here in Paris.'

'And I'm a student.' They had begun to walk in the direction of the river. She was aware of the length of his stride beside her.

'But you are not living here?'

'No, in England, except that I'm here for a year just now.'

'Then you *are* living here!'

'Just for a year.'

'But a year is a long time. Who can say where any of us shall be next year?'

17

She thought he meant the crisis over Czechoslovakia.

'Yes, it was a pretty close thing, wasn't it? For a moment I thought the whole world had gone mad.'

They had reached the quay where the portable bookstalls lined the Seine beneath the sad elm trees. A carpet of fallen leaves in russet, brown and gold crunched underfoot. He stopped walking and stood looking down at her. A faint, somewhat ironic smile hovered on his full expressive mouth. She thought suddenly that his was a most arresting face, strongly defined by an almost Slavic bone structure and a broad, high forehead. His hair was cropped short in an untidy thatch the colour of faded old gold. She judged him to be in his late twenties, but would have been surprised to learn that he was actually thirty-one.

'Would you meet me again?'

His question took her so much by surprise that she laughed.

'I could perhaps buy you lunch.'

'I don't eat lunch.'

'But you should. This is not good for you.'

She laughed good-humouredly. 'Well, sometimes I take sandwiches. If I'm at the Bibliothèque Nationale.'

'You eat in the library?'

'No, in the Palais Royal gardens, if the weather is fine.'

His voice was low and serious. 'Yes, I know the gardens. We could meet there. Tomorrow, perhaps?'

She found herself agreeing, enjoying the look on his face. They arranged to meet at 12.30 at the Palais Royal and parted amiably, turning in opposite directions along the towpath below the Île de la Cité. She had scarcely reached the Place St Michel when she heard pounding feet behind her.

'You didn't tell me your name,' he announced breathlessly.

'It's Diane.'

'Diane! Like the beautiful Diane de Poitiers? I like this name very much.'

'I'm pleased. It's the only one I have.' He laughed. 'And yours?'

'Ah, mine? It is Dieter, yes, Dieter.'

'Then I'll see you tomorrow, Dieter.'

'Yes, indeed, I will wait for you there.'

She dodged between the traffic to the far side of the square, but when she looked back he was still standing there. Amused, she raised her copy of Hemingway in a kind of salute.

She was early, but he was even earlier. He was waiting, pacing up and down the paths of the formal gardens, looking awkward and impatient in a cheap blue suit and white shirt. It seemed he had tried to make an effort to impress her, although she thought he had looked better in the casual jersey and jacket of the day before.

'Hello, Diane!' He broke into a smile the moment he saw her. 'Why, you look quite marvellous today.' He took her possessively by the arm and guided her through the garden. 'This is the most interesting place. I have looked it up. Did you know, Diane, that Charlotte Corday bought the knife to kill Marat in a shop right here in this place? That is why Paris is so fascinating. Always there is something to interest us. I think I love this city.'

'More than Switzerland?'

'Switzerland? My dear Diane, I *detest* Switzerland. Now, shall we walk or shall we stay?'

After the austere mustiness of the library, Diane said she was glad to walk. He kept a firm hold on her, talking constantly. His French was fluent, if

19

eccentric, and he was persistent in his questioning but she noticed that he rarely chose to talk about himself. Even when she asked him, he seemed curiously evasive about his past, his present and more especially about his future. By the time they reached the Tuileries she had learnt little more about him than the fact that, inexplicably, she liked him a lot.

They sat by Le Nôtre's circular pond and shared her sandwiches, ham and cheese, in a split baguette loaf that required both hands. Dieter's contribution was a small flask of cognac, which he offered her the top to sip from. A chill wind was rising from the river, scattering the fallen leaves. The gardens were virtually deserted.

Their picnic finished, Diane suggested they examine the paintings in the Orangerie, and they spent an hour among the Impressionists, the time passing so quickly that it hardly seemed worthwhile for Diane to return to the library. Playing truant did not bother her, but she wondered about him.

'Don't you have to get back to your work?'

His voice sounded troubled. 'Diane,' he took her by the hands,'Diane, I have not been quite honest with you.'

'No?' She wondered what was coming.

'I have not told you the truth about myself. We were strangers. I have learnt to be guarded, even with friends. But you – you are no longer a stranger.'

'Dieter, you don't have to tell me anything you don't want to.'

'But I want to, Diane! For the first time. It is important to me. Can we go somewhere for coffee? I could talk to you then. There is a café we could go to, a special place where my kind of people meet and talk.'

'Your kind of people?'

He gripped her hand with unnecessary force.

20

'Germans,' he replied, his voice little above a whisper, 'Germans.'

The Café de la Rose became their regular meeting place, but Diane never quite overcame her first impression of excitement, of the unexpected, of danger lurking just around the corner. There seemed very few French among its varied clientele. There were Austrians, Poles, Russians, Spanish, yes, and Germans, but few native Frenchmen. French, however, was the lingua franca that made communication possible. At scattered tables the refugee population of Paris conducted business, legal and illegal, gave vent to their fears and neuroses, and exchanged news of homelands far away.

The flotsam of Europe swept by a wave of war and persecution had temporarily settled on the shores of the Seine to await events. The Munich crisis had caused a tremor of naked fear and, as Dieter revealed, a number of suicides amongst those who could not face the prospect of being forcibly returned to their native countries to jail, or prison camp, or even worse. This shifting, desperate population of 'displaced persons' was living on borrowed time.

The discovery that Dieter was a well-known figure in this exotic world gave Diane a sense of unease. In the same afternoon that he revealed he was in fact German and not Swiss, she learnt that his full name was Hans Dieter Haas, born in Frankfurt thirty-one years before, a journalist by profession, a liberal by conviction, hounded out of the Reich three years before to live by his wits how and where he could.

'My story is not unusual,' he assured her. 'I live in the margins. I work where I can find it. I frequently change my address. I avoid situations and places where I am asked for my papers.' His watchful blue eyes compelled her attention. 'I am a non-person

21

here in France. Diane, they could send me back at any time.'

Diane was shaken by the strength of her feelings of alarm and pity. That there was another side to this strangely disturbing, engaging, magnetic man did not surprise her. She had known there must be some mystery behind his lonely, intriguing figure, but she had never suspected that he was on the run without a *permit de séjour* or even a *carte d'identité*. For three years he had lived an underground existence, surviving on the generosity of friends, the odd German lesson or job for the Refugee Committee. Since France had closed her borders to new immigrants, he had come and gone illicitly, without passport or papers.

He looked at her with luminous, passionate eyes and stretched out to seize her hand across the table.

'I tell you this because I trust you, Diane, because we are friends. And perhaps will be more than friends.'

3

Beyond the window the frosty glitter of the moon peppered the empty street. The fifth-floor apartment on the Boulevard St Michel afforded a wonderful view over the city. Inside, the gramophone was playing 'Spread a Little Happiness'.

'Who is this *type* Diane is bringing?'

'I don't really know,' Simone confessed. 'Someone she met at a student café. She's been quite secretive about him.'

'Well, so at last our little virgin gets herself a man!'

'Christian!'

'What's so wrong with that? I'm surprised someone hasn't snatched her up long ago with her looks –'

Simone flashed Suzanne an anxious glance, wondering if Christian was just taunting her or callously unaware of her standing behind him, a tray of canapés in her hands. She set down the tray among the mandarins and roasted chestnuts with a resounding clatter and instantly retreated to the kitchen.

'You really are a bastard.'

'*Tiens, tiens*, dear Simone, Christmas is supposed to be a time for fun. Lucien, you don't object if I borrow your glamorous *amante* for a dance, do you?'

Lucien, preoccupied opening another bottle of wine by the stove, gave a vague wave in their direction.

'It's nice to know he cares,' Simone grumbled and reluctantly surrendered to Christian's arms as a Jean Sablon number began to play.

At that moment Gervais arrived with Diane and her unknown escort in tow.

'We met in the lobby,' explained Gervais, depositing his armful of well-wrapped presents on to the nearest chair and unwinding vast lengths of red woollen scarf from about his neck. Diane and Dieter pushed into the apartment behind him.

'Well, well,' Simone heard Christian comment as their dance was abruptly cut short.

'Don't just stand there. Let me help with your coats,' she offered vigorously.

'This is Dieter,' Diane announced, removing her jacket and turning to give him an encouraging smile.

Dieter, caught with one arm in and one out of his overcoat, blinked and made a cautious little bow to the group which only emphasized his obvious Germanic origins.

'We've heard so much about you,' said Christian, coming forward boisterously and offering his hand.

'Christian and Suzanne,' Diane explained, hanging on to Dieter's arm. 'And this is Lucien, and Simone, of course.'

'Don't let's be so formal,' Lucien complained as the bout of handshaking subsided. 'Have a drink, you two. Red or white?'

'We've brought a couple of bottles, too,' added Diane. 'I'll just put them in the kitchen.'

Dieter stood deserted in the middle of the room, his long arms hanging awkwardly by his sides. His eyes strayed anxiously after Diane and he looked acutely out of place.

'Try a canapé,' Simone suggested, taking pity on him. 'Suzanne made them herself. They're delicious.'

He obligingly picked up one of the concoctions, grasping it carefully between his fingers but not venturing to eat it.

'You're at the Sorbonne, I hear,' Lucien began.

'No, actually.'

'No? Oh, I thought Diane had said –'

24

Simone judicially cut into the interrogation. 'Lucien is doing postgrad work there, and I'm at the École de Médecine.'

'Ah, yes, Diane told me. It must be very interesting for you.' He seemed unable to make up his mind whether to call her '*tu*' or '*vous*'. He looked acutely uncomfortable.

'Is this your first Christmas here in France?' Lucien was asking, but Dieter was saved from replying by Diane's return with Suzanne from the kitchen.

The moment he saw her his eyes lit up and relief flooded his face. Looking at them together, Simone was left in little doubt of their attraction for one another. Diane's eyes were shining as she laughed up at him and hung on his shoulder as though afraid to let him go.

The gramophone began to play the latest Charles Trenet song, which flooded the apartment with waves of emotion.

'Oh, I love this!' cried Diane. 'Come and dance.'

The others also took their partners as the strains of '*J'Attendrai*' made everyone grow sentimental. Gervais calmly helped himself to another glass of wine as the couples swayed gently around the room. The lights of the city winked in the close darkness of the December night.

As Simone turned in Lucien's arms she contemplated her friend dancing with the enigmatic stranger at their side. He was quite different from what she had expected. Diane was barely twenty, and it was obvious that Dieter was five or more years her senior. But more than that, it troubled her that he was out of the ordinary run of students. If he *was* a student. And she had never once hinted that he was an emigré, a foreigner, and with that accent and those looks probably an Austrian, or worse, German.

25

There was such a look upon her face. Simone felt a strange tremor of envy. She doubted whether she could ever reveal her own feelings quite so nakedly, doubted perhaps her capacity for such intensity.

As the record ended and they all joyfully attacked the food laid out on the side table among the Christmas candles, Simone noticed Christian moving into the attack.

'So what is it you actually do, *copain*?'

'I'm a journalist as a matter of fact,' Dieter answered levelly.

'A journalist! Who do you write for? *Le Matin*? The London *Times*? Don't tell me, *Der Stürmer*?'

With great restraint, Dieter replied, 'No, none of those.'

'No? I must have read something of yours, surely?'

With a strain in her voice, Simone said sharply, 'Christian, leave him alone.'

He drew on his Gauloise nonchalantly. 'But I'm interested. After all, Diane's one of our little group now and someone should be concerned that she's running around with some Hun refugee *parasite* –'

'Christian!'

Suzanne had gone pale, spilling wine down the front of her velvet dress. Lucien stepped forward, seeing the muscle move in Dieter's cheek, but he was instantly in control of himself. With cold deliberation he put down his plate, picked up his overcoat and headed for the door.

'Dieter!' Diane ran after him.

He scarcely looked at her but his sharp eyes surveyed the room with acrimony.

'I won't stay where I am not welcome. They are your friends, Diane. Don't spoil your evening on my account.'

Hurt and anger swept through her. She stared bleakly at the closed door and then seized her own jacket and flung out of the apartment after him.

The yellow plane trees in the boulevard were stark and bare in the lamplight. By the time Diane caught him up, Dieter had already reached the corner of Barbusse and L'Abbé. His coat collar pulled up, his hands thrust deep in his pockets, he turned a frozen face to meet hers.

'Dieter, I'm so sorry –'

'It's not for you to apologize for your friends. They only want to protect you.'

'Christian is a bigot and a fool.'

'Don't you see?' he said in a hoarse whisper. 'They are suspicious of me and my intentions.'

'I don't care what they think!'

He looked down at her face pinched with the cold and gently touched her cheek with his fingertips. He spoke so quietly she could barely hear his next words, 'Diane, *Liebling*, I love you, and for a man on the run there is nothing worse. I have to tell you this is impossible. I have no future here, perhaps not anywhere. It is too late, you see? Too late for us.'

Suddenly he moved his arms and pulled her towards him. Briefly his mouth brushed hers, and the next moment he was walking briskly away as quickly as he could, appalled by her tears.

Diane sat in the Rue de Rennes with her knees drawn up to her chest and her arms wrapped around them, waiting for Simone to return. It was some time before midnight when she heard her key in the lock and she was thankful to see Simone was alone.

'Oh, Diane!' Simone came and folded her in a tight embrace. 'Diane, it's not as you think. The party broke up after you left. Lucien, Gervais and I have been at the Bonaparte, talking. Lucien tore a strip off Christian. You should have heard him! We were all so ashamed –' She suddenly caught sight of Diane's stricken face. 'Didn't you catch up with Dieter?'

To Simone's horror, tears began to roll down her cheeks.

'He left me. Oh Simone, he walked away and left me! He's on the run, without papers. He's an illegal, and if they catch him they could send him back to Germany at any time.'

'Why didn't you tell me?'

Diane replied in a small, wistful voice, 'I didn't know, I didn't realize until now just how much – how much he means to me.'

'*Pauvre petite*, I understand.'

'I love him, Simone. What can I do?'

'Oh, *chérie*,' Simone said gently, 'I wish I knew.'

Christmas passed and the New Year of 1939 ushered in a period of bitter weather. Simone had intermediate exams coming up and when Diane offered to help her revise she gladly accepted, pleased to see her friend stir out of her depression. They sat curled by the stove surrounded by medical textbooks, drinking mugs of steaming hot chocolate while the rain lashed down outside.

For two weeks Diane had seen nothing of Dieter. She might have gone to the Café de la Rose in search of him, she might have left a message for him there or sent him a *pneu*, if only she had known what to say. But time had sobered her first rash impulse to run to him. He had said he loved her but he was afraid to hurt her. He, who had seen so much more of life than she had, who had known unimaginable terrors and uncertainties. He wanted the best for her, everyone wanted the best for her, but no one seemed to have taken into consideration her feelings for Dieter.

28

Just after New Year she received a letter from her parents in the wake of the Munich Crisis. Her mother was the writer, although the sentiments she expressed were very obviously her father's. He had always been opposed to her 'adventure' in France and the scare over war seemed merely to confirm his view that the whole escapade was 'dangerous nonsense'. He appealed to her to come home 'while she could'. The threat of war was very far from over, he believed.

She could have gone home, she could have just given up and turned her back on everything, writing up the experience as bad luck. But she knew if she did go back she would never again be as brave. This was her one chance to make a break for independence and if she meekly surrendered now she knew she would be trapped in English conformity, perhaps never daring to risk anything ever again.

However hard it was, however foolish she might appear to her friends, she determined to see it through. She felt infinitely older and more mature than the raw girl who had arrived on the boat-train less than six months before. She did not believe for one moment that war was coming – the business at Munich had surely dealt with that – but even if it came to war she was in no greater danger here in Paris than she would be in London, and at least she was free to make her own mistakes.

When the university reopened in January Diane determined to make a greater effort to put her unhappiness behind her. Every morning she and Simone separated in the expanse of the Place St Sulpice and she turned south towards the Jardin du Luxembourg. She enjoyed the walk whatever the weather. The wind moaned in the old trees. Their skeletal forms and the empty flowerbeds did not depress her. She remembered the children who had played there in the sunshine, in particular the little

29

girl with plaits flying who had tried bravely to stifle her tears.

In the second week of the new term grey clouds hounded her steps through the gardens and before Diane had gone twenty yards it began to rain. She pulled a scarf from her pocket and quickly tied it over her hair. When she looked up again she was suddenly rooted to the spot as the rain slanted down. Beyond the round pond, his coat already soaked, its grey turned to black, Dieter stood watching her.

She did not move as he strode down to meet her. He stopped just yards away and they stared at one another. Then, without saying a word, they fell forward into each other's arms.

She felt his arms crushing her against him as, hungrily, he sought her mouth. An agony of need opened up inside them and they kissed with passion and desperation, without restraint. Breathless, Diane was laughing and crying all in the same instant as he smoothed the hair from her rain-streaked face and kissed the corners of her mouth.

'I tried to keep away –'

'Don't say anything. This isn't the time for talking.'

And clasped in the fold of his arm, she drew him away, retracing her steps to the empty apartment on the Rue de Rennes.

As they lay holding one another in the early afternoon, the rain drummed relentlessly against the half-open shutters. The room was washed in opal colours and filled with the noise of water. The journey they had made together had brought them to this unknown shore, this point of no return. No words needed to be spoken. It was taken for granted that from now on they would be together, stay together, whatever the cost. If time was their enemy then every hour together was a moment to savour and cherish.

30

Held in the crook of his shoulder, she whispered, 'How little I know about you. And yet I know everything I'll ever need to know.'

'I want to take you away with me. I want to keep you safe.'

Seeing him so troubled, she raised herself up on one elbow, looking down on him. 'Why should we ever be parted?'

He took her face in his hands and for a moment the look of anguish in his eyes terrified her. He released her and pulled himself up on the pillows.

'We have known each other for only a few months. These months, Diane, almost made me forget. I have lived dangerously near the edge. If they caught me now –' He closed his eyes as if to ward off the thought. 'Now I must learn to live a different way, more cautious. I cannot be sent back again.'

'Again?'

'*Liebling*, when I escaped from Germany I knew I could never go back. Not as a free man. I came to Paris believing I was safe here, but in weeks the police had found me. I was put in jail. "Unauthorized entry," they said. Then they took me to the border, but the Swiss sent me back. The next time I was not so stupid, so naive. I bought myself a false passport, I learnt a false name. I became Austrian.' He sighed ironically. 'Then came the *Anschluss*, and suddenly Paris was full of Austrians. The police took us to Colombes by the vanload –'

'Colombes?'

'It's a camp. Yes, the French have their camps as we Germans have Dachau. At Colombes the police burnt my expensive new passport in front of my eyes. Then they took me again to the Swiss border.' He drew her close and held her lovingly. 'But I came back, Diane, and this time they will not find me.'

31

Diane trembled in his arms. She knew how much it had cost him to speak about his past. Although she had seen the refugees at the Café de la Rose for herself, she realized she knew nothing of their desperate lives. She was filled with outrage and alarm at events she could never even have guessed at before she met Dieter.

'We will never be parted,' she told him in an urgent whisper. 'Whatever happens we will be together.'

He shook his head in wonder and smiled at her.

'We must be crazy, you know. There was never a worse time to fall in love.'

'There was never a better.'

'Then come away with me.'

'What, now?'

'Yes, now!' he insisted, enthusiastically pulling off the covers. 'Pack a bag, Diane! We're going for a trip to the country!'

Chéramy delivered the *plat du jour* to the little group at the corner banquette. It was a subdued trio without Christian's presence and acid sense of humour. Simone sat between Lucien and Gervais and fitfully picked at her *cassoulet*.

'Come on,' Gervais grumbled, raising his glass, 'this is supposed to be a celebration, not a wake! Your exams are over, enjoy yourself!'

'She's worried about Diane,' Lucien explained. 'It's a week now and there has been no word of her.'

'But she left you a note.'

'Yes, she left me a note but I can't help worrying. Just going off like that. With Dieter. I know he's all wrong for her.'

'You're not responsible for Diane,' Gervais pointed out between mouthfuls.

'I *feel* responsible. She's so young, so inexperienced. And Dieter – well, how long can he survive like this, living on the run? It's all going to end in heartache.'

Gervais exchanged an anxious look with Lucien, but it was not connected with Simone's pessimistic prediction. They had both caught sight of the newcomers who were fast approaching their table.

Lucien laid a warning hand on Simone's arm. She turned abruptly in her seat and let out a squeal of joy.

'Diane!'

Diane warmly embraced her friend and hurriedly drew Dieter into the circle.

'Meet M'sieur and Madame Dieter Haas!' she announced triumphantly, gripping his arm. 'Yes, it's true, we got married!'

4

Events in Europe moved apace as winter turned to spring that year of 1939. The Civil War in Spain came to a brutal end as the legitimate government of the Republic crumbled. The ragged remains of the international army who had tried in vain to stem the tide of Fascism poured through the snowbound passes of the high Pyrenees into France seeking sanctuary. The French, panicked by this fresh wave of unwanted humanity, hastily set up a number of detention camps near the border and promptly forgot about their existence.

Lucien Caristan, who at one time had seriously considered offering his services to Spain, lamented his decision to finish his thesis first, as if aware of a great opportunity lost. In an attempt to make amends, he plunged himself into work for the refugee committees and after a trip to Perpignan to see for himself, returned to his friends with harrowing tales of the primitive conditions suffered by Spanish refugees.

Then, on 15 March, the German Army entered Prague and the last fragments of the tainted Munich accord were shattered. In France Daladier reacted immediately and obtained full emergency powers to introduce a number of sweeping measures. In the interests of national defence the government abolished the forty-hour week that had been fought for over decades and finally introduced by the former Popular Front Prime Minister, Léon Blum. To many people such measures bore the stamp of potential dictatorship. It was not as though France had been immune to her own native brands of Fascism from the *Cagoulards* and *Action-française* to the *Parti populaire française*.

'Time is running out,' Dieter confided to his young wife. 'Soon there will be nowhere left to run to.'

She placed a finger on his lips to silence him.

'Whatever happens, we'll be together.'

Diane discovered he had nightmares. The first night they spent as man and wife at the Rue de Rennes, by courtesy of Simone who readily vacated her tenancy of the bedroom, Diane was woken by his restless dreams. He cried out loud and she tried to comfort and reassure him, but it was several minutes before he could remember where he was and that, for the moment, he was safe.

Theirs was the most unusual situation. They were married but they were forced to live as though they were not. Diane kept the apartment with Simone, and Dieter kept on the move from room to room all over the city. They dared not move in together, they dared not even establish any kind of pattern to visits for fear of drawing unwanted attention to his presence. They were particularly cautious of Madame Laclos and her suspicions.

Simone tried to express her fears to Diane, but as she groped for the right words she was afraid she would say something she might afterwards regret.

'How long can you go on like this? It's no kind of life, is it?'

'It's all the life I want.'

'And what will you do when your year here runs out? Your parents are still expecting you back in London.'

'I won't leave, not without Dieter. And how can he go without a passport?'

Simone looked at her friend with barely veiled despair. The past months had only reconfirmed her

35

doubts. But every time she tried to talk seriously to her, Diane was evasive, blindly refusing to face reality. She was so completely absorbed, so very obviously happy with Dieter that nothing else seemed to matter.

It was as though the mood of the country was somehow contagious. There was a kind of madness in the air, a desperate gaiety. They all lived through that summer blind to the possibilities of approaching war, seeking a last chance for happiness before the whole world caved in around them.

That last wonderful summer! The weather was glorious, the sky a pure eggshell blue, Simone's exam results had been good and the university year ended on a high note of optimism. The group made the round of fêtes for the Bastille Day celebrations together. Even Christian was forgiven and reabsorbed into the circle of friends as they toured the local balls until the early hours. In the large carefree crowds Dieter danced openly with Diane. There was an electric tension between them that was undeniable.

Suzanne and Simone watched them from the sidelines, and Suzanne was less than enthusiastic.

'What does she see in him? Oh I know he's wildly attractive, but to marry him, a German, at a time like this —'

'She wouldn't listen to anyone.'

An orange moon hung over the river as they wandered homewards along the quais. The lights of the city strung out along the Seine like a necklace of garnets.

'Was anything ever so perfect?' Diane wondered out loud. 'I've never been so happy.'

They had the apartment to themselves for once. Simone had gone back to Lucien's rooms in the Eleventh near the Père Lachaise because Gervais had

36

found himself a girl with a place in Vincennes. The Rue de Rennes was in darkness as they crept upstairs hand in hand. Once safe inside they dissolved into one another's arms long before they found the bedroom door. It had been more than a week since they had been together.

'My love, my love,' he murmured, taking her face in both his hands as she came to him, their bodies locked together, her lips seeking his. It was so easy, this harmony, this togetherness. They complemented one another so perfectly, seeking new ways of delighting each other, finding pleasure in each other's satisfaction and fulfilment.

He lay in bed in the morning watching her brush her hair. His concentration was so complete, so intense, that she wondered what he was thinking.

'When I look at you, I am storing up memories for the future,' he told her.

He did not add the words: for the time we are no longer together.

They spent the long summer days like tourists in the museums and gardens of the city. They preferred to avoid places where they might be stopped by the police and asked for their papers. Once, Christian got hold of a friend's car and they all went out to the beach at Nogent-sur-Marne and enjoyed a lazy picnic by the river. In the evenings they haunted those clubs and bars of the Left Bank that had not closed early for the *fermeture annuelle*, in July not August, as though afraid that this year August might not happen.

It was a summer for memories: the café on the terrace, the chanteuse at the piano singing '*J'Attendrai*'; the brass bands playing the Marseillaise on the Pont Neuf; the gas lamps glowing in the romantic half-light on the place Fustenburg. Did they guess even then that such simple pleasures would soon be

37

relegated to the distant past? Everyone lived in the pathetic hope of another Munich, another last-chance effort to avoid the inevitable impending holocaust.

The end of August brought an increase in tension as Germany's rapacious appetite turned towards Poland. Daladier's government was in crisis. Suspected Communists and leading opposition figures were arrested as the whole city lay under an epidemic of infectious fear. Crowds hung around cafés to catch the latest announcements over the radio and newspapers were sold out the moment they hit the streets. The Louvre was closed and its treasures being taken away to some safe and secret destination. Posters began to appear to advise on blackout regulations. Already a procession of cars was making its way to the Porte D'Orléans crammed with frantic and panic-stricken families eager for exile in the south.

Lucien and Simone had their own fears. Lucien had had a close escape the year before when France threatened to mobilize. Now there seemed to be no possibility of a reprieve. The dreaded news came late on September 1st. The *Appel Immédiat* was called for 1 a.m. the following day.

As they walked back through the brilliant moonlit streets, Lucien voiced his doubts about the future.

'I'm twenty-five. If we have a repeat of the last war I'll be almost thirty before it's over. *If* I come through. Would you wait for me that long?'

Simone was evasive. 'I don't believe it will come to that. Germany won't attack us. The Maginot Line will stop them.'

'I don't know, Simone, I can't help thinking that we're all too complacent. We've concentrated on the Maginot and yet our boys have rifles forty years out of date!' He took her in his arms and tilted her face up to meet his. 'I just know I'll come through safely if you will wait for me.'

'Lucien —'

'Promise me, Simone.'

She wanted to say something to reassure him. She knew in that instant that this was not love. It was nothing compared to the white heat of emotion she had seen between Diane and Dieter. Whatever Lucien felt for her, she knew in her heart that she was deceiving herself, and him, to call it love. But it was easier, kinder, to stifle her guilt and still pretend. After all, he was going away into danger and she might never see him again.

'I promise,' she murmured and raised her head for his kiss, trying to hide her guilt.

Diane and Dieter were in the Bois de Boulogne enjoying the late afternoon sunshine when they heard that France had declared war. All day Saturday everyone had been anticipating a reaction to Germany's invasion of Poland. When it had not come, hope was foolishly renewed and Sunday crowds flocked to parks and gardens. In the Bois, families were picnicking under the trees, taking lunch at the restaurant or rowing on the lake. Diane sat with Dieter on a mossy bank, tilting her brown face to the sun. The lake shimmered in the yellow sunlight, the wind was drowsy in the trees. For several minutes they remained blissfully unaware of the disturbance going on by the boathouse. But suddenly a mother nearby had leapt to her feet anxiously calling for her son, and her husband was frantically scooping up child and picnic basket and rushing like a madman towards the exit.

Diane sat up, meeting Dieter's troubled gaze. She called out to a group of young people hastily following the example of scores of others leaving the Bois.

'What is it? What's happened?'

'They've just announced it on the radio. It's begun! The war's begun!'

Dieter pulled her roughly to her feet. She began to gather up their things, but he took the basket out of her hands.

'Diane, you know what this means. They are bound to intern me. We'll be separated.'

'No! You'll be safe. I won't let anything happen.' She clung to him desperately as if she feared they would come and drag him away at any moment.

'Diane, Diane,' he gently chided her, 'whatever happens we have had this time together.'

The face of Paris had been transformed. Roads out of the city continued to be choked with traffic, while the eastbound railway terminals were crowded with troops and their wives and girlfriends locked in emotional farewells. Many Métro stations were inexplicably closed, or worse, blacked out. People stumbled blindly along in the new blackout conditions, the streets barely lit by the dull blue lamps which cast a sickly glow on the nervous faces of passers-by.

Shops had their shelves stripped of food in spite of government appeals not to hoard, foreign restaurants bore notices declaring they were French-owned, and the sandbags continued to pile up outside public buildings. The pond in the Luxembourg Gardens had been drained and stank abominably, the radio played Chopin's *'Polonaise'* interspersed with news and official announcements, and by night the sirens wailed their false alarms.

On the Monday night Simone and Diane were busy hanging thick blue curtains to black out their

40

windows when the sirens went again. Madame Laclos came pounding on their door as part of her new duties as air-raid warden for the house. When Simone looked out on to the landing, the concierge was hurrying on her way down the stairs to the cellar already wearing her gas mask.

Diane followed Simone to the door and laid a hand on her sleeve. 'Don't let's go down. It's bound to be another false alarm, and besides I need to talk to you.'

Something in her voice alerted Simone to a new note of anxiety and seriousness she had not detected before. They came back inside and Simone refilled their coffee cups. Diane had turned off the lamps and drawn back the blinds. It was a fine starlit night and the room was filled with a calm silvery light.

'Simone, I think I'm pregnant.'

The words fell like heavy stones into the silence. With difficulty Simone struggled to overcome her first reaction, an irrational sense of fear.

She looked searchingly at her. 'Are you sure?'

'No, not sure. I was hoping you could tell me for certain.'

Oh God, thought Simone, I should at least have warned her to be more careful. She tried hard to sound bright, but she heard the waver in her own voice, 'Don't worry, it's probably a false alarm.'

Diane flashed her a look of surprise. 'Oh, I'm not worried. I *want* it to be true. I want a baby.'

'Have you told Dieter?'

'Not yet. It wouldn't be fair, not until I know.'

She had missed her period, it was three weeks now. She had noticed a couple of other signs – swollen breasts and nausea when she woke in the mornings.

It could not have come at a worse time, thought Simone, didn't she understand that a child would merely complicate everything? But when she looked

41

at Diane's face as she confirmed her belief, she saw only joy and radiant, blind happiness.

Simone did not know whether to envy or pity her. In the time they had been together they had become closer than friends, as close as sisters. She did not want to see Diane hurt, she did not want her to suffer.

'I think I must be the luckiest woman alive,' said Diane, hugging her. 'I hope one day you and Lucien will —'

'It's not the same.' She broke quickly apart. 'It's different between us. Oh, I do love him, of course I do. In my way. But I've thought about it a lot, seeing you and Dieter together, and I don't think I'm really capable of that kind of love —'

'Simone —'

'I suppose you think me a hard bitch.'

Diane looked stricken. 'No, no, of course I don't! You're too hard on yourself.'

'I just don't feel the same way about Lucien as you feel about Dieter.'

'But you have your work. It's understandable, Simone. You have a direction to your life. You're doing something really worthwhile, you're going to be a doctor! I have nothing but Dieter – and now, the baby. They're the whole world to me. But you could never be satisfied with just that. You're meant to do something really important with your life.'

Simone stared at her friend and tears pricked at the corners of her eyes. She shook her head. 'Diane, you are truly amazing, you know that?'

Diane laughed. '*Imbécile!* Go and put on the coffee. There goes the All-Clear.'

A kind of paranoia hit the capital. Every night the sirens were set off for non-existent air raids. Everyone had been issued with gas masks in expectation of diabolical poison gas attacks that never came. The police started checking the identity cards of every able-bodied man under sixty, convinced that if they were not at the Front they must be foreign agents, a Nazi Fifth Column preparing the way for invasion. One could no longer even make a simple telephone call at the post office without showing identity papers.

To compound the problems facing Dieter and other illegals, just two days after France declared war the government issued a decree reversing all naturalizations since 1927. This meant, in fact, that even legal residents in France, long since French citizens, now discovered they were back on the Aliens List. Many Frenchmen considered the decree a sensible measure. All the incipient nationalist racism came openly to the surface. The fear of denunciation was very real now. Dieter reported panic among the refugee community. Those who could do so were getting out.

Dieter knew his options were limited. Even if he had the money, it was doubtful whether he could find good papers these days. The best of the forgers had deserted Paris weeks ago. The Café de la Rose had been abandoned. Of course, he might have tried a clandestine escape from one of the ports, or south to neutral Spain or Portugal over the Pyrenees. Or there was always Switzerland. But he was a cautious and, God forbid, an honest man. He knew he could not walk out on Diane in an attempt to save himself, not now that he knew about the child.

He had tried to make her see sense, to get back to England while she still could. Her family would look after her there. He would be easier in his own mind just knowing that she and the child were safe. But she was such a stubborn little thing and she adamantly rejected any such idea.

43

'What makes you think England will be any safer than France?' she had argued. 'England is in this, too. And in the last war the Germans even bombed London with Zeppelins.'

'I'm thinking of you and the child.'

'And so am I. What kind of future do you think we would have without you? I don't want my baby to be brought up never knowing its father.'

In the face of such determination Dieter resolved to hide his fears, to make things as easy as possible for her. He kept to himself the alarming news of friends who simply disappeared off the streets, of the suicide of Manuel Esteves, his wife and daughter. It was said even foreign businessmen were being arrested and sent to Colombes.

'I'm worried about you. At the moment the British are safe, they're allies, but things could turn around. If France makes a deal with the Nazis —'

'But they won't do that!'

'With this government anything could happen. Diane, all I am saying is you would be safer with dual nationality, with French papers.'

'And I'm concerned about you.'

'Then don't be,' he told her lightly. 'I'm an old hand at all this, remember. I'll always find a neutral corner.'

He hoped he had convinced her. For the past day or so he'd had the uneasy feeling that he was being followed. He was taking a chance even coming to the Rue de Rennes, although he had taken precautions and come in the blackout.

'I don't think we should meet again for a few days, Diane. No, nothing's wrong,' he lied, 'it's just that I need to see a few friends in St Denis.'

'Can they help us?' She was still banking everything on finding him papers so that they could live openly together.

'I hope so. We'll just have to be careful.'

'But when will I see you again?'

'Soon. As soon as I can, I promise you.' He put his arms around her and kissed her with what should have been reassurance. But something in that kiss alerted her and a real doubt was raised in her heart as she watched him slip away down the stairs and out into the darkness.

There had been no electricity for the past three days. Fortunately the mild September sunshine continued, but Simone and Diane had to take their meals in the Bonaparte. The dazzle of lights inside the café hurt the eyes after the blacked-out street. Little hurricane lanterns brightened each table and the warm fug of gas heaters and cigarette smoke gave the place a close murky atmosphere.

As the two women took their seats at a table near the door, a swarthy young man was watching them from the bar. As soon as they were settled, he put down his copy of the evening paper and came over to join them.

That moment was to live for ever, frozen like a perfect photographic image, in Simone's memory.

'I have a message for Diane.' His accent was unmistakably Spanish.

'Sit down,' Diane suggested, covering her surprise.

'No, I cannot stay.' He eyed the door with suspicion. 'It is about your husband. I'm afraid he was taken last night. They have caught him, Madame.'

And as Diane gripped Simone's hand with whitened knuckles, the messenger had already fled the café into the anonymous night.

5

For three days they kept him at the Préfecture. Dieter found himself in the company of a large group of Spanish Republicans who had arrived in the same Black Maria. At first he was looked upon with suspicion because of his German accent and German looks. The French police were rounding up his countrymen regardless of their politics, Fascists and anti-Fascists alike. But fortunately someone from a fresh influx of detainees soon recognized him from the Café de la Rose and by nightfall that first day he was finally accepted.

His main concern was for Diane. He could be strong until he thought of her. Had she heard by now? Did she know what had happened to him? Once he allowed the nightmare to invade his mind, his resolve began to falter. Never to see her again! Never to see their child, or hold them in his arms!

The future seemed suddenly unendurable. He sank forward, cradling his head in his hands, struggling to overcome the waves of black misery that threatened to engulf him, finish him. He had seen too many brave men – men who had resisted the most terrible beatings – succumb to torture of their own making. Somehow he knew he had to shake off this deathly despair and begin to fight back. He had a wife and child to live for now.

By day they were kept in a hall, the Salle Lépine, where films had been shown in the days of peace. They slept curled on rows of seats or sat and talked, trying to understand what was happening. At night the *flics* forced them all down to a large cellar under the Préfecture, a place used to store coal for the boilers. They emerged the next morning, blinking into the daylight, black as sweeps from the coal dust.

Occasionally one or two of their number would be picked out for questioning, hurried along by blows and curses, but Dieter was left alone. He sat with his friend from the Café de la Rose, a Spaniard called Julio Gonzales.

'What will they do with us all? Even they cannot have so many camps.'

'I hear others have been taken to the Vélodrome d'Hiver.'

'The Vél d'Hiv? What happens when they run out of sports stadiums?'

'Eventually, *companero*, they will have to admit their mistake. They cannot treat Nazis and anti-Nazis alike.'

'I'm not so sure,' Dieter commented sourly.

'I worry about my wife. What if they've taken her, too?'

'I got a message out to mine.'

'How did you manage that? I could suffer anything if I knew Marisa was safe.'

'Look,' said Dieter eagerly, 'let's make a pact. If one of us gets the opportunity, let him try and get word to both our wives.'

'*Espléndido*! I tell you Marisa's address, you tell me your wife's. If one of us is released before the other —'

'If.'

'I cannot believe even they would be so stupid.'

Dieter's mouth twisted wryly. 'I hope you're right, Julio. I have no desire to see Switzerland again.'

After the first immediate shock had worn off, Diane tried hard to maintain a strong, hopeful face in front of others. Only Simone really understood her pain. She worried about her state of health, she guarded

47

and protected her like a bustling mother hen. She kept repeating, 'Things will come right, *chérie*. This war can't last for ever.' But Diane's eyes continued to hold a haunted, inconsolable light.

The worst was not knowing the details of his arrest, or where he was being held. She only knew he was one of thousands who had been rounded up in police raids, who had disappeared without trace.

The reaction of many people was that the refugees must have done something wrong or they would not have been arrested. But surely the police would soon understand they were holding many innocent men, men who, far from supporting the Nazis, were their avowed enemies and had suffered and been persecuted at their hands? Diane had to believe that before long Dieter would be released and soon be with her again.

But alone at night she fell prey to all kinds of fears. Across the city glowering copper-tinted clouds carried the threat of an autumn storm. She tossed and turned in the restless darkness, reliving every moment of their last night together. There was a sudden flash of lightning and the room was lit up with an electric-blue glare. A cry of pain and despair came from her crumpled figure, drowned by the low rumble of thunder overhead. Why had she allowed Dieter to leave her that night? She still saw his face caught in the narrow shadows on the stairs, upturned for a last goodbye.

Beyond the shutters the heavens released their burden of unshed tears in sympathy with her. How had the police known where to find him? Had he been betrayed, denounced? Or was it just bad luck, pernicious Fate?

The noise of water drowned her tears. The rain gushed down gutters, cascaded from the roof in weeping waterfalls. She could not but remember that

48

day they had been caught in the rainstorm and returned to the apartment to be together. Tears coursed down her face and neck and rolled back into her damp hair. She cried for Dieter and all she had lost. She cried for their future and the keen injustice of it all.

She lay on her back, her hands touching her stomach. The baby was all she had of him now. Simone was right. It was the baby that she had to think about now. She had to learn to be strong, to look after herself for the baby's sake.

She rose from the bed and threw a shawl around her shoulders. A flash of lightning in the street was reflected in the rain puddles and then plunged once again into darkness. She shivered and turned aside. Her mother had written on the outbreak of war, begging her to return to London. She was so young, she reminded Diane, she should be with her family at times like these. Her mother meant well, but what she did not understand, could not understand, simply because Diane had never told her, was that Dieter was now all her family, Dieter and the child who would be born in the spring

Simone had lavished all her savings on a new bicycle costing over 700 francs. She proudly displayed it to Diane and Madame Laclos in the yard of the Rue de Rennes, looking very sportive in her pleated skirt and long woollen sweater.

'It's an investment. Now they are sending me to the Salpéthiére for my practicals, I'll save a fortune on fares!'

Diane looked at the shining green bicycle with unconcealed envy. It would be many months before she saw herself borrowing Simone's bike. She already felt ungainly and enormous. She was aware she had begun to attract curious stares in the street about her 'condition'. On Simone's advice, she had purchased a cheap plain ring to ward off casual inquiries. Madame Laclos had already been initiated into Diane's whirl-wind romance and secret wedding, although they were happy to let Madame Laclos think that her missing husband was one of the many at the Front.

The following week, cycling back along the Boul' Mich from the hospital, Simone encountered Suzanne Drouot. It was several weeks since they had last met, perhaps even months. The boulevard was looking glorious with the trees in their riotous autumn colours in the cold watery sunlight. Simone was well bundled in an ancient duffle coat which made it difficult to steer the bicycle, but as she recognized Suzanne she pulled over to the kerbside.

'You look stunning!' She examined Suzanne with a jaundiced eye. She was wearing a smart cream and black tweed coat and a little black pillbox hat with a veil that gave her a coquettish air. Since war had been declared it was not done to appear too well dressed. Even the most fashion-conscious of Parisien grande-dames were conscious of the new trend and tried to 'dress down'. And yet here was Suzanne looking as though she had stepped straight out of Chanel's salon! Simone's first thought was to wonder where she had found the money. 'How is Christian?' she asked casually.

'Ah, Simone, he's doing so well! He's got a job now, did you hear?'

'You mean to say he's dropped out of university? Without even getting his degree?'

'Some things are more important.' Suzanne's dark eyes flicked away. 'He's working for a government supplier now.'

Unlike Lucien and Gervais, Christian had somehow contrived to escape military service.

50

'A government job? That must pay well,' Simone said carefully, aware with sudden resentment that she really meant safe.

Suzanne raised a hand and pushed a stray hair back into place. She was wearing a pair of gold stud earrings Simone had never seen before.

'Have you heard from Lucien?'

'No, not for some time. The mail is slow.'

'I can't understand why he didn't ask his father to find him something. His family own some kind of transport company, don't they? They must have government contracts.'

Simone shifted uncomfortably astride her bicycle.

'You know Lucien doesn't have much to do with his family.'

'But I would have thought in the circumstances –'

'I'm sorry, Suzanne, I'm a bit short of time just now. Perhaps you'll come round for a chat one evening?'

'Oh yes, I'd like that.' Under the carefully applied make-up her face brightened. Suddenly she appeared much younger than her twenty-seven years. 'I'm often on my own these days. Christian's work takes him away, you see.'

Simone felt almost sorry for her. Christian's little forays were nothing new; only the excuse was original. It seemed that the war had a lot to answer for.

'So we're all on our own. You heard that Dieter is interned?'

'Yes, Christian told me. How is Diane taking it?'

'She's under a lot of strain.'

'What a situation to get into. She should have taken your advice and dropped him long ago. That's what I would have done.'

Simone struggled to control her sharp tongue. After years of contending with Christian's bad behaviour, she wondered that Suzanne had not more understanding. She found it hard to believe even she could be so insensitive.

She quickly made her excuses and pedalled back to the Rue de Rennes fuming with righteous indignation. It troubled and alarmed her to think how much all of them had changed in the past year. Last September they had been so optimistic, so relieved in the aftermath of the Munich agreement. There had been so much hope for the future. They were all young, with the world their onion. But now – Lucien and Gervais were soldiers at the Front, Christian had sold his soul for a safe government post, while she and Diane – so much had changed! Who would have believed last September that within a year Diane would be married to a German and having to bear his child alone while he rotted in an internment camp?

As she drew into the shelter of the courtyard at number 55 she wondered sourly what other tricks Fate had in store for them.

France had been at war for almost three months. The men manning the Maginot Line's underground fortresses and away in the Zone des Armées, the border areas with Germany, were hoping for Christmas leave. In his infrequent letters Lucien spoke more of boredom than of danger. The expectation of air raids and gas attacks had long since given way to a sense of anti-climax, of complacency. *La Drôle de Guerre*, they were calling it. Even in England, Diane's mother reported, they had a name for it: the Phoney War.

Winter came early and proved the hardest of the century. With the cuts in electricity they noticed the cold more keenly. There was a shortage of fuel everywhere and Simone and Diane tried to conserve whatever they could get hold of to keep their little stove working. Food, too, was in short supply. Simone would fawn and bargain with the butcher and grocer to secure something extra for Diane. She was anxious about her friend's health and conscious of the needs of the baby.

'You must eat,' she urged Diane. 'You must think of the baby.'

It was hard to keep her spirits up. As the weather grew worse Diane thought constantly about Dieter and what he must be suffering. Wherever he was, the cold must be to him a deadly enemy. She longed for another message from him, just to let her know he was still in France at least. She would have given anything to know he was all right.

One night in the new year Diane awoke to the unearthly glow of snowlight in her room. The roofs opposite were frosted blue-white with a fresh fall and the early traffic was dulled in the street. Silver barrage balloons hung limply in a sky the colour of burnished steel. The beauty of the city held her entranced against her will. As dawn broke, the morning clouds were tinged with pink and saffron above the snow-swept landscape.

Paris was entombed for a month in snow and ice. The yard of their apartment block was banked in high drifts and rows of yellowing icicles encrusted the outside pipes and shutters. The streets of the capital turned into a quagmire of ruts and slush, remaining uncleared for weeks as labour was in short supply because all the men were at the Front.

In February Simone returned home to discover an unexpected visitor ensconced with Diane by the stove drinking coffee. Her sharp pang of disappointment soon evaporated as she gave Gervais a quick embrace.

'They gave me a forty-eight-hour pass,' he explained. 'I've been to see my mother, and now I

53

thought I'd drop by to see how you two are managing.'

It was strange to see Gervais in his uniform as a common *poilu*. His unruly mop of hair had been ruthlessly cropped back, exposing his boyish face and large ears. He looked well, but different, as though the experience had somehow tamed him. He sat and talked about his life at the Front, the tedium, the daily round of senseless tasks, almost wistfully. He seemed oddly out of place in the confines of the apartment.

They played a hand of *belote* and drank the wine he had brought as hailstones rattled the windows. They assiduously avoided all discussion of missing friends. Only when it was time for him to leave to catch his train did he pause and take Diane by the hand, blinking at her with his dull blue eyes full of concern.

'Are you worried about the birth?'

She gave him a cautious smile. 'A little.'

'You're lucky to have Simone with you. I know everything will be all right.' He gave her hand a gentle squeeze.

Simone accompanied him to the station across the city. The glass dome of the Gare de l'Est echoed to the vibration of conversation, slamming doors and the shunting of steam trains. Simone sat with Gervais in the brasserie under the painted stare of the generation of 1914 setting out to 'the war to end all wars'.

'I'm sorry, Simone, I'm sorry it wasn't Lucien who got leave.'

'Don't be foolish.' Simone was embarrassed in spite of herself for she had been thinking exactly that.

She walked to the train with him among all the entwined couples and tearful farewells. As he heaved his kitbag aboard and the shrill whistle signalled departure, she reached out and dropped a chaste kiss

54

on his cold cheek. She saw a flash of surprise in his eyes and, curiously, something more she could not read. Then he was lost in the billowing steam and the slow train grunted its way down the track and out of the yawning mouth of the station.

Spring brought a slow thaw at last. The chestnut trees were already a delicate haze of pink and white blooms before the streets were entirely clear of the sallow remains of the snow. There were new regulations controlling food rationing. Cafés and restaurants were now permitted to serve only two courses, only one of which could contain meat. Pâtisseries were closed three days a week, and there were entirely 'dry' days when alcohol was supposedly unavailable.

Simone accompanied Diane to the Mairie to collect their ration cards. Diane had registered in the autumn using her student identification card from the Sorbonne and judiciously dropping the 's' from her name, becoming Diane Clément. As she moved down the line of waiting women she was very conscious of her rounded stomach under her smock. The male clerk peered at her over his spectacles and began to fill in her new card in a slow deliberate hand. When he came to the section on 'status' his pen poised in mid-air and he looked across at her conspiratorially.

'Marriage lines?'

Diane hesitated. She knew they had decided it was out of the question to show her marriage certificate. There was too great a danger that the police would be informed and she might risk internment herself as the wife of an 'enemy alien'. But as she stood among the curious, attentive crush of women and clerks, she felt a rising tide of humiliation.

'No.'

'I'm sorry?' The clerk was clearly enjoying himself at her expense.

'I said no.'

'*Bien*. "Father unknown",' he said aloud as he wrote out her card. There was an answering titter of amusement in the crowd behind them.

Simone glared around at the queue furiously. 'Just remember,' she snapped at the clerk, 'to give her the extra ration.' She tapped threateningly at that part of the form which entitled expectant mothers to an additional allowance. She watched closely as he completed the formalities and then snatched up their cards. 'Come on, chérie,' she announced, 'let's get out of here.'

Outside in the street Diane gripped her arm and laughed.

'Oh Simone, the look on their faces! For a moment I really thought –' She stopped abruptly in mid-sentence and suddenly doubled over.

'Diane! What is it?'

Diane shook her head, her face white with acute pain.

'The baby?' cried Simone. 'No, it can't be! Not so soon!' she looked around in consternation. 'Oh God, I have to get you to the hospital.'

Diane clung to her arm. 'No, no, not hospital. It's going away now –'

'But, Diane, if you've started –'

'It's probably just a false alarm. Please Simone, let's go home.'

Simone looked doubtful but Diane was insistent, and it was true that it was two or three weeks earlier than either of them had expected. But by the time they had reached the Rue de Rennes at Diane's cautious pace, the pains had come again.

Simone sat her down on the bottom flight of the staircase and started to panic as Diane's face contorted with strain and she gasped for breath.

'I'll fetch a taxi.'

'No, Simone, don't leave me!'

Madame Laclos, hearing the noise outside the *loge*, came running out and threw up her hands in horror at the sight that met her eyes.

'*Mon Dieu, mon Dieu!* What are we to do? She can't have the child here!'

'We have to try and get her to hospital –'

'No, no,' Diane argued, her head shaking vigorously, her hair damp with effort. 'I'd rather have the baby here than in the back of a taxi.' She gripped Simone's arm, her face drained of colour. 'Help me get up to the flat while I can.' She stood up, steadying herself with one hand held in the small of her back. 'Thank God you're here with me, Simone. At least you know what to do!'

Over her head Simone exchanged a look with the appalled concierge. Somehow it did not seem quite the time to mention that she had dropped out of last year's Obstetrics class. As they struggled up the stairs together she was trying to recollect whether she still had the relevant textbook or had lent it to one of the other students.

Before they had reached the second floor landing Diane felt the next pain creep around from her back and she stopped, gripping the handrail of the staircase.

Less than ten minutes now, perhaps even five, thought Simone, trying to keep calm.

'Can you go ahead?' she asked Madame Laclos, handing her the key of the apartment. 'We'll need some towels –'

'And hot water.' The concierge looked positively eager. She scampered up the stairs ahead of them as

Simone watched Diane and summoned up her best professional smile of reassurance.

'You're doing fine, just fine. Try and relax.'

'Relax?' gasped her patient. 'You must be joking!'

By the time they finally reached the apartment Madame Laclos had the bed ready for her. Simone helped her remove her coat and shoes and slip into a clean nightdress.

Diane looked up at her friend, suddenly uneasy. 'Is it all going to be all right?'

'Of course it is. You'll have your baby safe in your arms before very long. Come and get into bed.'

'No, I can't – here it comes again.'

The contractions were coming at four minutes now. It looked very much as though Diane would have the baby, with or without Simone's 'expertise', before the afternoon.

'Be a brave girl,' she said brightly, wrapping a shawl around Diane's shoulders as the waves of pain receded. She hugged her, then looking at the concierge said quickly, 'Madame, would you stay with her a moment? I'll be right back,' she reassured Diane.

In the living room she quickly consulted her text-books, gnawing her nails and scanned through the relevant pages. It could not be too complicated a procedure, surely. After all, it was all perfectly natural, wasn't it? Women all over the world were having babies every day –

'Simone!'

She came rushing back, wiping her damp hands on a towel.

'Simone, it's coming! It's coming!'

Madame Laclos stood at the foot of the bed in her morbid black dress muttering, '*Mon Dieu, mon Dieu!*' and crossing herself. Simone looked at her in exasperation and concentrated on Diane.

'Now calm down,' she bluffed, taking charge, 'you have to keep calm. Take big breaths. Yes, that's it.' She glared at the concierge. 'The hot water, Madame, have you got the hot water?' After Madame Laclos fluttered off to the kitchen, Diane began to moan again, squeezing her hand. Simone mopped her forehead as she strained and pushed down, pressing back against the pile of pillows at the head of the bed. 'That's it, that's terrific, Diane.' She felt her fingernails digging into her hand. Diane looked exhausted already, her hair sticking to her red and sweating face.

Then, all at once, the water broke and, laughing with relief, Simone cried, 'One big push now, chérie, here comes the darling little head –'

'Oh Simone!'

'Yes, the head is through! Right, now stop pushing –'

'I can't!'

'Yes, just keep saying that.'

'I can't, I can't –'

Simone suddenly received the slippery child out into her arms. 'It's a girl! It's a girl, Diane!'

'Is she all right?' whispered Diane, tears on her cheeks.

'Just wonderful.'

'Oh, Diane!' exclaimed Madame Laclos. 'You have a beautiful daughter, *quelle petite*!'

An indignant, healthy wail of outrage came from the new arrival. Triumphant and almost bursting with pride, Simone presented the red-faced squealing bundle into her mother's eager arms. She and Madame Laclos exchanged self-satisfied smiles of congratulation as though this miracle was all entirely their work.

Diane cradled her baby in the fold of her arm. She was perfect, she was beautiful! She wriggled in her

59

large white towel and her tiny eyes opened and stared, unfocused, up at her. Diane felt an overwhelming surge of joy and recognition.

'What will you call her?' asked Simone in awe.

Diane could not draw her eyes away from her daughter's.

'Michelle, I'll call her Michelle,' she whispered breathlessly. Her baby, hers and Dieter's! She clasped her protectively to her breast. She was theirs! She was all she had left of Dieter.

6

In early May, just as the chestnut flowers were beginning to wilt and drop, the German Army made a three-front attack on Holland, Belgium and France. The event so long anticipated, the day they had thought would never really come. After eight months of *La Drôle de Guerre* the officers of the General Staff put away their white gloves and swagger sticks and prepared to face the reality of war. For years they had made studies of the defeats and victories of the war of 1914–18 when France had lost a million and a half men. The huge defensive underground wall called the Maginot Line had been the result. But on 13 May the German Panzers came to the River Meuse and the town of Sedan, and suddenly all their confidence in the infallibility of the Maginot Line crumbled. Sedan was an ominous name in French history, the town which had witnessed the great Prussian victory which led to the fall of Paris in 1870.

After the first numb shock the citizens of Paris reacted strongly to the invasion. The news of the bombing of Rotterdam reached them on the evening of 14 May. The city centre had been destroyed by wave after wave of German bombers. There were said to be a thousand dead. With such an example before them, it was hardly surprising that once again all roads south were soon thronged with a tide of desperate, terrified refugees ready to abandon their homes for the chance of safety beyond the reach of the invader.

The German breakthrough at Sedan had outflanked the defences of the Maginot Line. With almost unimaginable speed their tanks thrust towards the Channel, cutting off a vast pocket of French and British Expeditionary troops. Rumours were rife. The Belgians had surrendered, the French were on the run.

Simone took a coffee in the Café des Trois Mousquetaires on her way back to the apartment. As usual, the radio behind the bar was half-drowned by the constant clamour of conversation, barked orders and clattering cups and saucers. Simone irritably requested the patron to turn up the volume so that she could hear the news. She had been desperate for information ever since she realized Lucien was caught by the German pincer manoeuvre north of the Seine. She drained her *café-filtre*, waiting impatiently. Her eyes took in the blank blackboard on which the day's menu was usually chalked up, the empty counter normally stacked with fresh ham and cheese, pâté and quiche. In the past few days food had simply disappeared from shops and cafés; even milk was now a thing of the past.

On the hour the radio news bulletin came through with its usual bombastic fanfare, the announcer smoothly treading through disaster after disaster with deceptive optimism. The patron exchanged a jaundiced look with Simone as the bulletin finished, to be replaced by Maurice Chevalier singing 'Paris Reste Paris'.

Simone began to believe the real situation was even worse than they could imagine. The radio said one thing, the newspapers another. She had had no word from Lucien for weeks. Perhaps the refugees streaming through Paris from the battlegrounds were right: perhaps their army had collapsed, their officers hastening to save themselves, abandoning their men to the advancing tanks and the screaming Stukas.

She looked at the clutter of strange vehicles pouring over the Seine bridges and choking the great boulevards to the southern 'gates' of the city. Weary, filthy, stern-faced men and women inched their way forward in the fierce heat. There were cars and trucks and tumbril-like handcarts piled high with chairs, iron baths, bundles of bedding, even poultry. Simone watched the solemn procession with a sense of foreboding. Today her class had been half empty. Even her friends were giving up, getting out while there was still time. She heard Christian and Suzanne had left days ago.

Would she go? Would Diane and the baby? Perhaps there was still time to get them out of the country, to get to England. Though if the rumours from Dunkerque were to be believed, the Germans were already in control of the Channel ports.

At the apartment she discovered Diane changing Michelle on the bed. The baby kicked contentedly, unaware of the mounting crisis that threatened them all.

'I can't leave Paris whatever happens,' Diane said solemnly. 'Dieter would never know where to find us.'

'That's a point to consider. It's the only place where we can be reached.'

'I can't believe Paris could be in danger. The whole world has gone crazy.'

But on 4 June German planes bombed the northern industrial districts of Paris. A curfew was imposed. The government came to the momentous decision to abandon the capital and declare it an 'open city' to avoid the fate that befell Rotterdam. People stood on street corners listening to the radio announcement, tears of shame and anger in their eyes. Paris was being surrendered without even a fight. This was the end. Within days the Germans would enter Paris.

The ministers fled to Tours leaving the city in the throes of hysteria. The exodus of refugees continued relentlessly, until it seemed that no one would be left. Suddenly the streets of abandoned Paris were as deserted and bleak as the wings of a theatre in daylight. Incongruously, the weather continued gloriously hot and brilliantly untroubled. News came that the government had fallen back further south, to Bordeaux, which had been France's fallback capital during the Prussian occupation of Paris in 1871. The last remnants of the open city huddled behind closed shutters listening to the low rumble of artillery in the distance. How could the days dawn so full of promise when the whole world was falling to pieces?

The end when it came was peaceful enough. Most Parisians were still asleep as the first motorbike side-cars of Von Kuechler's 18th Army scouted the wide, calm boulevards at 5.30 in the morning of 14 June. It was barely five weeks since the invasion.

The unnatural silence of this new Paris was suddenly shattered mid-morning as the Germans marched in as conquerors. By noon Radio Paris was playing Wagner and already broadcasting in German. A flurry of garish scarlet and black swastikas appeared like a rash on public buildings and monuments from the Arc de Triomphe to the Tour Eiffel.

The curious ventured out of doors to view their new masters. The sight of the smartly turned-out German troops swaggering confidently down the length of the Champs-Elysées became one of the fixed daily routines of the new régime. The clash of cymbals, the throbbing drums and a chorus of 'Wir Fahren gegen England' won some admirers. Faced with a fait accompli there seemed nothing else to do except make the best of things. Within days everything in the stores disappeared as a grey plague of locusts stripped Paris bare. Wehrmacht lorries bore away booty from Les Halles to trains bound for Germany, the first of many. The invader paid generously in new Occupation Marks, but the euphoria and greed of the storekeepers soon turned to fury when they realized this paper money was just that, worthless paper.

By 21 June the worst was over. Eighty-four-year old Marshal Pétain had stepped into the breach to end the 'useless fighting' and bring about 'peace with honour'. On the morning of the 24th the people of France gathered around their radios to hear the Marshal's speech to the nation.

'I make to France the gift of my person,' he began. 'In these painful hours I think of the poor, destitute refugees walking along our roads. I offer them my compassion and my solicitude. It is with a heavy heart that I tell you today: we must stop fighting. Last night I approached the adversary to ask if he were willing to seek with me, soldier to soldier, after the battle and in good faith, a means of ending the hostilities.'

'Thank God, it's all over,' Simone commented in the stunned silence that followed. 'Now perhaps Dieter and Lucien will come home.'

But a further shock was in store for Diane. As part of the conditions of the Armistice, France had agreed to German demands for the extradition of refugees. All internees of German origin were to be returned to the Reich.

This news was brought to the Rue de Rennes one day early in July by an unexpected visitor. Marisa Gonzales was a small woman with a thin harassed face and sleek, neat black hair cut in a short bob. She stood nervously on the doorstep looking over her shoulder, her dark eyes red-rimmed from sleepless nights.

'I have a message from your husband,' she explained, taking a seat in the living room with the two astonished women. Her French was rapid and almost without an accent. Only her olive skin and exotic colouring gave any hint of her Spanish origins. 'My husband Julio is in the same camp as your husband. They have been together since September.'

Diane could barely control her excitement. 'Where?' she demanded.

'In Brittany. But that doesn't matter now.'

'No? Why not? I don't understand.' Diane looked anxiously across at Simone standing by the stove.

'Because they are moving them back to Paris.' She caught the immediate gleam of hope in Diane's eyes. 'No, not to release them.' She hesitated, and they could hear the terrible strain in her voice as she continued in a low whisper, 'The Nazis are shipping wanted men back to Germany.'

Diane sank back in her chair. Her hands were visibly shaking, but her voice was controlled as she said quietly, 'When?'

'I don't know,' confessed Marisa Gonzales. 'I only got word last night. I would have come straight here except for the curfew.'

'You're very kind,' Simone said quickly.

At that moment Michelle let out a plaintive wail from the bedroom. Diane leapt to her feet and hurried in to pick up the baby.

'Ah, you have children.' There was a look in the Spanish woman's eyes of infinite pity.

'Just one. We were only married a short while before –' Her voice trailed off. 'Dieter has never seen his daughter.'

As though upset, the visitor got to her feet. 'I must go now. I am sorry I had to be the bearer of such news.'

Diane stood in the middle of the room cradling Michelle. Simone took it upon herself to walk Marisa down to the front door.

'We want to thank you for coming.'

'*De nada.*'

'Do you know where they are being held? Or where they are leaving from?'

Marisa shook her head. 'There's nothing you can do. There's nothing anyone can do for them.'

'But you do know?'

'I heard – they said it was at Pantin, the railyards at Pantin. But it's useless to go there. You will never find him. There are too many.'

'We can try,' said Simone bleakly, watching the woman walk quickly down the street. 'We have to try.'

Pantin freight yard lay across the city on the north-eastern approaches, the nearest point of departure for Germany. Simone and Diane arrived there in the early afternoon, having left Michelle in the care of Madame Laclos until her next feed was due.

The railyards were a cauldron of noise and steam as lines of rusting cattle cars snaked their way down the junction, shifting and clanging together as they jostled for position. Where do we start? Simone wondered, moving anxiously along the track, aware of the enormity of their task. Each iron train was composed only of windowless freight wagons. There was not a passenger car to be seen.

'I don't understand it,' Diane was saying. 'Are you sure we're in the right place? If these are the trains, then where are all the prisoners?'

Behind them, one of the heavy locomotives suddenly started to move. It hissed and snorted dramatically, engulfing both women in clouds of filthy black smoke as its pistons churned past. In the clamour of sound and steam, Simone and Diane stood in awe watching the seemingly endless succession of trucks pick up speed.

At last the train cleared the track and in the abrupt stillness, Diane turned to her friend in horror.

'You don't think they put them in —'

'In the wagons? No, how could –' But she stopped short as the truth hit her with all its force.

'It must be true!' cried Diane desperately, her voice breaking. 'Where else could they be? Look, don't you see the doors are padlocked? My God, don't you see!'

Simone stared at the lines of iron cattle trucks and it was as if a veil had been lifted from her eyes. She suddenly saw the heavy bolts, the chains and padlocks securing the doors. She heard the soft moan of human, living creatures from inside. She smelt their presence, felt their desperation and misery in her very soul.

I think I'm going to be sick, she thought, but this was neither the time nor the place for weakness. She saw Diane's fierce determination with growing admiration and struggled to control her own feelings of pity and revulsion.

They stumbled blindly down the length of the train under the glare of the sun. Every wagon was sealed. A faint moaning came through the burning metal sides of the cattle cars. Down near the engine, panting on the track, impatient to be off, they saw their first German troops. They were standing nonchalantly smoking in conversation with the stoker. The Frenchman was mopping his face with a rag, his greasy skin gleaming in the heat. He turned round all at once and became aware of the two women watching him. His eyes were white and wide with warning in his sooty face. Although he kept talking to the enemy soldiers, he made a quick sign for the women to be careful.

Simone and Diane withdrew several yards and waited. They saw the Germans climb aboard the engine and the *cheminot* began to walk calmly down the track.

'What are you two doing here?' he hissed sharply. 'Don't you realize this is a restricted area?'

'We heard there were prisoners here, detainees,' Diane said quickly.

'You can't stay here,' the *cheminot* insisted, glancing desperately over his shoulder. 'There are *Boche* everywhere.'

'I have to know,' cried Diane, laying an arm on the grimy sleeve of his *bleu de travail*.

'They're all foreigners, all Germans,' the stoker said defensively.

'One of them is my husband.'

He looked from Diane to Simone, sweat running in long white furrows down his black face.

'They're sending them back to Germany,' he admitted. 'It's got nothing to do with us.'

'They're sending them back to die,' Simone insisted.

'You must help me, M'sieur. I have to know,' Diane begged him, her voice wavering. 'My husband has come from a camp somewhere in Brittany. Do you know if anyone from Brittany has gone yet?'

The *cheminot*'s eyes filled with sudden pity. He shifted uncomfortably from one foot to another and then turned abruptly towards Simone. In a gruff, guilt-ridden voice he told her, 'Take your friend home, Madame. It's useless her waiting. The men from Brittany – they were here last night. They left on the first transport out this morning.'

7

The perfect July weather only seemed to mock Diane's grief. Simone watched her friend with a growing sense of helplessness and despair as Diane sank further and further into depression. The bitter hours she had suffered seemed to have destroyed all her natural optimism and vitality. She took no trouble over her clothes or her appearance and she scarcely ever left the house these days. All her time was centred around the needs of her child.

'Diane, you can't go on like this. It's helping no one. Dieter wouldn't want you to grieve for him like this.'

Diane looked up sharply, her dark eyes threatening further tears. 'I know I shall never see him again.'

'No!' cried Simone, going over to clasp her firmly in her arms. 'You have to believe he will come back. You told me how many times they had sent him away. But he always came back.'

Diane shook her head blindly. 'This time it's different.'

Simone held her, at a loss for words to comfort her, so strong seemed her belief. But there was still a chance, surely, that Dieter had survived, that he still lived in a camp somewhere in Germany.

'I shall never see him again,' Diane repeated with chilling conviction.

'But you have his baby. You will always have Michelle.'

Little Michelle had never seen her father. Diane often wished that she had a photograph of Dieter that she could show her one day. It did not seem right that Michelle should grow up never knowing him. Diane felt so inadequate. She felt that the child was being deprived, having such a mother.

Sometimes, at night, she allowed herself to think of Dieter. She sat in her room as Michelle slept and tried to conjure up the memory of his face, the sound of his heavily accented French. She was quite distracted when she could not remember exactly the shape and expression of his mouth, or the irony of his smile. She would sit there in the darkness suddenly terrified that she had lost him, that even her precious memories were slipping away and lost for ever.

Michelle was Dieter's child, the child he had wanted so much. She had her father's fairness, her father's eyes. Standing over the baby's cot watching her as she slept so peacefully, she tried to relive those few months of perfect happiness, to remember their talks, their walks and their laughter, even to torture herself with the vivid memory of his touch.

The sky in the east was thin and blue as the stars clung to the last receding reaches of the night. She stood a long time watching as her daughter stirred and began to play with her toes. Simone was right. She owed it to Michelle to try and pull herself together. She owed it to her to try harder, to try and be a better mother. Dieter had been cruelly taken from her, but she would always have Michelle. She was Dieter's future.

The next morning she was looking better, clear-eyed, with more colour in her cheeks. She had also made an effort with her dress and her hair was washed and neatly brushed.

'Simone, I've been thinking about the future – our future – and for Michelle's sake, I have to get some work, make some money.' When she had Simone's firm attention, she continued seriously, 'I'm twenty-one. I've no real qualifications, no profession. More

72

importantly, I have no work permit. All I have is my student's card for the Sorbonne, and I can't afford to study any longer. Anyway, what use is Art? I wish I had been sensible, like you, and taken a more practical subject.'

She had always envied Simone's vocation and the single-minded way she set out to make a career for herself. Diane, on the other hand, had been frivolous, taking each day as it came, toying with sketching and an interest in painting that held no prospect at all of future remuneration. She was only twenty-one; the rest of her life was before her. She owed it to Michelle to make a secure home, to give her a decent chance even though she did not have a father. The little money she had saved from the allowance given her by her parents had almost run out, and the war had cut her off from further funds. She had heard nothing from her family since that first letter at the outbreak of war, and although she had written with the news that they were now grandparents, she could not be certain that it had ever arrived. Now she had the rent to find, and food and clothes were becoming increasingly expensive and difficult to find. She knew she had to come up with a scheme to make money, and quickly.

That afternoon she took Michelle to the Luxembourg for the first time in days. They met Simone on her way back from the Ecole de Médecine on the last afternoon of the term and walked home together. In the yard of the Rue de Rennes they were stopped by Madame Laclos who asked Diane if she had any news of her husband.

Simone, thinking quickly, answered for her. 'No news, not yet, Madame.'

'Such a tragedy!' declared the eager concierge. 'So many young men. They say *les Boches* are putting them into camps in Germany.'

73

'Yes, so I've heard. We must hope for the best, Madame.'

Madame Laclos looked Diane over and sadly shook her head.

'I will pray for you and the child, *ma petite*,' she pledged grimly, and scuttled back to her *loge*.

Diane met Simone's eyes. Hearing her lie for her when she had heard nothing from Lucien and must have her own worries, Diane felt grief and gratitude well once more to the surface.

They both lived through that summer in close isolation. Simone was facing her final examinations that autumn and spent her time reading and revising. Although she was highly motivated, there was still in the back of her mind the nagging fear that the new authorities might not permit her to practise, however well she did.

Diane was pleased to help with the mountain of revision, plying her with questions on symptoms and treatment, feeling that she was repaying in a small way her friend's kindness and support.

They were both young, with their whole future ahead of them, but now suddenly they felt their lives were slipping wildly out of control. Everything they had hoped for, longed for, was threatened. In two brief years they had both grown up, perhaps too much. Would they ever find that old spirit of eager anticipation and heady, youthful optimism when the whole world seemed to be at their feet? Or had that hope gone for ever, their lives to be mapped out for them, their youth wasted, sacrificed to the cruel caprice of the times?

It was the so-called 'honeymoon' period between the occupied and their German occupiers. An uneasy calm reigned in the streets of Paris. The crowded sidewalk cafés on the Champs-Elysées were frequented by Parisiens and German troops alike, giving an illusion of peace, but it was a frail truce. In August a Wehrmacht military post in the Bois de Boulogne was blown up. In retaliation the German authorities closed the Bois to the people of Paris. The bombing was said to have been carried out by a group of student *résistants*, either hot-heads or patriots depending on your own particular viewpoint. But either way it was proof that there were people who were willing to fight back.

Diane found the Sorbonne alive with rumours. A secret organization was said to exist among certain students and members of the staff. The attack on the military post was just the beginning.

Diane had gone to the university to put up a notice advertising her willingness to type students' theses and dissertations. It was Simone's idea, a way that Diane could make some money and still be at home with Michelle most of the time. She got hold of an ancient typewriter from a friend and Diane had been busy trying to revive her old skills in a new language. She had great hopes that the scheme would provide the solution to her problems.

She was just walking back through the precincts when she almost collided with a young man going in the opposite direction. In astonishment Diane recognized Gervais Rousseau.

'Gervais!'

'Diane!' His pale blue eyes blinked foolishly back at her and he looked genuinely delighted. He was wearing an open-necked shirt and an old pair of faded slacks, quite a contrast from the last time she had seen him.

He clearly saw a difference in her, too. He asked about the baby and wanted to know everything about her. He was very solicitous and kind, and never once referred to Dieter. Diane thought it was most sensitive of him.

She wanted to know about the Front and listened avidly as he outlined the rout that had broken the unit, scattering half their men behind enemy lines and leaving the rest to fend for themselves. He had managed to slip away undetected, but many of his comrades were taken as prisoners straight away. Gervais had stripped off his uniform and headed for Paris across country, avoiding the main roads.

'And Lucien? Did he make it back?'

'There's been no news, none at all.'

'Poor Simone. But it's early days yet.'

Diane had a bright idea. 'Gervais, you must come to dinner! Yes, please come. We would both love it and you would have the chance to see Michelle.'

He gave her a quick, uncertain smile. 'Well, if you're sure?'

'Of course!'

'Then I'd love to come, yes, sure.'

He arrived at the Rue de Rennes with a contribution towards the meal. There was wine, some macaroni and a loaf of bread. These days such gifts were gratefully received. The evening made a pleasant break for both women. Not since his last visit had they had a man to supper at the flat.

Gervais enjoyed playing with the baby until it was time for her to go back to bed. He was surprisingly good with her, crawling on the floor and making her gurgle in delight.

Simone insisted that Diane show him some of the little sketches she had done of Michelle. They were just pencil drawings, but Gervais' eager reaction echoed Simone's own opinion that they were surprisingly good.

'You ought to sell them,' he suggested. 'You could show them at the university. They would soon be snapped up.'

Diane was secretly pleased. It was not such a bad idea if it would bring her a little extra money.

'Where are you staying?' Simone asked Gervais as he prepared to leave before the curfew hour.

'Not in the old place. I wasn't sure it would be safe. No, I'm staying at my mother's. She's been sick, you see.'

'I didn't know about his mother,' said Simone after he had gone. 'It's surprising how little we really know about him.'

'He seems so lonely,' Diane commented. 'I can't help feeling sorry for him.'

Simone's examinations coincided with a marked turnaround in the attitude of the German authorities. In a series of midnight arrests many leading figures among city councillors, deputies and trade unionists were seized and taken to the prisons of Mont Valérien, Fresnes and La Santé: names that would soon become ominously familiar. The summer idyll was over.

At the university an underground leaflet was circulated attacking Pétain and the Vichy partition of the country. Diane obtained a copy and brought it home in the thesis she was typing on Miró. Within days the leaflet was followed by a secret student newspaper called *Université Libre*. The paper warned of plans by the Germans to ban women students from the university. Simone was suitably outraged. These days she was living on her nerves, waiting for news of Lucien and for the results of her examinations.

On 30 October Professor Langevin, said to be a leading member of the resistance group, was arrested in his laboratory. There were spontaneous protests against his arrest and messages began to appear throughout the university calling for staff and students to demonstrate for the release of all those who had been arrested.

'11 November — All to the Etoile!' read the chalked notices. It would be the first mass demonstration against the new régime and no one knew how the Nazis would react. Simone and Gervais announced their intention of going, but assumed that Diane would not.

'Because of Michelle,' Simone explained.

'It could be dangerous,' warned Gervais.

But Diane waved aside their objections and was determined to go with them. She said she would ask Madame Laclos to look after Michelle.

The day had been deliberately chosen because 11 November was Armistice Day, marking the anniversary of the end of the last war. In France this had always been a special day, la Fête de la Victoire, but for Germany it was a day of shame and bitter humiliation. At five in the evening by the clocks now set on German time, crowds of students and young schoolchildren began to gather on the Champs-Elysées from all over Paris and the suburbs. There was a wonderful atmosphere, as though for a carnival, complete with tricolour flags and badges bearing the immortal words Liberté, Egalité, Fraternité. Some children even carried flowers in red, white and blue.

The demonstration set off from the Etoile singing the Marseillaise. The Champs which had been designed by Le Nôtre as magnificent gardens, where fashionable ladies in the time of Empire had paraded in their carriages, was now the daily focus of Nazi arrogance and the bombastic strains of a brass band playing 'Pruessens Glorie'. Now the great avenue rang with the full-throated fervour of the French

National Anthem, reclaimed from the Pétainist collaborators for one afternoon.

The parade was watched from the sidelines by small groups of nervous bystanders. The cheerful demonstrators eagerly urged them to join in, but there were others among these spectators who had other ideas. Before the head of the march had reached the Rond-Point halfway down the avenue there were catcalls and shouts of abuse from groups of jeering youths.

'Take no notice,' one of the stewards of the march told the demonstrators. 'It's just a provocation from the Croix de Feu or Jeunesses Patriotes. Keep calm.'

But further along the procession scuffles had already broken out. Children were screaming and the crowd scattered as punches were thrown and one of the pro-Nazi supporters fell back on to the cobbles, bleeding from a split lip.

Diane and Simone were caught up in the crush of demonstrators moving away from the fighting. Suddenly they were cut off from the mass of marchers and realized that Gervais had vanished. From behind them there came the shrill alarm of a police whistle and a hoarse warning, '*Les Boches! Les Boches!*'

Out of the Avenue Montaigne came the slow grinding roar of the grey-green armoured cars of a Wehrmacht detachment bearing down on the demonstrators. The Germans had been waiting within call.

As the marchers turned and ran, a line of steel-helmeted German troops began to spread out across the width of the Champs-Elysées, their rifles raised. There was a sharp crack in the air over the heads of the crowd, followed by a whole series of shots in quick succession.

'They've opened fire!' someone cried, but the warning was cut short by the screaming of terror-stricken children on all sides.

'Come on, let's get out of here!' gasped Simone. She had seized Diane by the arm and was trying to manoeuvre a path through the shrieking panicking demonstrators surrounding them.

A man crashed sideways into them, blood streaming from a flesh wound on his forehead. Somewhere ahead of them a hand grenade exploded among the crush of students and schoolchildren. Suddenly there were dead and wounded lying huddled on the ground and the moan of the injured among the trampling feet.

'Oh God,' sobbed Diane, faltering in her tracks.

I ought to stop, I ought to help, thought Simone desperately, seeing the carnage. But the frantic, thrusting crowd had caught them up, forcing them away from the avenue in a stampede of kicking and pushing.

On the edge of the Place de la Concorde, where Madame Guillotine had claimed her victims, the demonstrators scattered in all directions, running for their lives. Diane had fallen, ripping her stockings and taking the skin off her knee. Blood was slowly seeping down her leg as Simone dragged her to her feet and pulled her along, making for the bridge over the Seine. Behind them they could hear more shots.

'We have to get right away,' Simone was saying urgently. 'They're already arresting people.'

The streets to the south of the river were quieter, but the distant wail of police sirens seemed to follow them. Diane had difficulty in walking, but Simone helped her along as best as she could, hoping they would not draw too much attention to themselves. They cut down the length of the Boulevard St Germain, avoiding the German headquarters at the Hôtel Lutétia on the corner of Sevres and Raspail. By the time they reached the safety of the Rue de Rennes and the courtyard of the apartment house, Diane was white-faced and shaking, climbing the stairs to their flat in obvious pain.

'What about Michelle?'

'I'll fetch her in a moment.' Simone made Diane take a seat and she fetched some water to wash and dress her leg. 'It's quite deep,' she declared after examining the wound, 'but I don't think you'll need stitches.' Which was just as well, she thought to herself. The Germans were sure to have the hospitals watched.

After she had finished she went down to collect Michelle from Madame Laclos, happily reuniting mother and daughter and thinking they were lucky to get away so lightly from the afternoon's tragic events.

Michelle eagerly stretched out her hands and tugged at her mother's hair. To Diane's amazement the baby looked up at her and suddenly pronounced her very first word:

'Mama!' she said.

'Simone! Did you hear her? Simone, she said "Mama"!'

But Simone had not heard the remarkable news. She stood engrossed just inside the door, a crumpled envelope in one hand, a letter in the other.

'Simone, what is it?' The first thought in Diane's mind was that something had happened to Lucien.

'It's my results,' whispered Simone, her face suddenly lighting up. 'I've passed! I've passed and they are giving me a post at the Hôtel-Dieu as a registrar for the next two years!'

The day that had threatened so badly had ended well after all.

8

The wave of repression that followed the 11
November demonstration shocked and outraged
Paris. In reprisal, the Germans ordered the closure
of the university for more than a month, but if they
thought this would intimidate the young student
résistants they were much mistaken.

A group calling themselves Organisations Spéciales
carried out a number of daring raids on industrial
targets around the city. At Ivry machinery was sabotaged and oil tanks set on fire. In the railway stockyards supplies and food bound for Germany were
destroyed in mystery fires, and trains derailed. The
résistants were taking tremendous risks. The German
High Command had made it plain that any saboteur
who was caught would face the firing squad at Mont
Valérien.

That winter was even colder than the year before.
As the temperature plummeted, electricity cuts
became more frequent and with serious fuel shortages, Parisiens had to improvise alternative methods
of keeping warm. In the Rue de Rennes Simone and
Diane sacrificed their own comfort for the sake of
Michelle. She was teething and ran an alarming
fever, often crying continuously day and night. Every
evening Diane filled a stone hot-water bottle to heat
her cot, and in the morning it was still warm enough
to use to wash in.

Simone had begun her new work as a junior registrar at the hospital Hôtel-Dieu on the Ile de France
in the centre of the city. She cycled to and fro every
day until the snows came, and then trudged in to

work on foot. But, combined with her heavy schedule, this soon proved too exhausting and she often elected to stay over at the hospital rather than face the trek back home. That winter she was often on call for three or four days continuously and Diane never saw her at all. Then she would suddenly appear at the flat and collapse into bed for the luxury of a continuous eight hours' sleep without interruption while Diane slept in the living room with the baby.

It was on one such occasion early in February, while Simone was catching up on a week's sleep, that Diane got up from her typing to answer the door. To her delight and astonishment she found Lucien waiting outside.

With an uninhibited gesture of joy he pulled her into a bear-like embrace, almost swinging her off her feet. He seemed to take up most of the hallway in his vast greatcoat. They emerged into the living room arm-in-arm, where Diane had been attempting to type by candlelight. On seeing the baby propped up in blankets on the divan, Lucien gave another exclamation and immediately pounced on the child, grinning between his week's growth of dark beard.

'Yours, Diane? What's her name?'

'Michelle.'

'She's a beauty! And not at all afraid of me, you see?'

Indeed, Michelle seemed positively to welcome the stranger's hairy embrace. She was smiling flirtatiously up into his face and making crooning noises as she tried to grab his nose.

'It's your Uncle Luc, *ma petite*! What a clever girl!'

'Diane? What's all the noise?' Simone, in the doorway, was rubbing her red-rimmed eyes when she suddenly looked up and caught sight of Lucien. 'Ah, *mon Dieu!*'

83

Lucien deposited the baby into Diane's waiting arms and took up Simone instead. Diane felt like an intruder as the couple stood swaying together in the middle of the living room with tears on their cheeks. They made an incongruous sight, he in his filthy greatcoat and huge muddy boots, she in her thick tartan dressing gown and the bedsocks she wore for warmth.

When Diane produced a cup of their precious coffee, they all sat down and listened to his story. Diane noticed for the first time how he seemed to have aged and how thin he had grown. The easygoing boyish humour had gone from his eyes, to be replaced by a new wariness, a kind of haunted shadow that seldom left his face.

Their suspicions had been correct. Lucien was among the many thousands of French troops taken prisoner during the rapid German advance that summer. He had been taken to a prisoner-of-war camp, a *Stalag* not far inside the Dutch–German border. Just before Christmas the camp guards had grown careless and Lucien and two companions managed to escape from a work party on a neighbouring farm. One of his friends was shot and wounded, and the other picked up later by a patrol while foraging for food in a small town just inside the French border.

'There were times when I truly thought I would never see you again,' he asserted, reaching out and touching Simone's face.

Diane strategically withdrew to the kitchen to find him something to eat, leaving the two lovers on their own for a chance to talk. She recalled the night Simone had confessed her feelings of doubt over her relationship with Lucien and wondered whether she still felt the same now that he was safely back in her arms.

Lucien became a regular visitor to the flat, even when Simone was away at the hospital. He was living a semi-clandestine existence, much in the same way that Dieter had once lived, avoiding police patrols and having to explain his reappearance from the Front. But this time of enforced leisure soon became a burden to him and he railed constantly against the Occupation and those who had given in to the new régime.

It was not surprising therefore when one day he announced his intention of 'doing something about it'. He had by then heard of the exploits of the Organisations Spéciales and wanted to become part of the growing underground movement that was resisting the Nazis. Although Simone was afraid for him, she was not really shocked by his decision to take this dangerous path. Had he not told her that very first evening of his return that passive resistance was not enough? His experiences at the Front and on the road from the *Stalag* had taught him that. The time had come to fight back.

By the spring Lucien had become involved with a small group operating north of the Seine and came less and less often south of the river. He had found a couple of rooms in the Rue de Londres behind the Gare St Lazare where he was known as the mechanic Jean Chabanais. He had obtained false papers in this name and was actually employed at one of the garages in his father's transport company which was run by a member of the Organisations Spéciales called Antoine Delmas. For this purpose, and perhaps no other, he had become reconciled with his father. The old man, who was ill, was delighted to have his son back in whatever circumstances, and content to go along with his assumed identity in order to keep him safe.

The Caristan Company had been virtually commandeered by the German authorities after the invasion and assigned for Wehrmacht use. Now Caristan lorries were being used to transport German booty to the railyards where trains waited daily to bear it away, home to the Reich. Many of these transports worked day and night, providing excellent cover for saboteurs of the resistance going about their clandestine business. In Lucien's first month of operation three trains bound for Germany had been wrecked when a mysterious fire had broken out in the stockyards at St Denis at three in the morning.

It was inevitable that once Lucien had joined the *résistants*, Simone would also become involved. She sometimes attended meetings of the group at Lucien's flat, telling Diane she was on call at the hospital. Although she hated to lie to her best friend, it was for her own good. She did not want Diane in any way involved, for Michelle's sake.

Simone found a certain resentment against her participation in the group, not from Lucien, who might have been expected to object, or from Gervais, who had also been drawn into the circle, nor from Patrice Lamartine, a junior lecturer at the Sorbonne. It was Antoine the *garagiste*, the oldest amongst them, who voiced his disapproval of a woman in their membership. Fortunately he was outvoted, but Simone felt the need to prove herself worthy of their trust.

Her opportunity came at a meeting one evening at the beginning of April when Lucien announced an operation in liaison with a group working south of the river.

'We have a courier coming over with details. We have to find a secure exchange point. I don't want the garage to be involved.'

'What about the hospital?'

The men turned expectantly in her direction. Only Antoine was looking sceptical.

'I have the perfect cover. The courier can say there is a letter for me, a referal from some other hospital. They could mention the name of a patient. It happens all the time, believe me.'

'But what about passing the papers on?'

'If the contact was made in the morning then I could pass on the papers during my break at lunch-time. We could arrange somewhere close to the hospital. It's very central and there are a dozen places where we could merge with the crowds. Nôtre-Dame, for instance.'

'The Conciergerie –' suggested Lamartine.

'Or Sainte-Chapelle,' added Gervais.

'I don't like it,' declared Antoine sourly. 'It's too important to be left to a woman.'

'It's because I'm a woman that I'll get away with it,' Simone retorted. 'The people in the area know me. They won't see anything suspicious in my movements.'

'She has a point.'

'I want the chance,' Simone pleaded. 'I want to do my share.'

She got her way, but as the day of the mission dawned she found she was extremely nervous. All morning at the hospital she imagined what might go wrong. Perhaps she would not recognize the contact, perhaps she would have an emergency case and could not be found. But the morning proved a slow one, and the hours seemed to drag by. She stood at the window looking out over the twin towers of Nôtre-Dame whose bells had remained silent since the outbreak of war. In the hazy sunshine the Seine sparkled in two long loops around the island and a tug sounded its horn as it pulled its line of barges under the succession of bridges.

'Doctor? There's someone to see you in reception.'

'Thank you, nurse.' Simone tried to sound casual but her heart gave a leap and as she walked down the stairs towards the main entrance she hid her trembling hands in the pockets of her white coat.

She recognized Marisa Gonzales with a start. She was waiting calmly at the reception, the buff envelope in her hands. She was very correct, very businesslike, greeting Simone like a stranger and giving the key phrase – something about a patient called Perrault. Then the envelope was in her hands and Marisa was gone. No smile, no sign of recognition. Very professional behaviour, and yet Simone experienced a feeling of regret. She would have liked to ask Marisa about her husband.

At twelve thirty exactly Simone announced she was taking her lunch break. She left the hospital with the envelope in her handbag and strolled out into the sunshine. The Rue de la Cité was busy and she deliberately took her time wandering along the quai, trying to see if she was being followed. On the corner of the Pont St Michel and the Boulevard du Palais she stopped to buy a copy of the collaborationist newspaper, *Je Suis Partout* from a street vendor. His blind eyes seemed to scrutinize her as she crossed the street and entered the complex of ancient and historic buildings around the Conciergerie.

The famous clocktower at the corner, which had been working since 1370 and was now set on German time, told her she was on schedule. As she entered the square she glanced up at the graceful spire of Sainte-Chapelle where it pierced the sky like the outstretched sword of the Lady of the Lake. Not far from this spot Marie Antoinette had spent her last few hours before she was led out to the guillotine. It was not exactly an optimistic thought.

As she climbed up to the chapel Simone took her chance, deftly transferring the envelope from her handbag to the folded newspaper under her arm. As she entered the calm peace of the medieval gallery the sunshine was streaming through the high vaults of stained glass, casting dancing spotlights of colour across the flagged stones. Simone knelt to pray in a pew to one side of the chapel, casually laying the newspaper on the chair beside her.

She was aware of a German Luftwaffe officer with a guidebook studying the glass with absorbed interest, but she prudently bowed her head until he had passed on. Then, as she was beginning to panic again, someone moved into the pew behind her. Kneeling, he began to recite the Lord's Prayer in low, rapid tones. Fear welled up inside her as she recognized the voice as Lucien's.

She knew he was running the most tremendous risk in coming to collect the papers himself. She wondered why he had not sent Lamartine or Gervais instead. She would have been angry and rather alarmed if she had known that he insisted on acting as her contact in order to give her confidence on this, her first task for the group.

She scarcely even noticed as he got abruptly to his feet and scooped up the newspaper in one fluid movement. He had already disappeared by the time she sat up and glanced around. She felt rather let down. It had all been too easy. She retraced her steps down to the square without incident, and it was only when she walked out into the sunshine that a feeling of elation stole over her.

Later that afternoon she was taken aback to encounter Gervais in a corridor at the hospital. Her immediate thought was that something had gone wrong and Lucien had been arrested. But Gervais quickly set her mind at rest. He was at the hospital for purely private reasons: his mother had fallen and broken her hip and was now a patient in one of the public wards.

Simone accompanied him down the line of beds closely packed together under a picture of the Sacred Heart. His mother occupied a bed at the far end, facing a balcony covered by a metal grille to prevent suicides. The old lady was frail and in considerable pain. Gervais was distressed by her condition, obviously very close to her in a way that Simone found touching. She promised she would give her something for the pain and checked to see the schedule for her operation. She told Gervais that she would require a period of convalescence, preferably in a nursing home or somewhere where she could be looked after, but such places were expensive. Gervais said he would have to consider this and left the hospital looking very depressed.

That evening Simone returned to the Rue de Rennes bearing a scrawny chicken donated by one of her private patients in lieu of her fee. The date had not gone unnoticed, in spite of Simone's preoccupation with her mission. It was 5 April and Michelle was one year old.

They held a little party with Michelle staying up long past her normal bedtime. She was a bright inquisitive child and now that she had begun to walk she seemed to be everywhere getting into trouble. She finally gave in to her tiredness and fell asleep in an armchair with her thumb in her mouth, so blonde and angelic that her mischief was quickly forgotten. Altogether, it had been a memorable day.

That May Christian Fournier and Suzanne Drouot returned to Paris almost a year to the day since they had left the city one step ahead of the Germans. Christian turned up one day at Antoine's garage asking for Lucien. He had apparently got the address from Gervais who had taken pity on him. He was out of work and fallen on hard times. He and Suzanne could no longer afford the rent of their old place on the Boulevard St Michel and were living in a tenement near the cemetery of Montmartre. He asked Lucien to find him something, anything, in the transport company – 'just to tide us over' – and Lucien, without too much hesitation, agreed for old times' sake.

In June the world was riveted by the news of Germany's invasion of Russia. In Paris over twelve hundred suspected *résistants* were arrested in one night. Red and yellow posters began to appear on the streets and in the Métro stations bearing black borders announcing the executions of saboteurs for some new 'outrage'.

When two of their group were caught in a night raid at the beginning of July, Lucien took it upon himself to invite Christian to join them. He argued that Christian had changed radically from the brash and flippant student of the year before. His troubles had sobered him, and at heart he was a convinced anti-Fascist who could do well in the underground. It would be like the old days, with Lucien, Gervais and Christian all working together.

Suzanne soon discovered Christian's new interest. His night-time absences provoked a jealous rage in her that would not be appeased until he had confessed the truth. Suzanne was hardly reassured. She immediately sought out Simone to find out if she was aware of the dangerous games that their men were involved in and was horrified to find that Simone was a player, too.

'I'm not so brave,' Suzanne told her in confusion. 'I think I'd prefer not to know what is going on —'

'What is going on?' asked Diane, appearing suddenly in the doorway of the bedroom. She had heard every word and it appalled her to think that Simone had kept all this from her when even Suzanne was trusted.

'Diane, please don't be angry —'

'Of course I'm angry. I can't believe you didn't trust me enough to tell me what you have been doing.'

'It's not a question of trust. I just wanted to protect you,' Simone said quickly.

'Protect me?'

'You and Michelle.'

Diane could hardly contain her outrage. 'Who do you think you are? You have no right to treat me like some imbecile child! Do you think I would go round telling everyone what's going on?'

'I'm sorry —'

'If you are fit to be a member of the group, and Christian is fit, then don't you think that I deserve the chance to be included too? Don't you think that I might want the opportunity to strike back at the régime that took Dieter from me – that deprived Michelle of her father?' She was white-faced and shaking with emotion. 'I want to speak to Lucien,' she added solemnly. 'I want to strike back, too.'

9

That autumn it seemed all Paris had taken to the bicycle. The only cars on the streets were official German models. A few taxis, converted to gasogene, still operated at exorbitant rates, but for the most part they, too, had been replaced by bicycle-propelled rickshaws called *vélocabs*. Diane, like many other women that year, had discovered the benefits of wearing trousers when cycling. Skirts and dresses were abandoned as stockings became unavailable except on the *marché noir*. Trousers were cheap, comfortable, giving a newfound sense of freedom and confidence, and besides which they were warm. Fashion had bowed at last to the diktats of necessity.

Diane, using Simone's green bicycle, had become a courier for the group. She made irregular trips across the city between Antoine's garage and various rendezvous points in parks or on busy intersections where information was exchanged. With the expansion in resistance activities there was growing cooperation between groups scattered across the city in joint operations. Diane acted as liaison, passing messages along a chain of couriers from the north of the Seine to groups south of the river.

Antoine the *garagiste* made no secret of his opposition to the increased role of women in the group, but even he could not deny their success. He treated Diane with grudging admiration and strict professionalism, preparing the messages for her to carry coiled into the cylinder of a bicycle pump.

'You're early today,' he commented gruffly, handing over the pump.

93

'I've some distance to go. I can't afford to be late.'

She replaced the pump in its place on the bicycle and wheeled it out through the yard. Christian was working on an ancient Citroën and looked up as she passed, wiping his greasy hands on his *bleu de travail* overalls. He called out, '*Salut*, Diane!' but the greeting carried a false note of bravado. His new work still seemed to trouble him; it was quite a comedown from his old life.

The rendezvous point had been arranged for the Champ-de-Mars at three. As Diane set out to pedal down the maze of little back streets behind the Gare St Lazare she felt the familiar thrill of tension in her body. Her task was simple, but it was dangerous and therefore exhilarating. If anyone suspected the contents of the messages she carried she could face severe penalties.

Was she being reckless? Was it irresponsible for her to have become involved in the activities of the group when she had Michelle to consider? There was other work, less important but much safer, which she could have chosen instead, but she felt that would have been opting out, taking the easy way.

She crossed the Champs-Elysées at the Rond-Point and drifted down the Avenue Montaigne towards the Place de l'Alma. Everywhere there were signposts for the direction of German vehicles bearing daunting commands, '*General der Luftwaffe*' or '*Hauptverkehrsdirektion Paris*'. But there were also other signs, freshly painted overnight on walls and windows: V signs for Victory: a rash that had spread across Paris since the summer and reappeared no matter how many times the German authorities had them removed.

In the shadow of the Tour Eiffel Diane came to the lush greenery of the Champ-de-Mars. She pulled up on the south-east corner of the park, play-acting some problem with her bicycle. She was on time but her contact was late. There were no other cyclists in sight. She tried to relax, but in the back of her mind was the dread that someone else might offer to help her with the bicycle.

It was a lovely crisp September day and the brilliant sunshine caught the golden dome of Napoleon's Tomb. As she raised her hand against the glare, she saw a lone male cyclist cross the boulevard and enter the gardens, wheeling nonchalantly towards her.

'Are you having trouble?' He stopped and got off his bike.

'I think it's a slow puncture.'

They both knelt down to examine the rear tyre.

'Is everything all right?'

'No problem.' He straightened up. 'Let me try my pump. There seems to be a fault with yours.' He quickly produced the second bicycle pump and appeared to check her tyre. As he completed the task the two pumps were quickly exchanged and he bore the message away with him, giving her a friendly wave of his hand.

As was their brief, the plain-clothes men from the Avenue Foch continued to follow their suspect.

'Whatever happens, don't let him out of your sight.'

'What about the girl?'

'Leave her for now. She can easily be traced later.'

Simone was on call and sleeping over at the hospital. Diane was alone at the flat with Michelle, cooking supper. It was only offal and noodles but she had stood for two hours in a queue to get it and thought herself lucky. Most Parisians were subsisting on a strange diet now that rations had been cut to a bare ounce of meat, half an ounce of fat and less than a *demi-baguette* of bread per day. Only a few people could afford the prices of the black market racketeers, certainly not Simone and Diane.

Although she made some money from her typing, Diane knew she could not have managed without the proceeds of the sale of her sketches. They had proved surprisingly lucrative, and at times she could hardly keep up with the demand. She drew street scenes of women queuing for bread, of the vehicles like *vélocabs* and other typical curiosities of the Occupation. But her most popular subject was Michelle, now almost eighteen months old and more appealing than ever. But getting Michelle to stay still long enough to pose was a real challenge. She was the most inquisitive child, toddling around the apartment and constantly having to be rescued from imminent danger, or attempting to move every object in sight – regardless of size and weight.

There were other drawings which Diane did not sell. She showed these pictures to no one, not even Simone. They were an intensely private part of her life, pieces of a secret inner fear that she could not share with anyone. She drew these late at night while Michelle slept, and kept them hidden away in the bottom drawer of her wardrobe, only bringing them out on occasions such as this, when Simone was at work. She looked at these pictures with a mixture of guilt and aversion. They could not be more different from the romantic, sometimes rather kitsch sketches of her daughter. But they were part of her nonetheless.

They were all abstracts, curious anonymous cubist shapes in tones of grey and white. To other people they would mean little or nothing, surely. But to Diane these images, repeated over and over across the paper, were the very stuff of nightmare. Each picture was the ghost of a prisoner borne away in the sealed boxcars from Pantin. Each abstract was like a scream from the grave.

One day perhaps she would show these pictures to Michelle when she was old enough to understand.

She was stirred out of her private thoughts by an urgent hammering at the door. It was still light outside, but she could not imagine who could be summoning her so frantically. But in the moment that she reached out for the latch she heard Madame Laclos' strained voice out on the landing.

'Yes, she's there. I know she's there.'

Diane opened the door and three men moved quickly into the apartment past her. Diane just caught sight of Madame Laclos' pallid face as she scuttled away down the stairs.

'Who are you?' she began, but she did not really need an answer. There was no doubt at all about the identity of her uninvited visitors.

The men were already overturning the flat in a violent search. Diane quickly scooped Michelle into her arms and saw the fear in the child's blue eyes. She tried very hard to keep calm as she asked, 'What is it you want? I've done nothing, nothing.'

She might have saved her breath. The men made a thorough search, checking every cupboard and drawer and scattering their contents all over the floor.

'You are under arrest.' The leading officer regarded her with cold indifference. 'You may pack a bag. You have five minutes.'

Diane carried Michelle towards the bedroom.

'But leave the child,' he added as an afterthought.

'No!' She clung to Michelle, wide-eyed with alarm, afraid that he would seize her from her arms. As if on cue, Michelle began to wail.

'Very well,' he replied without interest. 'Then the child goes with you.'

97

Diane hastily packed a shopping basket with a few clothes for Michelle. There was no time to think of herself. She added the day's ration of bread from the kitchen, but the rest of their meal was abandoned. Then she and Michelle were manhandled out of the apartment and down the stairs. A Black Maria was parked out in the street. As Diane was pushed inside she thought she caught the movement of the curtain in the window of Madame Laclos' *loge*, but then the door slammed shut and the van jerked forward on its journey.

They travelled some twelve miles in the *voiture cellulaire*. The popular name given to this vehicle was the *panier à salade* or salad basket, because the interior was divided into a series of separate compartments to hold each prisoner. From her cell Diane could just see out of the grille in the rear door. As the van picked up speed the tree-lined avenues were just a blurr of rich autumn colours, but as they slowed at crossroads she could plainly see the crowded sidewalk cafés and clusters of pedestrians going about their normal lives in perfect liberty.

Oh God! thought Diane, could this really be happening?

She clutched Michelle tightly against her shoulder and hoped she would not realize that her mother was crying.

Beyond the Port d'Italie lay a barren district of desolate wasteland overgrown with weeds and wild flowers. Fifty years before this site had been chosen to build the largest and most modern criminal institution in Europe. Although Diane had never been here before, she had no trouble in recognizing the high walls and forbidding gates of the notorious prison of Fresnes.

From the moment that she set foot in Fresnes Diane felt that she was living a nightmare. The women in the *panier à salade* were ushered out into the fading light with shouts of '*H'raus!*' and '*Schnell!*' The crowded entrance hall was full of shuffling men and women, carefully segregated into separate lines for processing. Diane carried Michelle against her shoulder and looked about her in stunned amazement. She was not the only woman there with a child by any means.

She was ordered to follow a group of other women in the custody of one of the grey-uniformed wardresses. Later she would learn the prison slang for these SS guards: *les souris*, the grey mice. But at that moment she meekly did as she was told and tried not to attract attention. She had already observed what happened to those who stepped out of line when one of her fellow prisoners had been struck repeatedly about the head and shoulders.

A sour smell clung to the cold concrete walls. Along the length of the dank corridor the wardress unlocked cell doors one by one. When it came to Diane, the wardress looked at the child in her arms and frowned. Then she strode on down the corridor and pointed to the furthest cell.

'You! In here, *schnell!*'

Diane took a step forward and the heavy iron door of the cell clanged ominously fast behind her.

It was two days later when Simone finally returned to the Rue de Rennes ready to fall into bed for a long uninterrupted sleep. She unlocked the door and called out for Diane, but was met by an uneasy lingering silence and the alarming sight of the ransacked room.

She stood a moment in frozen horror, taking in the overturned chairs and the contents of the sideboard strewn across the floor. She forced herself to remain calm, firmly closing the door behind her, and moved

99

further into the room. In the kitchen she saw plates and cutlery set out as though for a meal and on the stove was a pan of boiled noodles and rutabagas covered by a film of green mildew.

A pervasive fear filled her body. She suddenly knew what must have occurred in the flat. Panic seized her and she ran into the bedroom, knowing already what she would find there. Drawers had been pulled out, cupboards emptied, with clothes and linen thrown across the bed. Among the debris were scattered drawings of Michelle, like fragments of a forgotten life. With a sob, Simone knelt on the floor and picked up the sketches one by one. But among the portraits she found other pictures she had never seen before. She stared at the harrowing images in her lap and knew at once what they meant.

Diane, Diane, what happened here?

She was crying now, feeling the sensation of panic begin to numb both mind and body. At the same time an insistent warning bell rang in her brain, telling her what she must do. Making a supreme effort of will she staggered to her feet, still grasping the handful of pictures. She found a small suitcase and seized a few of her own clothes and all the money she could find. On the top she placed Diane's pictures and then, slamming fast the locks, she took up the case and fled from the apartment as fast as she could. She could afford to take no chances. She had no idea who might be watching. The others had to be warned. As she hurried down the stairs and out into the apparently tranquil street, she knew she would never be returning to the Rue de Rennes.

In the night, with Michelle pressed close against her for warmth, Diane lay on the rough wooden bunk and thought of the city beyond the walls. Where were her friends? What had happened to them all?

She shuddered at the thought that they might have been arrested too, that in some other cell, in some other prison Simone was lying in the darkness and worrying about her. Perhaps far away in England, too, her parents were in despair, knowing only that Paris was occupied and she and their grandchild were living as enemy aliens under German rule.

She was not alone, that was one compensation. There were two other women sharing the cramped little cell. Sonia Dubois was a tiny woman of about forty, a black marketeer who had been picked up three months before after being denounced by an anonymous enemy. There was something almost Asiatic about the cast of her round face, the short bob of dark hair and the vivid black eyes that missed nothing. Her companion was a much younger woman, still in her teens. She had a wild beauty about her that was undiminished even in those drab, grey circumstances. Her name was Hélène Arnould and she made no secret of the fact that she was a street walker and this was her second time round in the confines of Fresnes.

That first evening both women had been kind and helpful, taking pity on Diane and the child. She had missed the last meal of the day, coffee at three in the afternoon, but Sonia, true to her nature, had hoarded a small piece of bread which she unselfishly produced for Michelle.

There was another occupant of the cell whom she had not seen yet. Another 'political', as Sonia described her. Nichole Léger had been discovered passing messages to a comrade in the men's section of the prison and was sentenced to a month *au secret*, in solitary confinement. There seemed to be some doubt whether she would reappear or not.

Diane soon came to understand the routine of her new existence in Fresnes. The days were broken into

101

the hours between the ritual of food. At six a.m. the inmates were woken by the rumble of the coffee trolley going the round of prisoners called to 'tribunal'. This echo of the French Revolution was a summons to interrogation in the dreaded Rue des Saussaies. Some returned to Fresnes, beaten or tortured. Others left and were never seen again. The women lay on their bunks and listened with dread to the distinctive rattle of the coffee wagon, wondering which of their number would be unlucky today.

At six thirty the rest of the prisoners received their ersatz coffee, a tepid acorn brew that was served in a metal mess-tin. At 10 a.m. they were issued with a ration of black bread, and at noon there was a niggardly serving of something that went by the name of 'soup'. The last offering of the day was another tin tray of coffee at three p.m.

Between waiting for food, some of the prisoners were recruited to work in the Sewing Room, repairing German uniforms. After ten days Diane did her first shift there, taking Michelle with her. The child sat on the floor at her feet and played with the scraps of material and cuttings, apparently amused by these new playthings.

Each day Diane dreaded the approach of the coffee wagon, terrified that she would be taken off for interrogation and separated from Michelle. As kind as the other women were to her, Diane knew it was only her presence that maintained a semblance of normality for her daughter. She thanked God that Michelle was too young to understand what was really happening.

One month to the day when she had entered solitary confinement, Nicole Léger returned to the cell. Diane had to contain her curiosity about this, her fellow 'political', for the first thing Nicole did on her release was to fall asleep for twenty hours in a way that poignantly reminded Diane of Simone.

Nicole Léger was a strong woman in her early thirties. She had been in Fresnes for more than seven months, ever since a night raid on her house in St Cloud. She had a certain reticence about discussing possible mutual acquaintances. In Fresnes there was always the fear of a Nazi stool-pigeon being planted to obtain information that could not be extracted by any other means. Diane, for her part, had no wish to discuss her own group with anyone, however much she longed to know if they were safe. Someone had blundered, someone had betrayed her, otherwise she and Michelle would not have been here.

Nicole had been twice to the 'tribunal'. She described her experiences to Diane in a cynical off-hand manner that barely hid the true horror that awaited visitors to the Rue des Saussaies. She assured Diane that it was better by far to tell the truth straight away rather than be foolishly brave – and dead.

'The Ukrainians are the worst,' she confirmed. 'The Ukrainians will turn you inside out and drain you of all hope.'

The four women, in spite of their diverse backgrounds, soon forged a close bond, the kind of intimacy that is encouraged by institutions like schools, hospitals or, indeed, prisons. Having Michelle there with them seemed to inspire the women to little acts of unselfish behaviour that made life more bearable for all of them. When Nicole received a Red Cross parcel in the week before Christmas she distributed the contents with perfect fairness and they all contributed a share of their rations to give a little extra for Michelle. Diane thought she would remember that strange Christmas in Fresnes for as long as she lived, not for the bitter cold or the sad

103

singing that pervaded the prison walls, but for the friendship and spirit of her three companions.

In January an influenza virus swept the prison. Diane gave up all her rations to try and keep Michelle strong. She sat on her bunk swaddled in a grey blanket, her little wizened face like that of an old woman, not a child less than two years of age.

Two days later in the icy pink morning the rumble of the coffee wagon ceased as it approached the cell door. The women lay unmoving, listening to the rattle of the key in the lock. The heavy door swung back with a clang and the *souris* pointed at Diane.

She had expected to hear the dread words, 'tribunal', but the SS wardress merely ordered her to pass her mess-tin to be filled with coffee. Diane's hand shook as she complied and her desperate eyes pleaded with the woman for an explanation.

'You will pack your things,' the wardress told her at length. 'Be ready to leave in ten minutes. You are going to Germany.'

In the stunned silence that followed Diane sank down on her bunk, the coffee forgotten. Michelle stirred beside her and opened her wide blue eyes.

'Maman,' she said, holding out her arms, wanting to be cuddled, 'Maman,' and she smiled.

'Not the child,' announced the *souris*. 'The child stays.'

Diane hugged Michelle as the other women cried in outrage. Diane stared at the wardress, unable to acknowledge what she had heard.

'I have my orders. The child stays,' the wardress repeated.

Diane screamed. She snatched up Michelle and retreated to the farthest corner of the cell. Sonia and Nicole moved in front of her as though to keep her safe, and Hélène spat a torrent of insults at the alarmed *souris*, who turned tail and left to call for assistance.

Beyond the window green and yellow buses were already waiting, engines running, panting in the frosty half-dawn. The wardress reappeared with two male guards. Outside in the corridor other prisoners bound for Germany were being herded down into the courtyard. As the men moved into the cell they knocked the women aside and set their hands on Diane. She screamed again and was struck brutally across the face, but she would not let go of her daughter.

'*Ruhig! Taisez-vous!*' shrieked the *souris*, horrified by the uproar. She tried to grab Michelle, but Nicole had stepped into her path and Sonia and Hélène were crying and shouting, receiving blows from the SS guards for their pains.

One of the men had seized Diane by her hair, forcing back her head. The *souris* grasped Michelle around her waist and pulled her free from her mother's arms, putting as much distance between Diane and her child as the confines of the cell would allow.

'We'll look after her,' cried Nicole. 'We'll look after Michelle for you.'

'*Ruhig!*' barked one of the SS guards as his associate dragged Diane towards the door, demented, beaten, sobbing.

Through the open cell door, before she was driven away to the cattle trucks that were waiting to take her to Germany, Diane's last glimpse of her daughter was in the unyielding arms of the Nazi wardress.

Part Two

10

There was not a dry eye in the house. As the cinema emptied into the afternoon sunshine Lydia noticed the women around her surreptitiously hiding away their handkerchiefs and smiling a little self-consciously. *Die Grosse Liebe* was the great success of contemporary German cinema. Its makers claimed that it had been seen by more than twenty-eight million women who identified with its strong emotional theme of lovers separated by war.

But Lydia Ulrich was not separated from her husband. She reminded herself constantly that she was a very fortunate woman to still have her husband at home after five years of war. Thanks to his position they even maintained a certain degree of comfort in their life together, and there were not many who could claim that these days. If it had not been for the one great sorrow in their lives, they would have been truly happy.

Lydia and Karl Ulrich had been married for almost twelve years, twelve years in which their marriage had grown so strong, so successful in every other way and yet —

No, don't dwell on it, Lydia rebuked herself. She had gone to the cinema to be entertained, distracted, not to be reminded of her own inadequacies.

The afternoon was warm and bright, a splendid day for mid-October. Unter den Linden was still the energetic heartland of Berlin, thronged with crowds of civilians and troops. It was almost possible to ignore the gaping spaces, like missing teeth, where buildings had once stood, to hurry past the mounting

109

hills of rubble and torn, charred stumps of trees that brought the war home to Berlin, the 'world capital'.

Lydia preferred the Tiergarten where the lime trees camouflaged the worst of the destruction. Whenever she could get away, in between air raids, she would come and sit in the gardens and watch the children returning from kindergarten or the Gymnasium.

Anyone seeing her sitting on a park bench enjoying the children play might well have mistaken her for a mother waiting for her own son or daughter. That was what Lydia liked to think. She hoped she merged in with all the other women awaiting their children. She had even, on occasion, fantasized about her own little girl or little boy, boasting about them to the other women she met in the park in a way that later made her ashamed and even more depressed than before.

Today she was wearing a neat suit of fine wool, the colour of warm burgundy. The outfit gave her an air of confidence and prosperity. Even the little hat, worn at an angle to shade her right eye and display her dark blonde hair coiled into a chignon, was exactly right for her. She cared a great deal about her clothes, especially in these difficult days. She needed to look good, to maintain her self-respect. Clothes gave her a sense of identity that was reassuring. They were, above all, a compensation, a treat she allowed herself in an attempt to make amends for other disappointments.

'Oh, hello there.'

Lydia looked up and found that the owner of the friendly voice was a woman she had met before in similar circumstances. She was a year or two older than Lydia but considerably heavier in build. Her ample figure filled out a double-breasted suit cut after the Bavarian fashion in a serviceable navy blue. Her shoes and lisle stockings were eminently sensible.

'You're waiting for your son?' asked the woman, flopping on to the bench at her side.

Oh God, thought Lydia in shame. She remembered everything now. The little blonde boy, five or six years old, such a charming rascal and so clever! Just like his father!

'What was his name now? Kurt —?'

'Karl. It's Karl. He's named for his father.'

'Ah, yes, that's it! I'm waiting of course for my twins. You remember the girls? Anne-Lise and Veronika. They love to come by the zoo. They're late today.'

What can I say? thought Lydia in growing confusion. I can hardly wait here for ever. What if she guesses the truth? I'll die of shame, I'll —

She suddenly blanched. She had noticed for the first time the little bronze brooch the woman was wearing on the high collar of her jacket.

'Is that the Mother's Cross?'

'Third class.' The woman shrugged modestly. 'But between ourselves – this time next year I shall be pushing a pram around these gardens as I wait for my little brood.'

Lydia tried very hard to smile, but she was gripped by an overwhelming feeling of bitter envy as she glanced at the woman's figure.

'My husband is delighted, of course,' the odious woman was saying. 'He is even learning Russian now, to get a better posting in Ostland in one of the manufacturing plants. He's so sensible.'

Lydia writhed uncomfortably on the seat beside her, wondering how she might escape her company. Then, fortunately, she was rescued by the arrival of Anne-Lise and Veronika in a rush of tartan pinafores and bobbing plaits, their bright round faces alike as

111

two rosy apples. Lydia survived the next few moments knowing they would soon be gone. She vowed to herself to choose some other part of the park for her future visits.

'I'm sorry I didn't meet your son,' the woman said to her with genuine regret. She even waved a hand as she guided her offspring away with her. Lydia was sunk in despair. The crisp autumn leaves scattered at her feet suddenly had the bitter smell of decay.

The injustice of life! It was so unfair! When she had married Karl she was so full of hope, she had such plans for the future. As Karl's career had flourished she had tried to be worthy of him, attending all the right courses, reading all the right books. As the years passed and nothing happened she had even attended all the right doctors. She tired of hearing relatives asking why there were no little Ulrichs yet, with the overtones or suggestion that she was too inadequate or too selfish to fulfil a proper wifely role.

She had become obsessed with her misery. She read again and again the novel by Carossa, *Der Arzt Gion*, where the heroine longs for a child of her own although she is dying of an incurable disease. The story held Lydia entranced. It inspired her to struggle against the depression that had held her in despair for so long. She tried to be the best wife a man could ever hope for. She concentrated on making her home the most comfortable, her dinner parties the most perfect, her appearance the most immaculate, the equal of any other woman in their circle.

Most of the time she succeeded in convincing Karl, if not herself, that she was truly happy. But how much happier would she have been if she had not had to lie and invent sad stories about a non-existent child of her very own?

112

There was every likelihood that the project would be finished on time. As the state planning committee broke up Karl knew that he had done well, consolidating his new position with the men of influence. As he rolled up his charts he caught Horst's wide smile of encouragement.

'You've made a hit with the board,' he congratulated him, as they walked the length of the ministry corridors together. 'You'll find that special works such as this new camp can pay high dividends.'

'You really think so?'

'I'm sure of it.' Horst Menzler glanced at his gold watch. 'I think I'll call it a day myself. What about you? Come and join me for a drink before you go home to the little wife.'

In Kranzler's they shared a bottle of hock and a good cigar. Horst Menzler had influence, there was no denying it. Although he and Karl were of an age, the lawyer had come a long way since he became an advisor to Speer himself. While Karl felt himself lucky to have attained the rank of SS-Sturmbahnführer, his friend was surely bound for the top. When he looked at Menzler, Karl knew he could not hope to compete. He was not really an ambitious man. He had only joined the Party in order to secure his position as a state-employed architect. But he valued Horst's friendship and patronage. These days one could not have too many friends. Times were uncertain, their leaders fickle. He had no desire to find himself suddenly posted to the Eastern Front away from the comforts of Berlin and Lydia, his wife.

His one regret was that he had no son to follow him in his profession, no son to carry on his name in posterity. Horst had once commented on the obligation of each member of the SS to father four children for the Fatherland. As Reichsführer Himmler had said, it was their duty to produce sons

113

of good blood for Germany. The problem was one he and Horst often discussed.

'Of course I'm not blaming Lydia.'

'Of course not. She's a fine woman, very fine. But in the circumstances —'

Karl looked up sharply. 'Divorce? No, that's something I could never contemplate. Not at all.'

'You have grounds.'

'I daresay.'

'Adultery, that's out. Evil repute, diseased mentality, the refusal to procreate –' Menzler recited the list in his analytical lawyer's voice, 'but infertility, yes, you have grounds.'

Karl twisted the stem of his glass, staring at the tablecloth. 'I know you'll think me rather old-fashioned, Horst, but I love my wife. Our happiness would be complete if only we had a child.'

'Yes, I understand, of course.' Menzler studied his friend for a moment as though trying to make up his mind about some hidden question. 'Well,' he declared, flicking an imaginary speck from his immaculate suit, 'as I see it, there's no real obstacle. Have you never thought about adoption?'

'No, we – I never thought —'

'Let me suggest an idea to you. Just a suggestion. What I have in mind is a purely private arrangement outside the normal official channels. You catch my drift? There are ways and means in everything, you know. For a consideration.'

Karl listened entranced as Menzler explained that he had knowledge of a woman who worked as a nursing administrator for one of the National Socialist welfare organizations in a children's home near Potsdam. The little orphans who were her charges were all, he was assured, of Aryan heritage and pure blood. The Party were encouraging the adoption of these children into good homes, to reliable SS families.

'Such an arrangement might be suitable in your case, Karl.'

Karl could hardly contain his excitement. A dozen different questions shot into his head.

'There would, of course, be administrative costs,' Menzler added. 'My contact has – expenses.'

Karl waved all that aside as unimportant. He would have laid out a fortune if it meant getting a child of their own!

'Horst, I would be for ever grateful —'

Menzler gave his arm a reassuring squeeze. 'Leave it to me, my friend. Trust me. I promise I will get back to you the moment I've had a chance to talk to my contact at the home.'

As Karl watched Horst drive off in his official Horch he felt like a new man. But he knew he must not tell Lydia yet for fear of raising her hopes. He must wait and trust Horst to help them find a suitable child. He could scarcely believe his good fortune.

Lebensborn was literally the Spring of Life. This was the name chosen by Heinrich Himmler for his new programme to build up the racial stock of the nation, to create a new super-race of Aryans. At its inception in 1939 the programme was designed to support large families and unmarried mothers, a charitable enough cause that attracted considerable support. But within a short period *Lebensborn* came to cover other, less savoury activities in the creation of the Master Race. Rumours of SS brothels and SS stud farms for the breeding of Aryan children had some basis in truth, but even these methods proved inadequate in producing the numbers of children required.

In the Reich the glorification of motherhood had become big business. Officials and administrators were assigned to the *Lebensborn* programme, working as far afield as Poland and the Ukraine in search of suitable targets. Specialist teams swept into towns and villages, raided orphanages and schools in the ruthless selection process that broke up families the length and breadth of the Greater Reich. For those children who might have been missed at source, there were officers who met the transport trains at the railheads and picked out likely candidates at the entrances of concentration camps, while the rest of their families went off to their fate.

The *Lebensborn* children were given initial screenings and those who passed as 'suitably Aryan' were sent to centres in Germany for further scientific tests. Children had to be 'pure Nordic': blond hair, blue eyes, the correct shape of head and nose according to specific measurements, uncontaminated by *Fremdvölkisch* or alien species. Even Slavs and Latin children sometimes fulfilled the Aryan ideal. Those who did not were callously disposed of.

The Führer had stated the aim of such a programme: 'When an enemy of ours says, "I will not join you," I say, "But your child has joined us already. Who are you? You will pass on. Your children are ours and soon they will know nothing except our new community." '

It was a bitterly cold December afternoon when Karl Ulrich arrived at the children's home in Potsdam. There was the bite of snow in the air as he stepped out of his Opel car and entered the well-appointed building. Klara Anders, the nursing administrator, was waiting for him as Horst Menzler had arranged. She was a tall woman with imposing features, already well into middle age. She regarded him with stern

116

appraisal, as though trying to weigh up his suitability as a parent for one of her charges. She wore a white coat over a dark suit and stockings and a pair of heavy leather shoes. Her footsteps echoed in the spotless corridors as she led Karl past a hall that resounded with the strains of 'The Lorelei' sung by a massed choir on the radio.

She took him first of all through a children's playroom hung with inspirational quotations by Party leaders. Next came a room for the very youngest children, where a neat row of cots were watched over by a portrait of the Führer. On each cot a white card bore a number, not a name.

'These babies have yet to be assessed and named,' explained Klara Anders.

Karl smiled back at her stupidly, taut with anticipation. Horst had warned him that he could not expect to get a child under two years of age. Babies were at a premium, and something of a risk as well. It was not always possible to certify precisely such a young child's true Aryan worth.

'I will be happy with a child of any age,' Karl had assured him eagerly, wanting no further delay.

'Well, none of the children are too old,' Menzler said smoothly. 'I would judge that a child of seven is already too old to be influenced.'

In the next dormitory the beds bore cards with children's names in precise Germanic script: Heinrich, Siegfried, Eberhard and other suitable names for the young males of the blood. In the girls' dormitory the names included Irmgard, Ingeborg, Edeltraut and Elfriede. Karl was uncertain how Lydia might react to a son named Albrecht or a daughter called Sieglinde. Of course none of these were the children's original names.

117

'If you'll wait in here I will have the candidates brought to you.' Klara Anders deposited him in a waiting room for what seemed like an endless time.

Eventually she returned leading a nurse in a crisp white uniform and three children. The boy and two girls stared at him in bewilderment but were very well behaved and quiet.

'The boy is more or less spoken for,' the administrator reported, 'although for a consideration something might be arranged. Either of the girls is available.'

Karl looked at the boy with regret, but he was older than he would have liked and Horst's warning rang in his head. Perhaps it was wiser to pick a girl after all. Lydia had always wanted a little girl whom she could spoil and pamper. Yes, a girl would really be ideal, and both of these children were remarkably attractive. The first was probably five or six years old, the second was younger.

'What is the background of the girls?' he wanted to know.

Klara Anders seemed taken aback by his question. 'We do not inquire into the identities of our children,' she said sharply. 'All our charges have been certified as racially pure by the very highest standards.'

Karl felt he had received a rebuke. His next question was more mundane. 'What are their names?'

'This is Hedwig,' Klara Anders explained, touching the elder girl lightly on the shoulder, 'and this, Jutta. They are six and four years of age respectively.' Her answer was competent and full of obvious authority, but there was no affection in her voice.

Karl looked at Hedwig for a long moment, taking in the short blonde hair and bold blue eyes. There was nothing wrong with the child and yet he was instinctively drawn to the younger girl. Jutta was more nervous, hanging back slightly and refusing to look at him. Her long blonde hair was neatly dressed in two plaits that sat like bell-ropes on her shoulders and her face still had the chubbiness of babyhood. Karl looked at Jutta and felt an immediate compulsion to reach out and protect her.

'I'll take Jutta,' he told the administrator without further hesitation.

Frau Anders looked pleased. She ordered the nurse to get the child ready and then she led Karl back to her office on the ground floor. He had expected a ream of papers to sign, but surprisingly there was only one.

'Dr Menzler did explain this was a private arrangement?' Klara Anders confirmed. 'Your signature is a pure formality.' She watched him closely as he scrawled his name at the base of the document. She seemed to be waiting for something more. There was, of course, the question of money. 'For the administrative costs, you understand. And a little something for the nurse.'

She named a sum that was considerably more than he had expected, but he was not about to argue. He was almost certain that she was cheating him, but suddenly it no longer mattered. As Jutta reappeared wearing a plain blue coat, he could only think how thrilled Lydia would be when he turned up with their new daughter.

The nurse gave him a small bundle containing a few extra clothes and then left her charge in his care. Karl took up the bundle and held out his hand to the girl, but she pulled nervously away.

'Jutta!' the administrator admonished her sternly. 'Be an obedient child. Say "Good Afternoon" to your new father.'

In a voice that was barely above a whisper the girl lisped dutifully, 'Good afternoon.'

She sat beside him in the front seat of the car during the drive back to Berlin, quiet as a little doll. Snow was falling heavily now and in the blackout they made slow progress back to Charlottenburg.

'Don't be afraid, Jutta,' he said gently. 'We're going to meet Mutti. Papa is taking you to Mutti.'

They were greeted outside the apartment by the sound of the gramophone playing 'Heimat, deine Sterne'. Karl could hardly wait to see his wife's face as she came to answer his assertive knock at the door. She would wonder why he had not used his own door key.

'Karl? What on earth –' Lydia stood in the open doorway and suddenly saw the child at his side. She looked from the girl to Karl and her eyes filled with tears.

'Yes, Lydia, yes, she's really ours.'

A cry broke from her and she knelt down and touched the child's cold cheek. She was laughing and weeping with joy, folding the girl in her arms and hugging her.

'Her name is Jutta,' added Karl with a catch in his throat as he watched them both.

'I'm your Mutti,' said Lydia, entranced. 'Welcome home, Jutta, welcome home.'

11

Lydia was devoted to her new daughter Jutta. She was a very serious four-year-old. She was obedient to a fault, excessively polite, but Lydia noticed how strangely guarded the child was in all her answers. She wondered about her background, about her unknown real mother. But she never questioned her husband's explanation of Jutta's adoption. The child was an orphan, a victim of this terrible war, and she needed loving parents.

That Christmas of 1943 was a very special one. Lydia dressed a fir tree with all the ancient baubles and carved wooden figures that had been passed down from generation to generation. Now they had a new significance. As she lit the candles on the tree and crib, Karl brought Jutta into the room and Lydia thought her happiness would overflow. The look of awe in Jutta's eyes as she saw the tree took her breath away. The little girl had never seen anything like it.

But the world was not as it used to be. When the *Pfannkuchen* and goose had been eaten, and the strains of 'Stille Nacht' had died away, reality intruded into their world with new ferocity. The sobbing sirens shattered the calm by day and by night. '*Achtung! Achtung! Eine Luftlagemeldung!*' were soon words as familiar to Jutta as the rest of Berlin children. The war that had given Lydia her child now threatened to destroy them all.

In the bitter cold of January and February the hours spent in the basement air-raid shelter of their apartment block were a purgatory. Lydia kept warm coats and gloves on a chair by the door together with a Thermos flask of hot soup ready to be snatched up the moment the first warning came. But it was one afternoon in early March, when the first glimmer of spring sunshine had tempted Lydia to take Jutta to the park, that they found themselves quite unprepared for the worst raid she could ever remember.

The wail of the sirens scattered the few remaining birds from the park. They took off into the brilliantly clear azure sky with a frenzied beating of wings. Lydia picked up Jutta and began to run, searching for the nearest shelter.

On the street she was turned away from the U-Bahn station by a warden who insisted she must find somewhere else. Lydia stared about her in growing panic, aware that the avenue had suddenly emptied. She ran on, panting as Jutta grew heavier in her arms. On either side of the street the shopfronts were boarded up, doors barricaded by sandbags. There seemed nowhere for them to go.

Lydia set Jutta down beside her, but kept a firm hold of her hand. She looked up at Lydia with her serious little face.

'I want to go home, Mutti,' she announced. 'We forgot the soup.'

'I know, *Liebling*, I know we did.' Lydia looked around her wildly, afraid that Jutta would hear the fear in her voice. 'Come on, we have to walk a bit now. You're not too tired, are you, sweetheart?'

Jutta shook her head but she looked uncertain. She tried valiantly to keep up with Lydia as she hurried on down the street. What a fool I was, thought Lydia over and over, what a fool to come out like this. If anything should happen to Jutta I would never forgive myself, I would— A shrill whistle cut into her thoughts. Running feet pounded the pavement and a red-faced boy appeared at her side furiously waving his arms. 'What do you think you're doing out here?' he demanded, the whistle flapping against the front of his Hitler Youth uniform. 'Are you crazy, or what? Get that child to the shelter immediately!' He gestured wildly to the corner of the block. He wore the armband of a *Blockwart*, although he could not have been more than fourteen. Lydia took offence at his tone but she did not stay around to argue. As she picked Jutta up into her arms and ran to the entrance of the shelter she heard the officious boy behind her muttering, 'Women! *Wie dumm!*'

The shelter was a basement cellar under a local bakery. Lydia hurried down the unlit stairs and found herself in a cavernous room some forty feet long. It was already very crowded with women, children and old men sitting on the rough wooden benches that had been set out in precise rows all facing the far wall, as if expecting some entertainment. Lydia squeezed on to one bench against the dusty brickwork, taking the child on to her lap. Again she cursed herself for being irresponsible, for being unprepared for a raid that might trap them here, so far from home, perhaps for hours at a time.

There was an atmosphere of almost unbearable tension in the shelter as everyone waited. A mother quietened her querulous son with a gruff exclamation and silence was restored. The occupants of the shelter were listening avidly for the now familiar wave of distant sound that indicated that the bombers were on their way.

In the eerie stillness there came at last the low droning vibration they had been waiting for. As it grew steadily louder and more intense, Lydia saw her neighbours exchanging fearful glances, wondering if this raid might prove to be their last.

Bombs began to fall across the city. The lights in the shelter flickered nervously, luridly lighting the wide eyes and taut faces around the room. The *Blockwart* was a chirpy Berliner in his late sixties. As the raid began he moved around the shelter setting out hurricane lamps and making cynical comic remarks about their ordeal. As he lit the last lamp they all heard a high-pitched whistle as a bomb fell somewhere nearby. The thunder of the impact seemed to reverberate right through the walls of the cellar and the lights in the ceiling swung violently and finally went out.

The fear was almost tangible in the shelter as mothers tried to keep the younger children and babies from crying. Lydia hugged Jutta closer, keeping her face pressed against her chest.

The bombs came eight to a cradle. Everyone was keeping their own private count as the rumble of the planes overhead swelled to a low note of danger and the bombs began to empty out, one, two, three, four. Each had its own particular screaming whistle. Five, six, coming closer. Seven. Too close for comfort! Eight. A thankful sigh of relief. But not for too long. Here came another plane, and another. The counting began again.

In the pale glow of the hurricane lamps Lydia noticed an elderly woman across the way busily knitting. The garment was something large and complicated, sagging on to her lap, and the ball of wool was hidden in her vast handbag, the typical *Hausfrau*'s *Einkaufstasche*. As the bombs came nearer her needles paused in mid-stitch as she counted them down, and after 'Eight' continued knitting.

'*Ach, mein Gott!*' sobbed a younger woman near Lydia as the shelter shook and clouds of dust enveloped them all. 'We will all be killed, killed!'

'Keep quiet there!' hissed the *Blockwart* promptly, but she took no notice.

'My sister and her family died in Hamburg last year, burnt to death with thousands of others—'

'Shut her up, someone! She'll scare the children—'

'The town was wiped out, wiped out, do you hear? And we'll die, too! We're all going to die here!'

The *Blockwart* had finally reached her and forced her back on to the bench. He shook her violently and threatened her to keep quiet. The woman stared at him as if he were mad.

'The fool,' whispered the woman at Lydia's side. 'Doesn't she realize she could be reported for saying things like that?'

Lydia thought it rather late to try and check the rumours that were spreading everywhere. It was not only Berlin that had suffered terrible destruction. The British and Americans had terrifying new weapons that could turn cities into whirlwinds of flame. She had heard of phosphorus bombs which exploded in green molten waves of red-hot liquid and could seep into cellars and seal up the entrances of air-raid shelters. The world was an evil place, incomprehensible, inhuman. She hugged Jutta closer.

Was she frightened? Many of the older children in the shelter were astonishingly calm, taking the raid in their stride. They had grown up with the war and had grown accustomed to living their lives among bombing and shortages. As Lydia looked down into her daughter's pale face she was taken aback by her composure. For a four-year-old child she showed amazing courage. Perhaps her early life with its unknown catastrophies and deprivations had prepared her to face the worst. She was no delicate, timid child. She had a natural streak of hardy and tenacious mettle, a plucky gift for survival that could only serve her in good stead.

125

After the All Clear had sounded the occupants of the shelter, shaken to find themselves still alive, staggered up into the early evening to see what was left of their city. Everyone remembered the memorable night the November before when a thousand acres of Berlin had been smashed into one vast bomb-site.

The survivors were greeted by a sight that took their breath away. The sky was scarlet as far as the eye could see. The unearthly cyclonic wind that always followed hard on an air raid whipped and scattered the stinging ash and thick, cloying dust. They coughed and covered their eyes, squinting against the fierce glow of a thousand fires. The whole street was transformed into a sea of burning wreckage and pools of glowing phosphorus. The air stank of high explosive.

Lydia blinked away the tears that turned the ochre blast dust on her cheeks to mud. She gazed in awe at the crippled landscape where only hours before had stood houses and shops. Above the skeletal remains there rose a heavy pall of dense black smoke to pattern the lurid crimson horizon.

How was she to find her way home? The whole area had been turned into a no-man's-land of rubble and craters. It bore no resemblance to the streets she had known so well. Even the poor trees were transformed into burning and charred stumps.

'Come on, Jutta,' she whispered urgently. 'We have to go home now. We must get home.' But what would they find there? she wondered desperately, and where was Karl?

She knew she had to head west. It should have been simple, it would have been simple a mere few hours before. But now it was no longer possible to tell where the houses ended and the main street began.

126

Lydia fought down her desire to panic and moved quickly away. Shards of glass like brittle ice fragments crunched underfoot. A tangle of torn electricity wires hung like a cobweb overhead. There was an ominous rumble and a wall caved into the street and showered them in plaster.

Ahead of them Lydia saw darting black figures picking their way through the smoking rubble, silhouetted against the flames. As she went closer she became aware of a group frantically digging in the ruins with their bare hands in the hope of finding someone alive. To one side there already lay a woman's corpse, yellow with blast dust.

Lydia felt a tug on her hand. 'Mutti, I'm tired.'

She looked down at Jutta's white face and took pity on her. She hauled the child up into her arms and began to walk on with a kind of desperation. Her back began to hurt and as she picked her way around the craters she almost stumbled and fell.

That walk back to Charlottenburg was like a nightmare come to life. She had to stop every few minutes to put Jutta down and rest, trying to judge her direction. It became clear that the central and southern districts had borne the brunt of the raid, where the ministries and administrative heart of Berlin were situated. Again Lydia found herself worrying about Karl. He had gone to the ministry that morning and she did not know when he would be home. It was already growing dark. If it had not been for the glow of the fires she thought she would never be able to see her way in the dangerous streets. It must be late. Had Karl survived? Was he at home now, waiting and worrying about them?

She recalled the many pathetic messages she had seen pinned to doors and even trees near bombed-out buildings. 'Ilse Baumann asks for news of her son Peter, aged 6, lost near here on 5 January.' 'The

127

Zintl family have moved. Contact c/o District Party HQ.' So many lost children. So many divided families.

Lydia picked up her daughter once again and set off westwards with new determination.

It must have been an hour or more later that she staggered into the familiar street in Charlottenburg. She sobbed with relief and thanksgiving at the sight of the apartment block standing whole and undamaged before her.

'We're home, *Liebling*!' she cried, setting Jutta down and watching as she ran eagerly towards the house.

She followed wearily, her breathing shallow as she thought of Karl. Jutta was already at the door of the flat, eagerly stretching up to knock, but Lydia did not really believe that Karl would be there before them.

She began to search frantically in the pocket of her jacket for her latch key while Jutta went on knocking. She could have sunk to her knees in sheer exhaustion and frustration as the key could not be found.

'Wait a minute, Jutta –' she began, but Jutta suddenly broke into a shrill squeal of delight as the door of the apartment opened.

'Papa!'

Karl caught the little girl as she flung herself at him in excitement. He stood in the doorway with Jutta in his arms and stared over her shoulder at Lydia where she stood in her filthy clothes, ready to drop from weariness. Then she, too, came into the circle of his arms and the family was once again complete.

12

By 1943 the *résistants* were no longer alone in their acts of sabotage against German targets. The RAF made bombing raids on the Renault works at Billancourt, the Citroën factory at St Ouen and the Panhard plant at 19 Avenue d'Ivry, all of which turned out military equipment for the enemy. The Paris blackout was peppered with vaulting searchlights hoping to trap the raiders and the night skies vibrated to the tune of anti-aircraft guns.

After each new 'outrage' the Germans took fresh hostages. It had become almost a daily event for people to be seized from the street, the Nazis making lightning raids and sealing off entire districts. Sometimes there was the chance to pass a warning by word of mouth – *'Rafle!'* – and the area would empty miraculously before the German cars could arrive.

The prisons of Paris were full. The southern resistance group suffered a severe blow when the Gestapo picked up almost all of their number. With the exception of Diane, Lucien's northern group had survived. Diane's contact had been arrested and tortured, so it was said. Diane must have been seen with him at the rendezvous and followed. They obviously thought she was a courier for the southern group.

Simone was heartbroken about Diane's arrest. She had tried to discover where she and Michelle had been taken, but without success. It weighed heavily on her conscience that she had been the one responsible for Diane joining the group, whatever Lucien and the others said to try and reassure her.

Simone was now living with Lucien in his rooms near the Gare St Lazare. She had not returned to the Rue de Rennes since that terrible day, not even for the rest of her belongings. She might have met Madame Laclos or one of their former neighbours, and the risk was too great. These days you never knew whom you could trust.

As winter turned to spring Simone could scarcely believe how quickly the months were passing since Diane's arrest. In an effort to dispel her guilt she plunged herself into her work. She had elected to leave the Hôtel-Dieu and found a new temporary post at a hospital a few stops on the Métro from Lucien's apartment.

With the scarcity of alternative transport the Métro was always crowded. It closed down all weekend and between eleven and three on working days, and finished before the midnight curfew. It was popular not only with Parisiens but with the Occupying Powers. Rowdy bands of German troopers would plunge into the Métro using the exit stairs, thrusting civilians out of their path. On the trains the ordinary travellers were strap-hanging in sardine-packed carriages while the Germans rode in comfort in reserved compartments marked *Nur für Wehrmacht.*

Simone learnt to bear this daily ordeal but she never quite got used to the frisson of alarm that overcame her at the sight of a spot-check at one of the exit points. As the passengers funnelled past the *gendarme* working in collaboration with his German colleagues, Simone produced her identity card and tried to preserve a calm, nonchalant appearance. But underneath she was pulsating with fear.

It was irrational, she told herself, she had nothing to hide. Her name was not on their lists. Not yet.

I'm losing my nerve, Simone thought angrily as she survived the security check with barely a glance

130

from the *flic* on duty. What use am I going to be to anyone if I go to pieces now?

There were other changes, too, which unsettled Simone. Suzanne had been deserted. Christian walked out on her one day in the autumn of 1943 and went to live with Paulette Guillot, a shop assistant at the Bon Marché department store. Suzanne was devastated. Simone visited her in the drab little rooms near Montmartre cemetery and found her almost suicidal.

'He left me for that little bitch–'

'He'll come back. He has before.'

'Oh yes,' Suzanne cried bitterly, 'but that was years ago! You don't understand. It's too late now, too late. He'll never leave that tart.' She raised her red and swollen eyes. 'Do you realize she is only nineteen? Nineteen! *Mon Dieu*, don't you know I was thirty last week?' She made it sound like eighty.

Simone was fast losing her patience. 'You have to get hold of yourself, Suzanne. Thirty's not the end of the road! What nonsense! You have your whole life ahead of you–'

'It's easy for you to say. You have Lucien.'

'You'll find someone else. In my opinion you were wasting your time with Christian. He was always a rat. You're better off without him,' Simone concluded. But she could see that Suzanne was unconvinced. Nothing she could say against Christian was going to make any difference once Suzanne had made up her mind to be miserable.

It was therefore with some surprise that Simone heard a month or more later that Suzanne had found herself a new man. The information came from Antoine at the garage, where he was taking a callous pleasure in taunting Christian with the news.

'I don't give a damn,' Christian declared. 'She's nothing to me any more.'

'No?' Antoine was enjoying himself. 'She was seen out having dinner downtown. There's no doubt it was her.'

'I'm not interested, do you hear?'

'Not even if the *copain* in question happened to be a *Boche*?'

Christian looked up sharply from the engine he was tuning. His eyes seemed to burn white in his greasy face.

'I'll kill the bitch,' he swore softly.

Simone, overhearing the exchange, wondered if it could possibly be true. She had told Suzanne to find herself another man, but surely even she would never consider going with the *Boches*? She wondered whether she ought to go round and see her, but having seen Christian's face, she thought better of it. Perhaps she had meddled enough.

The incident was soon forgotten under more pressing matters. Just before Christmas Simone was on duty at the hospital when a nurse brought a message that someone was asking for her at reception. As she hurried downstairs, the last person Simone was expecting to find was Lamartine's wife, Juliette.

'Ah, *Dieu*, thank you for coming,' she whispered, seizing Simone by the sleeve of her white coat. Her grey eyes flicked over Simone's shoulder. 'Is it safe to talk?'

'Come and sit down. You don't look at all well.'

Juliette agreed reluctantly, although she was shaking as if with fever. She sat on the hard wooden chair in the corridor, wringing her hands in her lap. For the first time Simone noticed that she was wearing bedroom slippers.

132

'What's happened?' demanded Simone in a breath-less whisper.

'It's Patrice. They arrested him this morning at the Sorbonne.' Madame Lamartine saw the horror on Simone's face and gave a sob of anguish. 'I didn't know where else to go! One of his students saw everything and came straight away to the flat to tell me. I got out at once and came here. I didn't know what to do!'

Simone put a hand on her shoulder and tried to sound calm. 'You did the right thing. Look, sit here a moment, will you? I'll try and telephone the garage.'

A look of panic leapt in Juliette's eyes. 'Don't leave me here—'

'It's only for a moment. The others have to be warned.'

'Yes, yes, of course.'

'I'll be right back. I promise.'

She could not find Lucien at the garage but she gave Antoine the bad news. 'What shall I do with Juliette? She can't possibly go home.'

Antoine thought a moment and then suggested a *cachette*, a safe house, in the working-class district of Levallois-Perret. 'She'll be safe there for a while. Can you take her?'

'Yes, I'll see to it, don't worry. *A bientôt*, Antoine, take care of yourself.'

She told the hospital she had an emergency call and would have to leave. She hung up her white coat and fetched her handbag and quickly got Juliette Lamartine out of the building before anyone else noticed her odd choice of footwear. She summoned a *vélocab* to take them to the safe house, unwilling to take a chance at the Métro checkpoints.

That evening when she returned to the Rue de Londres she found a meeting was going on in Lucien's flat.

133

'Thank God you're here.' Lucien greeted her with a quick embrace. 'How is Juliette?'

'Fine, for the moment. Did you discover anything?'

'Yes, they've taken Lamartine to La Santé. It doesn't look good.'

The group wanted to discuss the implications for a big transport operation that had been planned for the New Year. The Nazis were sending a major shipment of specialized military equipment from the St Ouen works via Pantin to Germany. The group had been working on plans to sabotage the train in the railyard ever since news of the consignment had been leaked by fellow *résistants* among the *cheminots* at Pantin.

'Surely we have to cancel now?' Simone had always regarded this particular operation with alarm. Pantin would always hold a special horror for her. She knew she would never be able to erase the memory of that tragic day when she and Diane searched the railyards for Dieter.

'Lamartine won't talk,' Lucien insisted. 'He's a good comrade. He knows how important this raid is. He'll hold out.'

'Yes,' Gervais agreed quickly, 'even if we did cancel the operation, Patrice wouldn't know that, would he?'

'Lamartine would suffer for nothing,' Antoine agreed. 'I vote we continue as planned.'

'Christian?'

'Certainly. I've been looking forward to this one for weeks. I don't see any reason for chickening out just because Lamartine got himself caught.'

You callous bastard! thought Simone, flashing him a look of contempt. You never change, do you?

'Well,' she said out loud, 'I see I'm outvoted. I just hope you're all right about this operation. Personally, I still think the whole thing is an insane risk.'

134

'Well, *you* don't have to worry,' Christian told her brutally. 'You'll be nice and safe at home.'

Lucien broke up the meeting and warned everyone to observe close security. He locked the door and came into the bedroom, placing his Mauser handgun, a souvenir of an earlier operation, in its usual place under his pillow.

Simone was sitting on the bed and he joined her, putting a comforting arm around her, when he saw what she was holding. Diane's drawings still retained a strange power over her that he failed to understand. The repetitive cubist shapes meant nothing to him, but he knew they made Simone deeply depressed, reminding her of her lost friend and filling her head with all kinds of illogical fear.

The day of the mission Lucien went to the garage in search of Christian. He found him in the yard working with Antoine on the engine of the truck they intended to use for that night's operation.

Antoine looked up at his approach. 'Is anything wrong, *chef?*'

'You better ask this *crétin* beside you.' He was staring at Christian with such cold fury that for once Fournier did not come back with some smart retort.

'What's happened?' he asked solemnly, wiping his hands.

'You went to visit Suzanne Drouot.'

Antoine turned to Christian and his face was murderous. 'You stupid bastard! What did you go there for? The woman is a security risk. She could sell the lot of us—'

'That's why I went to see her – about her being seen with that *Boche*. She denied it. She said it was just filthy gossip, someone wanting to get back at her—'

135

'Then she's a bloody liar as well!' Antoine exploded. 'And you're a worse fool if you believe her.'

'She wanted us to get back together again,' Christian added lamely. 'But I wasn't having any of that. I told her straight, "It's over," I said, "but if I ever hear of you playing around with any *Boche*—" '

'You threatened her?'

'She'll behave herself now. She's no risk.' He looked from one man's doubting face to the other. 'Look, I know her. She'll behave, all right?'

'She'd damn well better behave,' Antoine said savagely. 'No one is putting my life on the line, do you hear me?'

That evening there was still tension between the three men as the group gathered at the garage. The truck was all prepared with its portion of German supplies to camouflage the presence of a crate of explosives. Gervais would be driving, with Christian alongside him in the cab, and Antoine and Lucien hidden in the back.

'*Allons, les gars,*' Lucien announced as the curfew hour approached, and five minutes later the Caristan truck was on the street running through the yawning shadows of the blacked-out city.

Twice they were stopped by German patrols and Gervais handed over their travel warrants for inspection. In their big capes and helmets the *flics* flashed their torches over the driving cab and examined the first row of crates under the tarpaulin flap at the rear of the truck. Gervais and Christian sat still as statues, cold sweat freezing on their backs. But it was too soon to fear. Their papers were in order. The real danger would come later when they reached the railyard.

Pantin was a scene of great activity. As the truck joined the queue of other transport vehicles creeping into the yard, the whole vast area seemed to be alive with darting figures. Each truck pulled round to a depot where the driver alighted to get his papers officially stamped, then they reversed to the railhead where the supplies were off-loaded into the waiting boxcars. The vast length of the great train was proof enough of the value of this target. There must have been enough military supplies there to keep the German war effort in business for half a year.

There were also German troops at every strategic corner of the yard. As Gervais drove up in turn to the depot office he noticed a dozen guards on duty just in the immediate vicinity.

'You sit here,' Christian suggested, 'I'll see to the papers.' He clambered down from the cab and sauntered into the office, looking every inch the lorry driver's mate in his faded *bleus*.

'We've stopped,' Lucien whispered inside the truck. He and Antoine began to extricate themselves from their hiding place between the crates, manoeuvring the small box of explosives. There was enough there to blow the entire train to kingdom come.

They braced themselves just behind the tarpaulin flap, waiting for the truck to reverse round to the railhead. They were both dressed as *cheminots*. With luck on their side there should be no sentries at the boxcars to notice two extra workers unloading supplies.

'What's keeping them?' Antoine hissed impatiently.

Lucien thought about pulling back the tarpaulin an inch or two to look out, but he resisted the temptation. There was probably a queue at the depot that was holding everything up.

At last he heard the door of the driver's cab slam and their truck coughed into life. They rumbled forward across the cobblestones and Gervais began to manoeuvre into reverse, backing up towards the train. As Lucien and Antoine prepared to release the tarpaulin there was a sudden commotion.

'Get out, get out!' cried Lucien as the shouting outside and the sound of jackboots crashing on the cobblestones grew nearer. He ripped aside the tarpaulin cover and the yard was revealed under the harsh moonlight.

Lucien flung himself headlong from the tailgate and Antoine lost no time in following suit. From somewhere over on the right he heard someone scream 'Halt!' and as he ran and rolled into the deep blue shadows beneath the next truck in line he heard the first crack of gunfire.

A hot stab of pain made Antoine catch his breath. He lay awkwardly between the wheels of the truck and tried to wriggle backwards down the length of the vehicle. He could see the boots of the German troopers running past towards their truck but he had no time to consider what was happening back there. Sticky black blood had matted the shirt under his overalls. He thought it was just his shoulder, but it hurt like hell.

Antoine crawled forward on his stomach until he was almost directly under the driver's cab, praying that the truck would not begin to move. Ahead of him he could see the train and dozens of *cheminots* who had stopped their work at the sound of the firefight near the depot. To the left was a line of empty trucks which had already been unloaded and were preparing to drive off out of the yard.

Antoine did not hesitate. He slid out from between the front wheels of the cab and in a running crouch skirted the waiting trucks towards those at the front of the line. With all the attention directed away from the area, he was able to pull himself up into the back of one of the empty lorries near the front of the queue. Only once inside, safe behind the tarpaulin cover, did he chance a look back to see what had become of his friends.

To his horror he saw Lucien being dragged away between two Nazi troopers, his head slumped forward, obviously unconscious. Gervais was being manhandled towards the depot office, struggling and fighting his guards and shouting, '*J'vous emmerde tous!*' at the top of his voice. Christian was already standing up against the depot wall, his hands raised, a Schmeisser sub-machinegun pointed directly at his chest.

At that moment the line of empty trucks jerked forward and began to move out of the yard. Antoine slumped back, letting the tarpaulin drop into place, overcome with bitterness and pain.

Simone had not dared to sleep. She was sitting up watching the clock and drinking endless cups of ersatz coffee, longing for the night to be over. The knock, when it came, took her totally by surprise and for one dreadful moment she believed the Gestapo had come at last for her.

She shook her head incredulously at the sight of Antoine propped up against the wall outside her door. His face was drained of colour and he almost fell forward into her arms.

'You're hurt!'

She helped him to sit down and then began to explore the wound, her thoughts racing wildly.

'It was a fiasco. We were betrayed.'

'Lucien?'

Antoine grunted with pain as she probed the wound.

'I'm sorry, Simone. He was taken. They were all taken. They must have been waiting for us.'

'The bullet's torn right through. You ought to be in hospital.'

'Too dangerous. You do something.'

Simone went to fetch her doctor's bag. 'It will only be temporary. You'll need it dressed every few hours and take something for the pain.'

'I'll manage.' He grunted as she strapped his shoulder tightly to staunch the bleeding. 'That *salaud* Christian! He and his women! You were right, Simone, we should never have gone ahead.'

'You mean Suzanne?'

'The bitch betrayed us! We walked straight into their trap.' He suddenly gripped her arm. 'Leave that now. I have to get home. I'm moving out and you should do the same.'

'Will they come here?'

'Surely.'

'Oh God.' Suddenly the full realization of what had happened seemed to overwhelm her. She felt as though she had been struck in the stomach. First Dieter, then Diane and Michelle, now Lucien and the others.

'Get a grip on yourself,' Antoine said gruffly but not unkindly. 'Go to Levallois, to Lamartine's wife. You'll be safe enough there for the time being.' He stood up and tried to pull his overalls back into place. Simone moved to help him. 'I'll be in touch,' he promised. 'Thanks for this,' he indicated the dressing, and then he was gone out into the night just as suddenly as he had come.

13

Simone waited for weeks without news of Lucien. Not knowing was the worst. Juliette Lamartine had been through it all before, of course, but at least she knew where they had taken her husband. She had moved to the safe house at Levallois and no one but Antoine knew she was there. It troubled her that she might have missed a message by changing her address, and it was this desperate isolation that drove her to return to her work at the hospital, even though she knew she was taking a chance.

If the group had indeed been betrayed, Simone found it inconceivable that Suzanne had been responsible. She knew how upset Suzanne had been when Christian left her, but was she the type of woman who would take revenge on a faithless lover by betraying him and all his friends into the hands of the Gestapo? She did not believe it. She did not think Suzanne could be so cold-blooded.

And yet who else was there? Antoine had been certain that it was all a trap. He said the Germans had been waiting for them at Pantin, that they had clearly been betrayed. Simone felt appalled when she considered that all her friends had been arrested and she alone had survived. Who was she to get away when the others were rotting in some jail or prison camp?

She tried to bury herself in her work, volunteering for extra shifts at the hospital, putting her own health at risk. She was trying to avoid having time on her hands, time to think. She did not deserve her good fortune. She was racked by guilt, tormented by the thought that Lucien had cared more for her than she had for him, that she had not loved him well enough. She should have tried harder to get him to call off the mission that night. She should – well, there were so many things that she should have done and now it was too late.

Then one evening in March, just as she was coming off her ward rounds, she had a most unexpected visitor.

'You had better come in here,' said Simone, leading the way into a small treatment room off the corridor. 'We can talk in private here.'

It struck her as ominous that the news should have come from an outsider, not from Juliette or Antoine, her fellow members of the annihilated north Seine group. She could not find it in her heart to offer any welcome to Marisa Gonzales.

'You're surprised to see me? Well, it's been a long time.' She sighed and Simone detected an infinite weariness in her companion that seemed to echo her own feelings since Lucien's arrest. 'It is hard to be a survivor,' continued the Spanish woman. 'I think you understand what I mean.'

'We women seem fated to be survivors.'

'Then you know why I have come?' She paused. 'I'm sorry to be the bearer of such tidings.' She explained that the news had only reached her new group that morning. They had a contact who worked in Mont Valérien and smuggled out the names of those who had faced the daily firing squads.

'I was half expecting it,' murmured Simone, feeling a cold wave wash through her veins.

'They say he was in a bad way. Perhaps it was a blessing for him.'

'Poor Lucien.' Her words sounded hollow, even to herself. She knew she ought to feel shock, sorrow, anger, but there was nothing left to feel but cold, numbing emptiness.

The Allies had landed in Normandy! The news took Paris by storm. Expectations ran high that within days the Nazis would be pushed out of France for ever, that before long Paris, too, would be free.

The evening after D-Day the Germans made one of their most dramatic catches in months. Pierre Lefaucheux and most of the leading members of the *résistants* were captured at a top secret meeting in a suspiciously simple operation. In the weeks that followed hundreds of political prisoners were rounded up, shot or deported from Fresnes, Romainville and the other jails of Paris. There were rumours that transports were leaving Pantin day and night.

Simone shuddered at the thought of it. In the few months since Lucien's execution Simone had kept apart, maintaining no links with the resistance. She had changed and she knew it. She suddenly felt old beyond her years. It was hard to believe she was still only twenty-eight. Her youth had been squandered. The war had stolen away the best years of her life, destroyed her natural joy and hope for the future. She had lost her friends and her lover, leaving her with nothing. She would never have believed that she could have grown so cold, so indifferent to her own survival.

As the Allies advanced slowly towards Paris, the Germans seemed possessed by a kind of frenzied panic. They ransacked the capital for every movable item that could possibly be looted. Shops, hotels, art galleries – nothing was safe from their rapacious eyes. Their booty included furs, food, wine, furniture and works of art. Paris was being plundered. Germany's day was done. The Russians were advancing from the east, the British and Americans from the west. It was only a matter of time.

That August no one in Paris went on *vacances*. A heady vibrant heat had settled over the city. In the far distance came the dull thud of artillery, the most inspiring signal to the people of Paris. Colonel Rol, new head of the *résistants' Forces Françaises de l'Intérieur*, called on Parisians to 'wipe out the shame of 1940' and rise up against the Germans. If they waited for the Allies it could be too late, he warned. Hitler had given orders for Paris to be razed to the ground.

Overnight the FFI symbol appeared painted on walls all over the city. There were rumours of German vehicles seen unloading landmines and crates of TNT in the Palais du Luxembourg, the Place de la Concorde and other major historic sites. It was now or never.

On Saturday 19 August the first FFI commandos moved against German-occupied public buildings and attacked isolated enemy outposts. A large quantity of arms and ammunition was seized and distributed to groups eager to join in the fighting. Men and women wearing tin hats and FFI armbands took up the captured weapons, everything from Mausers to Schmeisser machine pistols. The word went out, '*A chacun son Boche*'.

Barricades were set up at important road junctions in an attempt to prevent the Nazis bringing up tanks or reinforcements against those positions where the FFI were holding out. The ancient cry of '*Aux barricades!*' evoked memories of the Revolution and the days of the Paris Commune. People brought out their bedsteads, old mattresses and furniture. Trees were uprooted, cobblestones ripped up. The barricade at the corner of the boulevards St Michel and St Germain earned a nickname, 'Death's Crossroads'.

After four days of street fighting food was in short supply in the capital. The FFI commandeered the remaining stocks at Les Halles and set up soup kitchens. One operated in the forecourt of Simone's hospital, offering *un plat unique* to staff and patients who might have starved otherwise.

Simone had not been able to get back to Levallois for three days. Fighting was intense. A burnt-out tank smouldered at the corner of the street outside the hospital and some enterprising person had put up a sign, warning in German, '*Achtung! Minen!*' to keep further tanks away. Nevertheless, casualties were high. Wednesday 23 August became known as 'Bloody Wednesday' and the hospital was filled to overflowing with victims of gunshot and grenade wounds. The dead lay in the cellars, the wounded wherever room could be found, including the corridors and floors. Simone was rushed off her feet, but at least she felt useful. No one knew where it would all end.

A dense pall of black smoke hung over the city. It was said that the Grand Palais had been set on fire by incendiaries. The Nazis would destroy Paris rather than let it fall into the hands of the *résistants*.

The question everyone was asking was, where were the Allies? The FFI forces were untrained, ordinary men and women holding out against tanks and storm-troopers with whatever captured small arms came into their hands. The odds were weighed heavily against them. If the Allies did not hurry and enter Paris the *résistants* could all be wiped out.

In their part of the city where the FFI forces had driven the Germans out, the local population took justice into their own hands. There were many public and private scores to settle. Well-known German sympathizers and collaborators were hunted down.

145

Revenge set the crowd afire and several of the worst offenders who had been responsible for denouncing friends or relatives to the Gestapo were shot out of hand. Others were arrested and held for more formal trials. In the four years of German occupation there were many bitter memories to be erased.

And the women were not forgotten. The men seemed to take a special pleasure in seeking out and humiliating those Frenchwomen who had been known to associate with their German masters. For years they had been secretly despised, or spat at in the streets for bringing shame to their less brazen and more scrupulous sisters. Now they would pay.

Simone watched aghast as the crowd jeered and paraded two women with their heads shaved through the street behind the hospital. Swastikas had been daubed in paint on their foreheads and one woman wore a placard announcing, 'I whored with *les Boches*'. Simone thought of Suzanne and felt sick in the stomach.

When her time for a break off duty came, she took her ancient green bicycle and set off resolutely to cycle to Suzanne's flat in Montmartre. It was not so far away, but she had no idea who might be in control of the district she was passing through. It was, perhaps, a foolish mission. She did not know if Suzanne still lived in the sordid little apartment by the cemetery, or if the stories about her were true, but she felt an overriding compunction to warn her, if it was not already too late.

In the Place de Clichy she was waved down by an armed FFI patrol. Two men and a woman surrounded her bicycle and demanded her business. The woman in particular startled Simone. She was wearing a pair of shorts and an attractive summer blouse, but she was brandishing a Schmeisser sub-machinegun as if she knew very well how to use it.

'I'm a doctor,' declared Simone, producing her papers. 'I'm going to the Rue de Maistre on emergency business.' She was grateful that she had brought her bag in the pannier.

'That area still hasn't been cleared. There have been reports of sniper fire,' explained the girl in the tin hat. 'So take care of yourself up there.'

'Perhaps one of our boys should go with you?'

'No, no,' Simone said quickly, 'I think I'll be safer alone. Perhaps I should carry a white flag.'

The trio looked at her with pity. 'That wouldn't make any difference to the *Boche*.' One of the men gave her bicycle a push. 'Watch out for yourself, Doc!'

On the hill to the right the marble dome of the Sacré-Coeur glistened in the hot sunshine. The whole *quartier* seemed ominously quiet. The streets were deserted, the shutters closed on the houses and corner shops. Simone got off her bicycle and began to push it, feeling she made a less obvious target that way. If some crazy German sniper was holding out in one of the buildings, she could at least try and roll into the gutter in time.

But she came to the house without incident. As she propped up her bicycle at the entrance she glanced up at the second-floor windows, wondering what she would find. She took her bag with her, thinking again of those hounded women she had seen with their shorn heads and bleeding scalps. She hesitated outside the peeling blue door on the upper landing, her footsteps creaking on the plain wooden floorboards.

'Who's there?' At last Suzanne's voice answered her knocking. The door opened a crack after Simone announced herself. 'Simone? Is it really you?'

Simone waited as Suzanne struggled to remove several heavy pieces of furniture set against the inside of the door. When the last obstacle had been dragged

147

aside, Suzanne pulled her quickly through the narrow gap and began to manhandle a tallboy back into place. Simone watched in horror and fascination, unable to believe the change in Suzanne. She was thin as a rake and her wonderful head of dark glossy hair had been shorn to a black stubble all over her scalp.

'Oh, Suzanne!'

She turned back to face Simone and tears coursed down her cheeks. She raised a pale hand and tentatively touched her head.

'I was afraid they would come back,' she whispered.

That night, on her camp bed at the hospital, Simone thought about Suzanne and her pathetic ordeal. Yes, she felt sorry for her former friend, even though she had made no effort to deny her relationship with a German lieutenant. She had to live. That was her excuse for going with the *Boche*. She knew no other way. She could not bear to be alone and unwanted.

It was plain to Simone that Suzanne had no idea what had happened that night at Pantin. She had asked after Christian, obviously still very much in love with him in spite of all that had happened between them. Simone broke the news of his arrest and watched Suzanne visibly disintegrate before her eyes. She was now convinced more than ever that Suzanne had not been the one to betray their group.

She made a pitiable figure. She had been deserted, humiliated and left with nothing. She was brimming over with fear and self-pity. What would happen to her now? Who would want her now? She was terrified at the thought of losing her beauty. She was thirty-two years old and she could not conceive of a future without a man. Simone felt compassion tinged with contempt. She was not the only one to have suffered, she was not the only woman in Paris who had lost her lover. The world would grind to a stop if they all behaved the way Suzanne did. Or was she being too harsh? Had she really lost all her softness, her tenderness?

None of that matters any more, she told herself sharply. There are men and women dying out there in the streets. The hospital is filled to overflowing, and here you are growing nostalgic for what might have been. Pull yourself together and try and get some sleep, Simone Blanchard, or you won't be an iota of use to anyone in the morning.

The first Allied tank to enter Paris approached via the Gare d'Austerlitz in the south-east part of the city. The Cross of Lorraine was painted in white on the side of the Sherman, and within seconds it was surrounded by a cheering, ecstatic crowd.

But across the city bitter fighting continued between the FFI *résistants* and the German High Command barricaded in the Hôtel Meurice. There was fierce fighting in the Rue de Rivoli and civilians as well as partisans had come under fire from German snipers in surrounding buildings.

As dusk fell Simone was finishing her ward rounds at the hospital as the radio crackled back into life. One of the nurses gave a whoop of joy and turned up the volume. Suddenly the strains of the Marseillaise filled the entire building from floor to floor: '*Allons, enfants de la patrie, Le jour de gloire est arrivé* ... From every open window and doorway there came the magnificent surging sound: '*Aux armes, citoyens ... formez vos bataillons!*' and soon people were joining in, singing with gay abandon and patriotic emotion, tears in their eyes: '*Marchons, marchons!*'

Then, in the stunned silence that followed, they heard another strange sound in the distance. They

149

turned and looked at one another as if uncertain what it could be.

'Bells – it's the bells!' whispered a nurse in awe.

In the distance church bells were ringing for the first time since the invasion. All over the city every church and bell-tower began to join in the glorious, abandoned eruption of sound. In the darkened streets the wild celebration announced to the world that freedom was coming, that Paris would soon be Paris once again.

By the morning even the Nazis holding out at the Hôtel Meurice knew it was over. The FFI made a concerted attack on the building and a furious crowd gathered outside. It was 25 August, the feast of St Louis, the day of liberation. As Choltitz and his officers appeared after their surrender the crowd went wild. Soon word spread all over the city. It was over, it was really over at last!

More Allied tanks rumbled into the city streets. They were greeted by a vast wave of joy and excitement. The French, American and British troops were offered cigarettes, wine and any precious food that had been hoarded. Women garlanded the tanks with flowers and kissed and hugged the astonished soldiers. They competed to invite the troops home for a meal. The day passed in a whirl of heady emotion.

As night fell, free Paris was flooded with light as the blackout that had operated since 3 September 1939 was abandoned for one special celebration. Looking out at the glorious expanse of twinkling lights, Simone thought she had never seen anything more beautiful. It was as though the city and its people had emerged out of the Dark Ages, out of a world of nightmare and horror.

Simone thought of all her dear friends, those who were known to be dead, those who were missing and those, like Suzanne, Marisa Gonzales and Antoine, who had survived. Looking out over the lights of Paris, Simone trembled in awe. It was time to turn to thoughts of the future, her future, to learn to live again. She just hoped she had not forgotten how.

14

By the winter the people of Berlin realized at last
that the end was coming. The Soviet armies were
advancing from the east in a relentless, vengeful
wave, eating up the miles week by week, country
by country. For years the propaganda ministry of
Reichsminister Goebbels had bombarded his fellow
Germans with reports of the sub-human Slavs, these
Untermensch who were little better than animals. Russian prisoners of war had been treated quite differ-
ently from their French or British allies, dying in
their hundreds of thousands from cold, hunger and
ill treatment.

To anyone who had a son or brother or husband
who had served in *Ostland*, the rumours of atrocities
came as no surprise. The war on the Eastern Front
had been fought without inhibition. The scorched-
earth tactics of the Soviets, the attacks by partisans
and the harsh, unyielding conditions encountered by
German troops had destroyed their last vestiges of
humanity. Villages had been razed to the ground,
thousands buried in mass graves, thousands more
transported to the camps. Was it any wonder that
now the Russians came seeking their revenge?

In November the Soviets had overrun the camp at
Majdanek. The horrors that they unveiled there had
won the German people few friends. If the Russian
Army took Berlin they knew they could expect no
mercy.

Karl Ulrich was under no illusions. Half of his
colleagues had already deserted their posts and fled

the city. Karl had no desire to stay on in Berlin and sacrifice his life for the Führer.

His SS rank, his work on the secret projects at camps that now threatened to become public knowledge, all convinced him that there was no future for him. His dreams of making a success of his career, of creating a secure home for Lydia and their daughter, had all turned to dust. Yesterday's men of distinction could soon become tomorrow's war criminals. *'Sauve qui peut'* was the order of the day.

Horst Menzler had already sent his family out of Berlin and made little secret of his own intention to leave. Those with means and connections had evacuated their wives and children away from the bombing and the Russian line of advance, but Karl had known that Lydia would never agree to leave him or even to send Jutta away on her own. As long as there was still hope Karl had refused to go. But as winter turned to spring, his hopes dissolved with the melting snow.

'Don't wait too much longer,' Menzler warned him bleakly. 'Only the madmen will be left.'

Already there had been some suicides. Professor Ernst Grawitz, head of the German Red Cross, had sat down to dinner with his family one night and released the pins on two hand grenades.

'Do you want that?' Karl railed at Lydia, trying to shock her out of complacency. 'Don't you understand? It's all over here.'

A feeling of complete helplessness washed over Lydia. She sat down and tried to stop her hands from trembling. That it should come to this! However terrible the past year had been, however frightened she had been, she had never really believed in her heart that it would come to this.

153

'I want you to pack,' Karl was saying firmly. 'I'll try and get a full tank of petrol for the car, but just concentrate on essentials.'

She raised her head and looked at him blankly. Did he mean she had to abandon the apartment and most of her precious belongings? Had she come through the air raids just to abandon everything to be looted?

'Don't you understand?' Karl repeated. 'We will be lucky to get away with our lives.'

On the evening of 15 April the Russian artillery began its bombardment of the eastern districts of Berlin. The sickening reverberation seemed to penetrate through the city streets and was worse, if possible, than the constant air raids had been. Zhukov's troops were moving to encircle the city and cut off all retreat.

When the shelling started many people began living day and night in their cellars and basement shelters, venturing out only to get food and water. Others moved down into the U-Bahn stations.

Heavy street fighting was reported in the eastern and southern sectors. As the Russians advanced there were rumours that they had been seen trying to break through German lines by using the subway tunnels and skirmishes had taken place.

At Kaiserhof subway station thousands of civilians had taken shelter. There were also several stalled underground trains of wounded soldiers blocking the down line, while occasional empty trains rolled through on the up line as if in some surrealist dream.

No one knew who gave the order. Someone had surely panicked. The stories of Russians in the subway tunnels had encouraged an SS explosives team to blow up the four-mile-long tunnel under the Spree and Landwehr Canal, regardless of the thousands of innocent human lives at risk.

As water began to flood the subway station a terrible panic ensued. There was an immediate rush for the exits, but many were blocked and barricaded against shell-blast or attack from the Russians. Men and troops pushed their way towards the emergency air shafts where ladders led upwards to street level. Women and children were pushed aside in the insane scramble. Many were trampled brutally underfoot or abandoned as the water came rushing through the subway tunnel from the fractured canal wall.

The air was full of screams and curses. In the stationary hospital trains the nurses debated whether to desert their patients and save themselves. The wounded men, sensing they were about to be abandoned, began to fight and cry out loud, seeing the water seeping through the corridors at their feet.

The force of the icy water carried a tangle of loose obstacles before it. As those trapped in the station began to lose their footing and started to swim in the current of the rising waters, they crashed into the debris that was bobbing, half-hidden, beneath the surface. Those who could not swim clung helplessly to the metal pillars that lined the station platform.

A woman and her small son hung tightly to the sign that read 'Kaiserhof'. As the swirling filthy water crept up to the boy's chin, his mother sobbed and cried out for assistance but no one took any notice of her. Within seconds the tide of onrushing water had borne away her child among a tangle of oil cans and dead bodies, and as the lights flickered and went out, she slipped beneath the slimy surface of the river without another sound.

The refugees flooded out of Berlin across the last surviving bridges to Spandau and the west. The roads

155

were choked by an undisciplined confusion of wagons and trucks, cars and civilians trying to escape on foot. The vast procession inched its way forward in a heated fever of anger, impatience and despair.

The fearful leaders in the back seats of their chauffeur-driven cars ordered imperative blasts on the horn in a foolish attempt to clear their way ahead. The silvered swastika badges on their windscreens no longer had any influence on the terrified, embittered mob that straggled the only exit road out of Berlin.

Abandoned vehicles and cars that had run out of precious petrol littered the highway. Here and there a wagon had broken down with a splintered shaft or a missing wheel, overloaded with alarming quantities of furniture, bedding and family heirlooms that had ironically sabotaged all hope of reaching safety. The fearful mass of ordinary civilians trudged ever onwards on foot, carrying a few essential items on their backs. Their expectations had all been stripped away. All that mattered now was to survive.

Among their numbers, their uniforms long since abandoned, were many deserters. There were few men of the age of military service who did not face the risk of being stopped by one of the gangs of marauding SS men seeking out traitors. Karl Ulrich was no exception.

As he saw the SS unit staked out across the road ahead, he slowed the car and placed his civil identity card at the ready. From a lamp post on the corner of the highway hung the gangling corpse of a hanged man. Tied about his legs was a notice which read: 'I deserted my Fatherland.'

The leading SS trooper leaned over the window on Karl's side of the car. His jaw was bristling with several days' growth of dark beard and his eyes surveyed the occupants of the car in deadly earnest.

156

'Get out.' He pointed a Luger Parabellum into Karl's face.

Karl felt Lydia stir beside him and hug Jutta more tightly on her lap. She was afraid for him, but he had already made it clear what she must do if anything should happen to separate them.

'Get away, get right away,' he had told her time after time. 'You have the child to think of. Don't stop for me, just go.'

The rear seat and boot of the car were crammed tight with items of food and clothing, blankets and a few small items of value that they could always sell if it came to the worst. Lydia wore her best fur coat and a pair of good leather boots. Under her gloves she wore her dress rings and the gold bracelet Karl had given her for the tenth anniversary of their wedding. She looked what she was: the wife of a well-connected man of means. He only hoped that it would not be held against her.

Karl tried to keep calm and to treat the SS troops with caution. He watched as his papers were minutely examined and a look of contempt was passed between them.

'So you're an architect?' the leader asked with derision. 'What is it you build? Opera Houses?'

'Houses, houses and barracks,' murmured Karl, hoping that the answer would pacify them.

The SS man looked beyond him at the gaunt ruins of the desolate city. 'You've a long way to go, you're way behind schedule.'

Karl did not know whether it was meant to be a joke. He kept a blank expression, knowing how unpredictable and crazy these battle-scarred men could be. Only the fanatics were left.

'Well, on your way, Architect.' The SS leader handed him back his papers. 'You won't get far in that crate,' he added, looking over the car.

'Thank God, thank God,' whispered Lydia as he sank back into the seat beside her and started up the engine. Jutta sat on her lap watching everything with her solemn little face. Nothing seemed to scare her. Perhaps she had already seen it all before.

In Spandau the press of bodies had brought the exodus almost to a standstill. It was as the SS man had predicted: within the hour Karl announced they would have to abandon the car.

Up ahead on the roadside verge lay a burnt-out ruin of a tank on its side. The charred body of a member of the crew was just visible hanging from the hatch. This area had been almost obliterated by shelling or a heavy air raid not long before. The air still stank of explosive, and fires were burning in a row of buildings flanking the street.

Karl had pulled the car to one side and was trying to help Lydia collect those items which they felt they could not leave behind. Lydia was crying softly with exhaustion and frustration. All her careful packing had been in vain. She could not imagine how Karl could expect them to manage on what they could carry between them.

'Don't cry, there's no time for that now,' he rebuked her. He was trying to tie a bundle of food and clothes together in a blanket. In the centre of the bundle he had contrived to hide a silver cigar box and several extra pieces of jewellery.

'Do you think you can manage to carry this?'

'What about Jutta?'

'Jutta will have to walk,' he said bluntly. 'She's a big girl now.'

'She's only five.'

'We'll manage, Lydia. Try and be strong. You don't want Jutta to be upset now, do you?'

158

He lifted his own bundle up on to his back. It contained all his life savings, his SS credentials and a quantity of antique golden coins hidden in a bedroll, and a spare set of clothes for Jutta. The remainder of their goods would have to be left behind. He carefully locked the boot and doors of the Opel, but he was under no illusions that he would ever see any of it again.

The fierce flames of the burning buildings turned the street into a furnace. A torrent of sparks showered down on the slow-moving mass of refugees and a ripple of panic seized the crowd. Those nearest the fire began to push forward to escape the worst of the heat. In the crush there was a good deal of screaming as some fell and were trampled and others were separated from their families.

Lydia and Karl had Jutta by the hand. As the crowd surged against them Lydia felt her feet slipping from under her. She clung desperately to Jutta and tried to keep her balance. In her left hand she carried the bundle tied around her wrist.

'Mutti, Mutti!' cried Jutta as the wave of humanity threatened to rip her out of her mother's grasp.

Lydia hit out with the bundle, fighting and thrusting at the tangle of backs and shoulders that were bearing down on them. She felt Jutta's hand slip in hers and screamed out loud. One minute the girl was holding her hand, the next she was gone.

'Jutta!' Lydia lashed out to right and left, attacking everyone in her path. The crowd had turned into a dangerous multi-headed monster totally without mercy.

Lydia felt how easy it would be just to let go and be swept along, but she knew that Jutta could never survive in that crush on her own.

'Jutta!' Her voice cracked as she called again and again. She tried to stem her rising tide of panic. Jutta was out there somewhere and had to be found.

Where was Karl? Did he still have hold of Jutta? As she fought the crowd, she felt as if her ribs would crack under the strain. She slashed blindly with the bundle and cut a path forward, suddenly bursting out into the wider space ahead which had once been a square. She stood to one side, breathing heavily, her eyes devouring the stampeding tide of men, women and children.

Then, caught between the dark legs of the crowd, she saw a flash of blue, the colour of Jutta's coat. As the tangle of men and women separated out into the square she ran forward and fell upon the tiny figure of her daughter, bruised and battered but very much alive.

'Jutta, oh Jutta!' She clasped the girl to her breast and touched her face over and over. 'Are you all right, darling? Do you hurt anywhere?'

Jutta kept her arms firmly gripped about Lydia's waist and shook her head. Miraculously, there seemed to be nothing wrong with her. But where was Karl?

Lydia and Jutta sat crouched at the edge of the rubble-strewn square waiting for Karl as the light died. The refugees were still stumbling past in the last lingering glare of the fires, black silhouettes against the smouldering embers. But none of them were Karl.

'We have to wait here for Papi,' Lydia had told her daughter when she still had hope that they would find each other, but that hope was fading fast.

He must have gone on, she thought grimly. We must have missed one another. She looked uncertainly round her. But what if he had gone back, thinking they had been left behind?

'Mutti, Mutti, I'm tired,' whispered Jutta.

'Yes, darling, I know you are.' She was probably also hungry but there was only a little food in her bundle and just a single blanket. The nights were still cold, but Karl had the bedroll with him and the keys of the car. She could not even go back if she wanted to, she realized as she looked at the never-ending mass of people pouring west. Anyone trying to move against that crowd would be risking death.

'Come on,' she said faintly, taking Jutta by the hand. 'You have to be brave, *Liebling*, we can't stay here tonight. We'll just go a little bit further, then I promise we'll find a place to sleep.'

Jutta stepped bravely out, putting all her trust in Lydia's judgement. Lydia felt the intolerable weight of responsibility heavy on her shoulders but her will to survive was still strong.

They were alone but they still had each other. We've come this far, thought Lydia desperately, we can't give in now.

15

Some fifty miles north of Berlin stood a small town on the Prussian plain where a group of lakes had made a popular prewar rendezvous for wealthy visitors. A number of elegant villas were dotted among the trees along the lakeside, but the visitors no longer came. The villas had been commandeered for the chief members of staff of a new work camp that was built on this site in May 1939. This camp for women was romantically named Ravensbrück.

The waters of the lake were veiled by a fine grey mist. The watchtowers rose black and stark on the bleak plateau, circled by dolorous birds. In winter the driven snow piled up against the electrified wire and settled on rank after rank of wooden huts where forty thousand women inmates occupied a camp designed for six thousand.

At the gates hung the ubiquitous sign reading 'Arbeit Macht Frei'. On entering the compound the main administration block lay to the right, the storerooms, post room and medical inspection room to the left. The main body of the camp lay beyond. The old huts lined a main 'street' where the *Appell* or roll-call was held each morning. Further to the right was the new camp, built more recently to take the increased number of women that had been transported there.

Appell in Ravensbrück was the one time when all the inmates gathered together. It was 5.30 a.m. in summer, but 4.30 a.m. in the bitter depths of winter. Thousands of women stood five deep to be counted while the searchlights picked out the swirling snowflakes in the primeval darkness. The women were Poles, Dutch, Norwegians, Belgians, French, Russians and British in origin, but in their tattered striped uniforms they all looked the same. Their shaven heads had a thin growth of stubble, their cheeks were hollowed out, the skin taut and leprous grey, the colour of chronic malnutrition. In her past life one of that number had been Diane Clements.

In almost three years inside Ravensbrück Diane had learnt very well how to become invisible, to hang back and merge with the mass, to keep alive. She was unrecognizable, unknown as Diane Clements or Clément, identified only by the number given her on selection at the railhead. The black row of numerals was tattooed on the skin of her arm, her passport to survival. The SS did not trouble themselves to number the women bound for the crematorium.

The same number appeared on the isosceles triangle badge sewn over her heart. Diane's triangle was red, marking her out as a 'political criminal' among the brown for gypsies, green for 'common criminals', yellow for Jews and purple for the *Bibelforscher* like the Jehovah's Witnesses. In the centre of the triangle each woman bore the letter of her nationality: 'R' *Russe*, 'S' *Spanier*, and in Diane's case 'F' for *Franzose*. In spite of all their bureaucratic red tape the SS could still make mistakes.

Each morning the women at *Appell* were examined by their guards. Those who stumbled or fainted were pulled out of line, instantly reclassified as lacking industrial value. They were no longer worth the rations to keep them alive.

The women guards moved along the main street flicking their leather whips, but their minions did all the real work. The *Kapos* were handpicked by the SS for their brutality. Many were Ukrainians or Latvians, but the Lithuanians were the worst sadists.

163

They had elected to join the ranks of the oppressors, they were not coerced. They took pleasure in turning on their fellow prisoners and demonstrating their newfound power. They were often blonde, blue-eyed; the Nazis loved them.

All through the *Appell* the counting of the work-force was accompanied by the rattle of the *charette*. This wooden handcart collected the dead from the huts and transported the corpses to the crematorium. The sick and disabled walked there themselves. At Ravensbrück women died from malnutrition, over-work, exposure, sickness and medical experimentation. The only way out of the camp was 'up the chimney'. The sickly sweet stench of burning flesh pervaded the air at Ravensbrück.

Once the numbers of the living and the dead had been assessed, the working day had begun. The *Kapos* herded their charges to their labours as military music blasted from the loudspeakers. The SS was a state within the State, with its own factories, its own workshops. The sewing shop, where they produced uniforms for the Waffen-SS, had a turnover in 1943 alone of more than nine million Marks. Slave labour was cheap, and easily replaced.

Diane had worked in the *Effektenkammer* repairing German uniforms for more than two years. It was the key to her longevity. She had discovered very quickly that the way to survive was to be allocated to the textile division, the sewing or weaving shops. Those women sent to fell trees, heave coals or make roads in temperatures of minus thirty degrees could count their lives in weeks.

Other tasks also suffered a high rate of fatalities. It was dangerous to be selected as field whores for SS brothels or as *Putzfrauen*, house slaves, to the families of SS officers. Death was even more certain for those women chosen for medical experiments

164

run by Dr Scildlavsky, the Senior Medical Officer in the *Revier*, the camp hospital. These female guinea pigs were known as 'the rabbit girls', but children were also used by Dr Percy Treite. The loathsome Matron Elizabeth Marschall supervised experiments for sterilization – without anaesthetic – and studies on the effects of gangrene poisoning, where the unfortunate victims were first infected with bacteria.

The watery sun touched the barbed-wire fence, glimpsed for a moment through the window of the Sewing Room. The women went to work in the dark and returned to their huts in the dark after fourteen hours, to where the ration of turnip soup awaited them. Those who fainted from weakness or hunger while at the workbench were taken for punishment to the *Bunker*. This was a complex of tiny little cells where the worst offenders were dealt with by SS wardresses.

Evening was the time when the prisoners were taken for flogging at the Punishment Wall. Dorothea Binz and Margaret Mewes used leather-covered whips, while Carmen Mory preferred a buckled belt to administer anything from twenty to forty strokes. Those who survived were left to stand all through the night up against the wall, crying and whimpering like animals in pain.

This was the misery of life in Ravensbrück that winter of 1944. Diane lay in the bottom bunk near the huddled bodies of her neighbours, too cold to sleep. How many days, weeks, months had she lain here fighting with her memories? Time and the world outside were factors she dared not think about. One day at a time, that was how she lived. Her whole existence was concentrated down into this narrow realm of unreality where women were numbers, where friends were a liability, and death waited for the unwary at every turn.

She wrestled with her memories, knowing them for enemies. She was afraid to let herself remember that any other world existed beyond the camp, to believe that people she had known and loved in that other life could still exist. If she once let herself dwell on those thoughts all her resolve would crack and she knew she would be lost.

It had been a hard lesson to learn. When she first arrived at Ravensbrück, after the terrible journey cramped in the slow-moving train, she thought she was going mad with the tumbling nightmares that filled her brain. The sight of those boxcars waiting at the Paris railhead had completely destroyed her spirit. She had screamed and fainted, and if it had not been for the other women who were her nameless companions she might never have lived to see Germany at all. The worst of her fears for Dieter's survival were now confirmed.

All her thoughts were of Michelle, Michelle as she had last seen her, pinioned in the arms of the wardress at Fresnes. 'Maman!' she screamed over and over in her head, her pinched little face twisted with anguish, 'Maman! Maman!'

Somewhere, she was somewhere back there. Sonia, Hélène, Nicole, were any of them with her? Looking after her, feeding her? She could not share the monstrous agony that she felt for her missing child. She wondered how many days and nights she would have to spend behind the wire at Ravensbrück, while the world turned without her as if she were dead.

At first it was unendurable. Her name was not the name Michelle called out when she was afraid or hurt. She would not be the one to comfort and hold her, to see her walk, to learn to run, to teach her to read and write and – the list was endless. Everything was happening without her.

Michelle was three, four, no – five. It was imposs-ible to accept. The small child of her memory, the baby who cried out 'Maman, Maman!' might no longer even remember her real mother's existence.

Why was she torturing herself like this? These thoughts were the way to despair and death. I will not allow this to break me! she swore to herself, she swore to Michelle. One day this war would be over and she would be free to find her daughter again.

Survive, survive, for Michelle's sake. This was her litany, the mantra she repeated over and over, year by year, to keep her hope alive.

The winter was slow to die that year. Spring was reluctant to visit Ravensbrück concentration camp. Before the last of the ice had melted from the main street turning all to mud, the camp was honoured by a visit from a top-ranking officer of the SS. Some said that it was Himmler himself. A few weeks later a team of 'experts' arrived to construct a new chamber on the site. There was no mystery about the purpose of this chamber being built close to the Youth Camp, where they kept the child workforce. The 'experts' had built similar chambers throughout *Ostland* for the purpose of processing the dead more efficiently, more economically. But this was to be no ordinary crematorium.

When the first stage of their work was completed, the team of 'experts' could be seen talking and smoking, looking over the massed ranks of women inmates at *Appell*. A number of pink cards were handed out. Only later did the women realize that these were the admission tickets to oblivion. The new gas chamber was now in operation.

There was an atmosphere of growing panic in the camp. Since the new year a series of firing squads had replaced the floggings at the Punishment Wall

167

for the slightest infringement. Rations had been dramatically halved, and then halved again. It was as though the camp authorities were set upon reducing the numbers of inmates by whatever means possible. And now the gas chamber had accelerated this 'task'.

Diane looked about her at the dwindling numbers at the morning *Appell* and kept her head low. To attract the attention of the SS or *Kapos* in any way was to court an early death.

I will survive, I will come through all of this, she vowed. I will outlive them all. For Michelle's sake.

Then something else very strange happened. A number of Red Cross lorries arrived in the camp to take away a certain number of the inmates. Diane discovered they were all Danes and Norwegians. It was the Swedish Red Cross rescuing Scandinavian prisoners – Aryan women. The chosen few were delirious with joy as they queued to board the line of white buses and ambulances. They knew nothing of Count Bernadotte, their saviour, and the deal he had made with Himmler himself to save their lives. The war was going very badly. The Scandinavian women were the fortunate bargaining chips in a last-ditch plan by top Nazis to save their own necks.

The Germans, the invincible all-powerful Master Race, had lost the war. The SS showed distinct signs of panic. The camp was full of rumours. The Russians were coming, they were already in the Reich. Suddenly, with the spring sunshine, the women of Ravensbrück learnt the meaning of hope.

But Diane was more cautious. She had been betrayed before. She dared not allow herself to think of the future. She knew that the numbers at *Appell* were decreasing alarmingly. The crematorium could no longer process the numbers of inmates who had succumbed from the lowered rations, tuberculosis and the typhoid and typhus that were sweeping the

168

camp. The huts overflowed with the dead and the dying. A mounting pile of corpses occupied one corner of the main street.

At last came the momentous day when the sky to the east cracked with a noise like approaching thunder. Only the panic on the faces of the SS guards told Diane that this was more than a spring storm. It was Nemesis herself.

Diane was one of the shuffling line of women who set off on a forced march west from the camp while the frantic SS troopers anxiously looked back over their shoulders. The Russian guns came closer by the hour.

Diane was faintly surprised to find there were still so many women left alive. They were packed eighty or ninety to a boxcar on the single-track railway that ran westwards through the forest. Their destination was unknown.

How long did they travel, sealed in suffocating misery, without food, without water? The prison train had the lowest priority. It was diverted time and time again into sidings and on to loop lines in order to make way for military transports and to avoid bombed-out sections, until at last the train ground to a final halt in a deep forest clearing and never moved again.

In the stinking cattle trucks the living jostled for air, trampling the bodies of their dead sisters in a futile struggle to reach the high vents near the roof. From the cars on either side came a faint sobbing, a wail of despair. Her throat gagged with the desire for water, her body burned with the heat of fever. All around her the women bore the unmistakable marks of typhus. Incubated in the camp, the disease had spread like wildfire in the boxcars. It was the end, she knew. Stalled in the gloom of the forest,

169

abandoned, forgotten, the train had become her morgue.

Paul Rafelson, captain in the United States Army, classified the German prisoners taken in his sector into two distinct categories. First, there were the serfs, the run of the mill, ordinary guys who had been drafted into the Wehrmacht and were now eager to give themselves up in their hundreds and thousands. The second category were a different breed altogether. These were the career soldiers and the ideologues, including the SS fanatics. Even after they had been captured, these men continued to believe themselves invincible. They openly sneered at their captors, convinced of their innate superiority over the Americans, whom they regarded as racial hybrids.

As the Allied armies had struck forward into Germany, Paul Rafelson, like many others, had been willing to give the German nation the benefit of the doubt. Yes, there were atrocities, but war was a filthy business under any flag. It was not until he had personally seen the first camp for himself that Rafelson understood how he had been deceiving himself. There was no comparison possible between an act of war and the cold-blooded, detached, bureaucratic process of torture and death as practised by the Nazis against their fellow human beings.

The discovery of Natzweiler, Belsen, Dachau and Mauthausen in the south, of Majdanek, Treblinka, Sobibor and Auschwitz in the east, and of Kulmhof, Sachsenhausen, Gross-Rosen and Ravensbrück could only harden the attitude of Allied soldiers to the German nation en masse.

No words could describe the obscenities revealed by the liberation of the camps. Rafelson had accompanied his commanding officer to confront the

170

inhabitants of villages who claimed total ignorance of what had been going on for years nearby. How could they deny all knowledge of what had happened there? The air was still rancid with the stench of burning flesh. The smoke stack of the crematorium was visible from their homes, the night sky glowed crimson from the furnaces. The villagers had been forced to walk through the camp at rifle point, to witness for themselves the abomination that had been carried out in the name of the German people by their elected representatives, so that none of them might ever deny in future that they did not know the stark truth.

With his unit Rafelson continued to round up small scattered groups of German troops who had deserted their posts. Eastwards along the railway line they encountered numbers of SS men, camp guards who had abandoned their charges in their frantic desire to escape from the Russian line, hoping for greater clemency among the American or British forces.

In this way Rafelson learnt of the existence of the prison train from Ravensbrück hidden in the depths of a forest siding.

There was a curious oppression about the clearing. The silence was the first thing that struck Rafelson and made his men uneasy. No birds sang in these trees, even the wind was still. There was an atmosphere of intense desolation as they suddenly saw the line of boxcars like so many coffins.

The doors, of course, were sealed. They had to find a jack to break them open, but they already had a presage of what they would find inside. On the wooden side of one of the cattle trucks someone had chalked the words of warning, '*Achtung*! Typhus!'

They found the boxcars piled high with corpses. Scarcely recognizable as women, the contorted tangle of human limbs, the stench, the spotted rash, all confirmed the presence of typhus. Ashen-faced, the troops opened up car after car and all they liberated were corpses. Until they came to the last few wagons.

Rafelson and his men could not hold back the tears as they pulled the first of the survivors from among her dead companions. She was no more than skin and bone, filthy and festering with sores and lice. Her fever-bright eyes surveyed the strange uniforms with curious detachment.

To Rafelson's astonishment Diane looked straight at him and said in perfect English, 'I waited as long as I could. Don't let me die now, will you? Don't let me die.'

16

'Please don't let me die,' she had begged him, and the look on her face and the sound of her voice had haunted him ever since.

They had taken her with three other survivors from the train to the local field hospital. The army surgeon had not given much hope for her survival, but Paul Rafelson was not prepared to listen to him.

'I don't care what you have to do,' he told the doctor, his words sounding harsh even to his own ears, 'you just have to save her. She's been through all kinds of hell. You don't give up on her now, do you hear me?'

A week later he heard that she had been transferred back down the line to a special hospital unit run by UNRRA, the United Nations Relief and Rehabilitation Administration. One of her fellow survivors had already died from typhus, but he was assured that these UNRRA people were used to handling cases from the camps. They were getting enough experience, after all.

At the end of the month he found himself back within thirty miles of the hospital. The war was over, the peace just five days old. On a forty-eight-hour pass he took a Jeep and drove south down the *Autobahn*, knowing he had to see her.

He found it hard to explain why he should have been so moved. She was only one among many women who had suffered unspeakable tragedies in the last five years. He had seen all kinds in the past few weeks: Polacks, Russians, Czechs, but the fact that she was English had made her stick in his mind.

173

What the hell was an English woman doing out here? What was her story?

He realized that he knew nothing whatsoever about her. Not even her name. She was 'the English woman' or 'one of the Ravensbrück women'. But he could not just walk away without knowing that she would come through, get safely home to her people, to her own family, if she had one. He had been the one to find her. Now he felt a certain sense of responsibility towards her that could not be denied.

The hospital proved to be a collection point for the flotsam and jetsam of every camp and prison within a hundred and fifty miles. In the weak sunshine Paul passed a number of walking ghosts shuffling around the neat rectangle of the front garden, their eyes blank, dead to emotion. Looking at their thin wraith-like bodies, Paul was conscious of his own robust, almost obscene good health. He felt like an intruder among these living dead, an interloper from an alien world.

The women's ward was on the first floor. He approached one of the nurses, a petite auburn-haired woman with a distinctive Scottish accent, and made inquiries.

'An English woman?' She looked at him curiously. 'There's no English woman here. Are you sure you've come to the right place?'

'Of course I'm sure.' His voice betrayed his panic. For a moment he thought she must have died. A cold hand seemed to clutch at his heart and he knew he should have prepared himself for the possibility.

'Which camp was she from?'

'Ravensbrück.'

'There were only three of them. A Pole, a French woman and a Belgian – but she died two days ago. "At least I have seen the Nazis defeated," that's what she said. Too weak, of course. That's the problem with all these cases. They can't take the food at first, it's too much for their systems.'

'The Belgian woman, did she speak English?'

'No, French. Luckily for us, Sister Channing is something of a linguist. She speaks French and German.'

Suddenly Paul thought he understood what had happened. He said, 'Could I see the other two women? It's very important to me. You see, I found them. I found the train they were on, just abandoned in the middle of nowhere.'

The nurse did not argue with him. Perhaps she understood something of the desperation he was feeling, perhaps she too had become involved with her patients. She led the way into a day ward where about twenty skeletal women in regulation hospital dressing gowns sat listlessly around.

'Waiting for the next meal,' the nurse explained. 'It's all they live for.' She stopped and indicated two of the women nearest the window. 'There they are. They sit like that all day, hardly ever saying a word, poor things.'

Paul moved towards the women with something approaching apprehension. There was nothing familiar about either figure in the plain blue gowns that were much too big on their angular birdlike frames. The first woman turned sharply and stared up at him, her brown eyes opening in alarm. Her long, yellow face was full of hollow shadows, but it was the face of a stranger. Paul gave her a reassuring smile but she glared back at him with that look of permanent suspicion and he quickly passed by to stand before her companion.

'Excuse me.'

The woman sat in a chair staring out of the window. The hair on her head was a bare half inch all over, an anonymous dark brown in colour. She turned around slowly, as if startled to hear the sound of English, and he took a sharp intake of breath as he recognized the woman from the train.

Even in extremity she had been beautiful. Since he had last seen her she had put on a little weight. Her skin was very pale, like ivory, with blue shadows under the eyes that watched him steadily. They were haunted, desperate eyes. She had been very ill, he could see that, but in those eyes was the same fanatical resolution to survive that he remembered from the train.

'Do you remember me?' he asked her softly.

She looked at him for a full minute, as if struggling to recall someone out of the mists of her memory. In the end he thought it was probably the uniform she remembered.

'You're American,' she whispered, but at least it was in English.

He sat on the arm of the empty chair opposite her, his cap in his hands. A feeling of elation stole over him. He wanted suddenly to know everything about her, but he knew he must tread slowly so as not to alarm her.

'What's your name?'

She blinked, a little startled by his question.

'My name is Paul,' he volunteered.

'I'm Diane.'

'Diane,' he repeated the name with great satisfaction. 'Diane what?'

'Clément.'

'So you're French? Diane, *vous êtes Française?*'

She seemed confused by his question, or perhaps by the change in languages.

'Paris, do you know Paris, Diane?'

A spark of life flashed in her remarkable hazel eyes.

'I want to go home. I want—'

176

'What? What do you want, Diane?'

She leaned forward suddenly and laid a feather-light white hand on the sleeve of his jacket. 'Do you have news? Do you know where they've taken her?'

'Who, Diane?'

'Michelle,' she said impatiently. 'They took Michelle. Where is she?'

When he did not answer a look of complete anguish came over her face. She withdrew her hand and her eyes widened. Before he could foresee the danger, she put back her head and began to scream.

Paul leapt to his feet, appalled. The other patients had all turned round to stare at them, but no one made any attempt to intervene. Diane rocked back and forth in her chair, crying out the same name over and over.

At last the little Scottish nurse arrived and, putting an arm around Diane, looked across at him reproachfully.

'I think you had better leave, Captain.'

'I want my baby!' sobbed Diane, still speaking English. 'Where's Michelle? What have they done with her?'

Paul did not want to leave her like that but the nurse was plainly blaming him. He obediently retreated to the door of the ward. He looked back, aware of feelings of guilt and pity intermingled with an even deeper sense of duty. He had little idea about Michelle, her missing child – surely a baby no longer? – but now he knew she existed, they both existed, he felt bound to her by a deep, humanitarian commitment.

Paris was still Paris, as the song had promised. It was just the people who had changed. Simone Blanchard was no exception. They were all so naive, so pathetically eager to make up for the years they had missed,

177

that they plunged headlong into the postwar mael-strom. The Germans had gone, only to be replaced by a floodtide of American troops filling the bars and pavement cafés or crowding on to the Métro. Gay Paris had not quite recovered from her years of deprivation. Rationing was still very much in force, not only for food but for fuel and clothing. The war was over but France was impoverished and there was a great deal of resentment that, although victorious, they had nothing to show for it.

In the long year between the liberation of Paris and the first heady days of peace in Europe, Simone and her companion Juliette Lamartine moved house twice. At first they found a large *atelier* near St Odile which seemed ideal, but the winter of 1944 was especially fierce and fuel was unobtainable. Weary of chilblains and triple layers of woollen jerseys, they moved that spring to an apartment in respectable Neuilly, just two streets from the house where Lucien Caristan's father had lived before his death.

Juliette was good company and the two women became firm friends, but as the Allied armies pushed deep into Germany news reached Juliette that her husband had been traced in a prison camp near Munich. The startling news opened up old wounds for Simone. She did not begrudge Juliette the joy of their anticipated reunion, but the fact that Patrice Lamartine had survived raised the phantom hope that others, too, might still be waiting to be found in the night and fog of the Nazi empire.

It was too late for Lucien, but there had been no word at all of the fate of Christian, Gervais – and above all, of Diane and her daughter Michelle. When Simone and Juliette had first read the newspaper accounts of the concentration camps they sat up all night talking of their lost friends. Simone would repeat the story of Diane's whirlwind romance with

Dieter and the trauma of his arrest and deportation. Juliette would live again the news of her husband's arrest at the Sorbonne and her own escape, with Simone's help, to the *cachette* in Levallois.

Following VE Day it was natural that people should have expected the immediate return of the thousands of deportees and prisoners of war being released from the camps. But the process proved disturbingly slow. All kinds of rumours came out of Germany about the death of internees while in the care of the Red Cross, from disease, from malnutrition and mistakes in overfeeding.

In September, unable to bear the waiting any longer, Juliette moved from Neuilly and went back to the Fifth *arrondissement* apartment she had shared with her husband to await his return. The trial and execution of war criminals seemed to take priority over the rehabilitation of their victims. The newspapers were full of the attempted suicide of Laval and his subsequent execution in October, and speculation was rife about the possible fate awaiting the great names about to face trial at Nuremberg, but the men and women from the camps seemed to have been forgotten.

The joy of victory and the high expectations Simone had once had for the peace were now clouded by doubt and disillusionment. As she approached her thirtieth birthday, Simone felt herself to be standing at the crossroads, and the future in all directions appeared unerringly bleak. Even her work no longer satisfied her. The challenge had gone, and she knew she would have to make a complete break from the dull routine to which she had settled if she did not want to be in the same job, the same rut, in another fifteen or twenty years' time.

It was in this mood that Simone returned one evening from the hospital and unlocked the door of

179

her empty apartment in Neuilly to find the message. It was just a slip of paper roughly torn from some notepad. It had been folded and pushed under her door to await her return, and as Simone bent to retrieve it she had no inkling or presentiment of what it could mean.

Then she saw the handwriting and a warning bell rang in the recesses of her mind. She read the three sentences over and over again before she could really take in the startling truth:

'I am back in Paris. I called but you were not here. I will come again this evening.'

It was signed, simply, Diane.

Simone had to sit down on the sofa and take a glass of straight spirits. Her hands shook and the alcohol went straight to her head, but her mind was already whirling from the shock.

She suddenly found she was crying, with relief, with thanksgiving for this reprieve. She had been so lonely, so lonely, and now Diane was back! She would no longer be the sole survivor of her memories. Now there really was a chance for the future.

But what kind of woman would she find? What kind of horrors had her friend endured all these years apart? Had she come out of Germany, out of some nightmare camp like those she had read about in the newspapers, seen on the cinema newsreels? How would an experience like that have changed her?

Then she realized that something was wrong. She stared once again at the message in her hands. Diane had written, 'I am back . . . I called . . . I will come again', with no mention at all of Michelle.

Where was Michelle? All these years, even in her worst nightmares, she had always imagined mother and daughter together. She had always thought, at least they have each other. But now it seemed she had been deceiving herself, creating a dream of false comfort with no real understanding of the stark and barren horror her friend really suffered.

She saw with alarm her tear-streaked face in the mirror. She did not want Diane to arrive and see her like this. She quickly washed and changed her dress, reminding herself that this was to be a celebration. She had to put on a brave face, not knowing quite what to expect. She opened a new bottle of wine and raided her food supplies to make a few hors d'oeuvres, wondering if she would expect to eat in or go out for a meal. But at that moment the doorbell rang.

In trepidation, steeling herself to face the worst, Simone opened the door.

The woman standing on the landing in a long dark coat was a stranger, and yet undeniably Diane.

'Diane, *ah mon Dieu*, Diane, it's you.'

The two women fell forward into each other's arms and silently buried their heads on each other's shoulders. Simone began to cry again as she felt how angular and thin was the figure she clung to, and yet how strong was the woman who stood comforting her. There were no tears on her gaunt pale cheeks, only a calm understanding that made Simone suddenly ashamed. She drew apart, quickly wiping her eyes, and with false gaiety said, 'Come in, come in, you can't stand out here! Let me take your coat.'

She was shabbily dressed, as if in other people's cast-offs. Her skin was almost transparent and the eyes unusually bright, all the signs of a long traumatic illness. Her hand was cold and frail as a child's and trembled as she accepted the glass of wine Simone thrust towards her.

'Your hair—' Simone began, and then stopped, quite overcome with embarrassment. She did not know what to say next.

'It's awful, isn't it?' Diane lightly touched the short dark boyish crop that gave her face an elfin quality. 'Perhaps I'll start a new fashion.'

She looked around the apartment, walking with the glass of wine in her hand. She sensed everything with a poignant delight, tracing her fingers over the fabric of the curtains, the feel of a china figurine. She was childlike in her appreciation and yet curiously wary, a little distant, apparently unable to relax. Simone watched her with growing unease, aware of her tension, the highly strung control of her emotions. Simone stifled all the questions she longed to ask, about the camp, about her release, about Michelle most of all. She knew she had to restrain her natural curiosity and wait for Diane to make the first move.

'You know, Simone,' Diane announced, turning abruptly to stand by the stove, 'it took me three days to find you! You moved around so much.'

'You've been back three days? And I didn't know —'

'I went first of all to the Rue de Rennes. It was only natural, after all. But even Madame Laclos had gone. There was no one there I remembered. It felt as though I had been away for forty years, not four. Then I went to the Hôtel-Dieu to look for you. They at least had kept records.' She gave a faint smile. 'I'm becoming used to this detective work.'

'But I changed hospitals, too.'

'So I discovered. You really led me quite a dance, you know! But I wouldn't give up —' Her face suddenly grew taut and the shadow of some unspoken memory seemed to unsettle her. She shivered and sat down.

182

'You're still not well —'

'No. I've been in hospital myself. They wouldn't let me come back until now.'

'Do you want to talk about it?' The words were out before Simone could restrain herself. 'I'm sorry, I don't want to intrude —'

Diane laid a hand on her arm and murmured, 'Oh, Simone.' The sleeve of her dress had drawn up to reveal a number tattooed in blue ink on her forearm. She caught Simone looking at it and realized at once that she understood what it was. All her reservations and control suddenly cracked and the words came tumbling out in a cascade of unrestrained emotion.

Through a long night Diane talked for the first time of her experiences, of Fresnes, of the sealed train, and Ravensbrück. She spoke of things she had pushed out of her consciousness, of events she had tried so hard to forget. She scarcely looked at her friend's face, she seemed almost mesmerized by the need to exorcise the ghosts of her past. In her heart she had vowed never to talk of this to anyone, but now she did not seem able to stop. The dreadful truth had a momentum all of its own. Diane could not rest until she had unburdened the weight of her memory to this, her oldest and best-loved friend.

'I've talked too much. I've told you things tonight I never want to tell anyone ever again.'

She ended on the hardest note of all, dragging the tormented image back to centre-stage: that winter's day at Fresnes when they forced her to separate from her child.

'I lied,' Diane confessed, her voice little above a whisper. 'I took three days to find you because first of all I had to look for Michelle.'

She had gone straight to Fresnes, haunted by the remembrance of her daughter pinioned in the arms of the Nazi wardress. 'But there was no trace of her,

183

no records.' She shook her head and began to rock desperately back and forth, hot tears starting to pour down her cheeks. 'Only the thought of finding Michelle kept me alive. She kept me strong. She gave me a reason to hold on.'

Simone hugged her, overcome and full of feelings of alarming inadequacy. She stifled her own story of the last few years out of concern for Diane, but her own life had been far from easy. She had no heart to mention her own troubles and the misery and loneliness of her present life. She wanted to help her, she wanted to find something to say that would pull her friend back from the abyss.

Diane whispered, 'If she is dead then I have survived for nothing.'

'No, no, she's alive, I know she is!'

Diane ran her hands over her strained white face. 'Do you think so? Can we find her?'

'Of course. We must. I promise we'll find her,' Simone swore fervently, unaware of how long and harrowing a journey they were about to embark upon.

17

Half of Europe was on the move that summer of 1945. When the Allied armies liberated the prisons and concentration camps they opened up the floodgates. Millions of displaced people had been forcibly dragged from their homes and transported halfway across the continent. Now they had but a single thought in their minds: to return home. The difficulties of getting transport, the fear of what they might find – or not find – when they finally reached their home towns and villages again, none of this could prevent the mass movement of slave labourers and deportees.

In Germany temporary centres were set up to house the former inmates of the concentration camps. In the beginning many died from disease and weakness. The inexperienced new authorities had little or no knowledge of the effects of malnutrition and a great many of their charges died from eating the large meals pressed upon them. As a result, rations in these centres were drastically cut, until they resembled nothing so much as the penal rations of the Nazi period. Rioting broke out, Allied troops and police moved in. The whole situation was growing increasingly dangerous and out of control.

Berlin in particular was beset by lawlessness. Marauding gangs of drunks roamed the ruins by night, homes and stores were looted, and in the morning the victims of murders and knife fights littered the streets. Since the Russian victory and according to the agreement previously signed by the Allies at Yalta, Berlin was divided into four sectors ruled by the Soviet Union, Britain, the United States and France. The demarcation lines between these little kingdoms were marked by multi-lingual billboards announcing the new ownership, but passage between the sectors was virtually uncontrolled. Many Germans who lived in the eastern part of the city now chose to move westwards, often to evade arrest and retribution from special Soviet squads hunting for SS war criminals. Also moving into the western sectors were thousands of homeless refugees who had fled the city for the countryside to avoid the shelling and bombing.

Among this number at the beginning of June was Lydia Ulrich and her five-year-old adopted daughter Jutta. Around them they found a lunarscape of rubble and ruins beyond all recognition. Every third building had been wiped from the face of the earth, and those that were left were often fire-blackened shells standing like accusing fingers in the dust-tortured wasteland.

In what had once been the prestigious suburb of Charlottenburg, where Lydia and Karl had their apartment, someone had chalked on one of the few remaining walls, '*Das verdanken wir Adolf Hitler*': for this we must thank Adolf Hitler. Bitterness was rife among the people Lydia encountered, bitterness against the Nazis who had lost the war and brought them to this state, and bitterness against their new masters whether British, American, French or Russian.

In the western sectors the Allies had commandeered many of the remaining buildings to billet their own troops and regiments of civil servants. These new *Herrenvolk* moved into the standing villas and houses of the former Nazi hierarchy and took over their privileges. The French, in particular, set out to exact reparations from the German people

186

and made it clear they intended to make the defeated nation pay for the four years of degradation and humiliation when France was occupied. The Germans had become the new *Untermensch* in their own land.

Life had certainly changed. Ever since Lydia became separated from her husband on the outskirts of Berlin in April she'd had to learn how to survive alone, relying on no one else for support or help. Of the few possessions she had managed to salvage from her flight from the city there was virtually nothing of value left. The astute farmers and villagers in the countryside outside Berlin made a quick fortune by preying on the desperate stream of refugees passing along their roads. For over a month Lydia and Jutta had survived by bartering away her rings and the several items of jewellery piecemeal for a daily ration of bread and potatoes. They slept where they could, in barns if they were lucky, under hedgerows if they were not. Common humanity seemed an outdated and superfluous emotion. Even a child of Jutta's age could not melt stoney self-interest and the desire for a quick profit.

How many times when lying in a huddle together in the outhouse of some farmer's field, stomachs cramped with hunger, afraid of being robbed or attacked, had Lydia longed for the support and strength of her husband. What had become of Karl? Had he escaped from Berlin or did he fall foul of some roaming SS unit pressganging men for a last-ditch stand in the name of a dead Führer?

Lydia thought with longing of the money and collection of old gold coins Karl had hidden away in his bedroll, especially after his silver cigar box had gone to buy two loaves of bread and a quart of milk for Jutta that had to last them the best part of a week. News of the surrender seemed like a blessed relief.

The refugee tide began to turn, and the roads became thronged with starving women and children eager to return home to Berlin.

Lydia traded her fur coat and sound leather gloves to a plump farmer's wife for enough food to see them on their way. Lydia and Jutta walked more than fifty miles in eight days, sleeping where they could and making their small supply of food last until they could reach Berlin, where they hoped to find better things. But they were to be disillusioned. They found the new Berlin a terrifying wilderness peopled by a ruthless, shifting population competing for food, for work and for somewhere to stay.

The day after their arrival, exhausted from a sleepless night spent watching over her daughter in the corner of a bombed-out church, Lydia queued at a British Army soup kitchen for emergency rations. All around her were grim-faced women and solemn, silent children waiting for charity. They made a strange sight, uniform in their drab clothes and broken-down shoes, probably the only outfits most of them had left. Women from every strata of society were now reduced to the same bitter penury, forced to come begging to their conquerors for a meal.

As Lydia and Jutta sat at the roadside industriously mopping up the very last trace of their soup, Lydia became aware that they were being watched by a woman she had first noticed talking to one of the British soldiers.

'She's a pretty girl,' said the woman, coming over and looking down at Jutta.

Lydia put a protective arm around her daughter and raised suspicious eyes.

'You needn't be afraid,' the woman said quickly, and there was a startling note of irony in her voice, 'I don't mean her any harm. It's just that she reminds

188

me of someone who is dead now. She was blonde, too.'

'Your daughter?'

The woman nodded. 'She was almost twelve, but she looked just like your girl at that age.' She looked at them sharply. 'You're new around here. I haven't seen you before.'

'We just got back from the country. I had hoped – well, I suppose it was foolish of me. I mean, there's nowhere left now, is there?'

'You don't have anywhere to stay?'

'Not any more.'

The woman seemed to hesitate. She had quite a tall, well-proportioned figure, badly dressed in a cheap cotton dress, but she had at least made an effort to look clean and tidy. Her red-brown hair was her best feature, falling just short of her shoulders. Lydia thought the style rather too young for her. She must, after all, have been at least forty.

'You could stay with me,' she announced suddenly, her eyes still fixed on Jutta. 'I've found a decent place. Two rooms, a roof overhead. It's not far away. What do you say? I could do with the company.'

Lydia could scarcely believe the offer. It was the first time any one of her countrymen or women had tried to help her. She regretted her hasty assessment of her new friend. She stood up. 'I'm Lydia and this is Jutta.'

'Renata, Renata Jansen.'

The 'decent place' proved to be a basement flat at the far end of what had previously been the smart Hohenzollerndamm. A fierce fire had wiped out most of the other houses on the block, and at first Lydia could see nowhere that seemed at all habitable. But although the rest of the block was little more than a burnt-out shell, by going round to the rear of the building Renata revealed a garden entrance that led down to her miraculously preserved new home. It was sparsely furnished, but at least it was dry and sheltered. To Lydia and Jutta it looked like paradise.

'You should have seen it when I first arrived,' Renata told them apologetically. 'I've only been here two weeks myself. I came over from Horst Wessel.'

So Renata had come out of the Russian sector. She told Lydia more about herself that night after Jutta had gone to sleep in the adjoining room. She had stayed in Berlin right through the May days, even after her daughter Helena was killed in the heavy bombardment of 28 April. She had been standing in a queue for water at the street pump and was killed outright.

'She was lucky,' her mother concluded, 'she escaped what came later.'

She said that the first Russian troops to enter Berlin had taken them all by surprise. They were expecting monsters, but these were highly disciplined crack units intent on moving against the Chancellery Bunker as quickly as possible. They shared their rations with the Berliners and gave crude, sugary sweets to the children. One of them had warned Renata to get away before the support units arrived. 'They are the very devils,' he told her, and so it proved. They were mostly men from the Central Asian steppes who, in common with the hordes of Genghis Khan, set about raping and looting with alacrity. Renata was no exception, but fortunately her rapist quickly discovered a conscience and began to bring her food and sing her songs. Best of all, he protected her against the worst excesses of his friends.

'How could you bear it? I would have died of shame,' Lydia said softly, genuinely shocked by her story.

190

'Oh, he wasn't so bad,' Renata disclosed. 'But I survived, and that's all that counts in the end.'

Lydia looked at her with newfound admiration. She was right, of course, survival was all that mattered. She had thought she could not manage without Karl, but when she had to she discovered a new strength inside herself, a will to live. In her heart she knew it was because of Jutta. Jutta was her life. She survived only for her. She would even make the best of these terrible conditions, find work, learn to begin again, for Jutta. Nothing lasted for ever and she had fared better than Renata. Her example gave her courage.

Berlin had become a city of women. The male-dominated society of Nazi Germany had crumbled to dust and the few men who were left were changed beyond all recognition, craven, cowed, hiding themselves away. The women were born survivors, revealing their own inner power and strength. They despised the men who had brought them to this disastrous state of affairs and now had deserted them to the threat of rape and hunger.

Every day Lydia saw gangs of women scrabbling about on the mountains of rubble. These were the *Trümmerfrauen*, working to clear the bomb-sites, salvaging and cleaning bricks that could be used to rebuild their city. The work was hard and laborious, but the women received top rations.

Famine threatened the city. Rations varied from a thousand calories a day for workers down to the 'Death Card' held by dependants and the unemployed. Even during the war Germany had never been self-sufficient. The Nazis had looted food and supplies from each of the occupied countries and sent it all home to the Reich. Harvests had been transported in their entirety, warehouses stripped, industries and fuel depots emptied.

France had been threatened with starvation, Russia and Eastern Europe had been crippled. Now these victorious powers wanted it all back. Whatever could be moved was commandeered and sent out of the Four Powers' zones. The German people would have to manage as best they could.

In those first few weeks Lydia had been sacrificing her own health for Jutta's sake. She gave her daughter most of her share of her scanty ration, telling Renata that she needed less food than a growing child. But Renata was not fooled. She herself had found another way to survive.

The Allied High Command had tried to prevent the 'fraternization' of their troops with local German women. The Americans imposed a sixty-five-dollar fine on any of their own men who were caught in compromising situations, but the soldiers were not deterred, especially when they saw their officers with the pick of Berliners. This 'sixty-five-dollar question' caused much amusement among the women who supplemented their rations with a little 'frat' on the side.

American cigarettes could buy food on the thriving black market. A packet of Lucky Strikes or Camels could keep a family for a month. There were even men who were reduced to following Allied soldiers around picking up their cigarette butts.

When Lydia informed Renata that she had been taken on as one of the *Trümmerfrauen*, Renata thought she was crazy. There were 'easier' ways to live, she insisted.

'You're still an attractive woman. You're too good for that kind of work.'

By contrast, Lydia thought herself too good for Renata's kind of work. The *Trümmerfrauen*, rough as their work was, as rough as they could be, were at least good-hearted, honest women who took one another at face value and did not care about the past. There was an easy-going kind of camaraderie among the gangs of workers on the bomb-sites that soon broke down reserve and inhibitions. There was an air of optimism and defiance among the women as they passed buckets from hand to hand, making outrageous remarks and cracking coarse jokes. In their dark dresses, overalls and head scarves, this army of women scuttled like so many stray cats among the dust-white skeletons of lost homes and the vast bomb craters strewn with wild flowers and weeds.

Lydia's only regret about her new work was the fact of leaving Jutta alone for long hours during the day. Renata assured her that Jutta was well able to look after herself. Once, when Lydia came home, Jutta had gone missing. Eventually she was found with a gang of street urchins playing with a pair of roller-skates on the bulldozed roads between the mounds of rubble. Although she scolded her, Lydia realized that Renata was right. Jutta was growing into a self-assured, independent-minded little girl of considerable resourcefulness. On another occasion she came home with a precious bar of chocolate given her by a British soldier.

It was one day in November that Lydia, while working on the bomb-sites, first heard of *Lebensborn*. One of the women had been talking about her sister who had come to Berlin from the country just the week before. She was full of stories of the displaced persons' camp set up by the Allies near her home town and what had gone on in the work camp there during the war. Some of her stories, if she was to be believed, made Lydia's blood run cold. She felt she had either been very naive or very stupid in blindly accepting so much at face value in the past. Had such terrible things really been going on for years? – the deaths, the tortures and all the other dreadful things she talked about?

To Lydia one of the most shocking things was her story about the children who were taken away from the women prisoners by officials of the *Lebensborn* programme. The children, said the *Trümmerfrau*, were regarded as orphans and given for adoption.

The thought of those children troubled Lydia all day. As she worked she kept returning to those orphans who were not really orphans at all. It made her reconsider their own adoption of Jutta, and she suddenly thought how little she really knew about the child's past life before Karl brought her home from the state orphanage. Of course it was quite absurd to think for a moment that Jutta should have any connection at all with what the woman had talked about. But nevertheless, she remained troubled by disturbing thoughts of Jutta's real mother, whoever she was, whatever might have happened to her.

That evening, as the light declined, Lydia was about to set off home when she was approached by an elderly woman in a long threadbare man's overcoat. It took her a moment or two before she recognized Frau Heilmann who had been a neighbour at her former apartment in Charlottenburg.

'I thought I knew you, Frau Ulrich! I saw you here yesterday and I had to come back to bring you this letter.' Lydia stared at the crumpled envelope Frau Heilmann held out to her. 'It came to the old address, but of course since the shelling we had no way of tracing you. Luckily, I found a place to stay quite close – by the church on Zeller Strasse, you remember? – and I kept the letter for you, just in case you turned up, you know. I suppose it will be from your husband?'

'Yes,' murmured Lydia, feeling quite stunned, 'yes, I recognize his handwriting.'

'Well, my dear, I see you are quite overcome. I won't keep you. I'm glad to know you are both alive and well. And your sweet little girl, she's still with you?'

'She's very well, yes. Thank you, Frau Heilmann, I can't thank you enough!'

Karl was alive! The letter, written on cheap lined paper, was more than three months old. She clutched it tightly in her hand all the way back to Renata's house, telling herself over and over that Karl was well, that Karl was alive and safe.

Renata was out when she got back, so she sat down with Jutta and opened the envelope. Karl's spidery handwriting filled less than half a dozen lines. At the top of the page was some sort of official stamp with some words in English she did not understand and a scrawling signature. The letter was alarmingly brief and written in a very detached and off-hand manner as though to a stranger. 'Dear Lydia,' he wrote, 'I hope you are keeping well. I am safe and in a British prisoner-of-war camp.' He gave the postal address. 'Give my love to Jutta.' It was signed, remarkably, 'Karl Langen.'

Jutta saw the tears spring to her mother's eyes and demanded, 'Is Papi dead?'

Lydia smiled and drew Jutta to her. 'No, *Liebling*, not dead. He's safe but he will be away from us for a little while longer.'

Lydia struggled to understand how her husband came to be a British prisoner of war when he had never been in the army. She knew that all German troops were required to serve two years in a prison camp, but it was regarded as a light sentence compared to the retribution awaiting those members of the old régime classified by the Allies as 'war crimi-

195

nals'. In fact, she had heard that the prisoners of war were very well fed and looked after in the camps, and probably faring much better than their wives and children left to fend for themselves.

But she was more disturbed by the change in name. Karl had plainly given the British a false name, a false identity, but why? He obviously thought it safer to be Karl Langen in a camp than Karl Ulrich, a man on the run. The war made it easy to disguise the truth. Thousands had been killed, their identities unknown. Records and official papers had been lost or destroyed in the bombing. It was a simple matter for Karl Ulrich to become Karl Langen, or for Lydia Ulrich to become Lydia Langen. If that was what Karl wanted, then it was what she must do.

At Christmas the Allies resurrected the traditional Berlin *Weihnachtsmarkt* for the sake of the children. In the bitter cold hundreds of women queued for hours to get a place on the *Karuselle* for their small children who could not remember a Christmas without war and deprivation. As Lydia stood with Renata in the glare of the bright white lights and watched Jutta shriek with joy on the giddy round-about, she regretted that Karl could not be there with them.

At least now she knew the truth. Ahead of her she had another eighteen months or more alone. Eighteen months in which she and Jutta must struggle to get by on their own, secure only in the thought that one day Karl would be home with them again.

18

In that winter of 1945 Diane was obsessed with the thought that her daughter was still somewhere in Paris. Throughout her time in Ravensbrück the belief that Michelle had been kept in France for a purpose gave her the hope to go on living. Everyday she saw the children of the Youth Camp driven by the *kapos* to work until they dropped and she told herself, at least Michelle is safe. They would not have separated us if they meant her to become one of them.

As she walked the boulevards and avenues of the city she loved so well, Diane thought more than once that she saw Michelle. She would rush up to the child in the park, an angelic toddler with laughing face and flying plaits tied with red ribbons, only to realize like a fool that the little girl was no more than three years old and that Michelle, unbelievably, was now almost six.

She began to search the faces of every blonde-haired girl in every crocodile of children shepherded to school. She had to remind herself that four years had passed. Would she even recognize Michelle now? More alarmingly, she began to wonder if Michelle would remember her?

Somewhere in this great city, in some garret or apartment, rich or poor, some other woman was bringing up *her* child. What kind of life had she had in these past four years? The people of Paris were hungry, had been hungry all through the Occupation. Does Michelle have enough to eat? Is she well? Is she loved? Is she happy?

These imaginary games kept hope alive. She resolutely dismissed all thought of the obverse side of the coin: the treacherous possibility that for four years she had been deceiving herself, that through some illness or form of neglect Michelle no longer existed, Michelle was dead. To succumb to those dark thoughts was to open up the floodgates of depression and despair, to take away her only reason for living.

If Fresnes retained no records of the children who had passed through its gates, it did not necessarily mean that her name was not registered somewhere. In the vast bureaucracy of the French civil service the Nazis had found ample scope to indulge their own passion for red tape. Each *préfecture* and *mairie* seemed to have its own lists of those arrested, of *déportés* and of those *résistants* sent for immediate execution as hostages and martyrs of the Occupation.

For weeks Diane and Simone trailed from one *arrondissement* to another, each time filled with fresh expectations and hope, only to be let down and disappointed. Simone was still working at the hospital six mornings a week, but often Diane could not bear to wait until she could join her and went ahead on her own, always feeling that this time perhaps she would be lucky.

That spring there seemed an abundance of flowers in the parks and gardens of Paris, more beautiful than Diane could ever remember. She felt acutely sensitive to her surroundings, feeling the first warmth seeping into her bones, into the earth, stimulating new growth and life. The sweet smell of the trees in bud, the vibrant colours of the plants and flowers filled her senses as though she saw everything around her for the very first time like someone who has been blind and now can see.

Yet she was living on her nerves. She still took each day as it came, hardly daring to believe that weeks could become months and months years. She took nothing for granted any longer. She still did not know if her parents were alive or dead. At Simone's bidding she had finally written to them, not knowing if they were still at the old address or even if they had come through the London Blitz unscathed. Such a chasm of bitter experience now separated her present from her former life that the gulf almost seemed unbridgeable.

It was one afternoon in the week before Michelle's birthday, the day when she would be six years of age, that Diane's self-control almost gave way. She had taken upon herself the chore of standing in the food lines to queue for rations for Simone and herself. It was arduous and time-wasting but Diane wanted to do her share of the housekeeping for the flat in Neuilly as she was no longer capable of paying her own way or contributing towards the rent.

Standing in the queue outside the local *boulangerie* she became aware of a mother arguing with her daughter, a plain child about four or five years of age. In a moment of temper the unknown woman suddenly struck the girl a resolute slap on the face, nothing very serious, but it was enough to send Diane into a towering rage.

'Don't hit that child! Don't you dare hit her!' she screamed.

The child looked up at Diane and immediately burst into tears. Her mother and the other women in the queue stared round at her in an appalling embarrassed silence.

Diane felt the anger suddenly drain out of her body. She saw the shocked faces and gradually became aware of what she had done. Without a word she slunk quietly away from the shop, wondering if she was going mad. How were they to know that she had seen something of Michelle in that child? That

199

when the woman struck her she remembered all the times she had hit out at Michelle in anger or scolded her for being naughty. Those were the really terrible memories that tortured her with guilt.

She hurried away, scarcely aware of where she was going. She and Simone had arranged to meet that afternoon to go through the card index kept at the Hôtel de Ville on the Rue de Rivoli. Did it really matter if she went ahead on her own? She found herself in the Métro and the line was direct from Neuilly to the centre. Why wait for Simone? What she needed was something to keep her busy, and perhaps this time – yes, this time she was sure she would find something, some clue to point the way to find Michelle.

The woman clerk was patient and sympathetic. It seemed to Diane that she recognized her as one of the Returned Ones, the ghosts of the concentration camps, searching for her past. Even though the children were not so painstakingly registered as the adults, the two women searched the calendar of months from 1942 to 1944 together.

Diane hoped that some name, some trace would explain what had happened to her daughter. Two years. It was not so long. Surely Michelle could not have just vanished from the face of the earth?

Diane trailed her finger down the pages of names, silently appalled at this record of betrayals and misery. How precise they had been! What thoughts had passed through the heads of the clerks with their neat handwriting as they inscribed the details of these lost souls?

What name would Michelle have been registered under? Clément for her mother or Haas for her father? No, that was impossible, surely. Michelle never knew her father and she was too young to reveal the truth. But there was nothing under

Clément, not even her own transportation, no clue at all.

Then, turning on, Diane drew in a sharp breath. The clerk looked up, her eyes alight with expectation.

'No, no, it's not her. It's just someone that I once knew.' She looked again at the name under her finger: 'Léger, Nicole, deported Ravensbrück, June 1942.'

Ravensbrück! She remembered very well her fellow 'political' from the cell at Fresnes. Had they been in Ravensbrück at the same time together and never recognized one another among the thousand other women? Or had she never reached that hell on earth? Had she perhaps died on the journey there, another victim in another sealed boxcar?

Poor Nicole, she was good to Michelle. They all were. How had she forgotten the kindness of those women, her good friends that bleak Christmas in Fresnes? There was Nicole, and Sonia, and little Hélène who had been a tart. What were their other names? Perhaps she could find them, if only she could remember – Sonia what? Hélène? Why couldn't she remember?

'If you've no luck there,' the clerk was suggesting, 'this is the record of those sent for execution as hostages.' She laid a thick ledger on the table before her.

Diane thanked her and began to turn the stiff yellow pages of the dead. She looked automatically among the 'Cs' for her own name first, and it was then that she came across an entry for the first months of 1944:

'Caristan, Lucien, *résistant*, executed Mont Valérien—'

Diane looked up sharply. 'Is this entry correct?'

The clerk looked over her shoulder. ' "Caristan, *résistant*," Yes, it must be. It's written down, isn't it?

201

The *Boches* were *salauds* – but efficient, God knows.' She suddenly saw Diane's face. 'Did you know him, too? You don't look well, *chérie*. Can I get you a drink, or a taxi perhaps?'

Diane got unsteadily to her feet. Her mouth was dry and she could only shake her head. She was appalled, not only by the discovery of Lucien's death but by the fact that Simone had never told her.

'Are you sure I can't get you a taxi?' asked the clerk.

'No, really, I'll be all right. I think – I think I'll just get a breath of air.'

Did Simone even know? Did she know that Lucien had faced the firing squad at Mont Valérien? Or was she trying to spare Diane the news, not wanting to add to her burden when she thought she had suffered enough?

Outside in the fresh spring sunshine Diane almost collided with Simone as she arrived at the Hôtel de Ville.

'I came to find you. I guessed you must have come on ahead.'

Diane gripped her arm. 'Why didn't you tell me? Why didn't you tell me what had happened to Lucien?'

Simone met her eyes and saw the tears brimming once again to the surface.

'You know, don't you? You know that he's dead?'

'Yes,' Simone replied gently, 'I've always known.'

'All these years! Why couldn't you come to me with your troubles? Didn't you think that I would understand?'

Simone's self-control suddenly gave way. She wrapped her long arms around Diane and her words came out in a rush: 'You had your own worries, worries enough. Nothing that happened to me seemed at all important by comparison.'

'Oh, Simone.' Diane clung to her, and the two women were weeping and supporting one another in the middle of the street, oblivious to the stares of the passers-by.

The UNRRA people had passed Diane Clements' new address to Paul Rafelson but he hesitated about just turning up at her door out of the blue. It was amazing to think that nearly a year had passed since he had last seen her at the hospital in Germany, but he could not contemplate the thought of leaving Europe without seeing her once again.

Paris took him by surprise. He had been expecting a glittering array of expensive stores and fancy restaurants; instead, he found a shortage of even the most basic items and rationing still very much in force. The men and women looked shabby, down at heel, and not so very different from the mass of ordinary Germans he had been dealing with for months past. He wondered what a contrast he would find when he got back to the States; it was four years since he had been home.

He decided to announce his arrival in Paris with a brief note to the Neuilly address. He was just passing through, he wrote, and perhaps she would like to meet him for dinner one evening before he returned to New York? He did not want to impose. He had no idea about her family; she had only ever mentioned her daughter Michelle, who was missing. He turned up at the apartment on the evening he had suggested feeling very nervous and not a little apprehensive about what he might find.

If he had known how reluctant Diane was to meet him, he would never have come at all. When she received the letter she told Simone it brought back all the terrible memories that she had been trying to stifle and control. She thought Simone would understand, but to her surprise Simone took the opposite point of view.

'He saved your life, didn't he? He's only asking you out to dinner. You owe it to him, and I think it would do you good, too. So go.'

Finding a dress had been a greater problem. Nothing of Simone's would fit Diane any longer, but by pooling their clothing coupons they were able to scour the shops for something to fit her. It was not exactly elegant, but the watery-green dress was at least the new longer length that had come back into fashion, and the colour brought out the highlights in her hair. It had now grown to curl in a neat crop just below her ears, giving her the appearance of one of Botticelli's angels. She stood for a long time in front of the cheval mirror just staring at herself.

'He's here!' Simone announced from the other room. 'And he's come in an army car.' She came to the doorway. 'What's wrong? You look terrific.'

'I suppose I'm just nervous. I feel awkward. It's been such a long time since—'

The doorbell shrilled and Diane exchanged a quick look with Simone, who said encouragingly, 'Off you go, *chérie*. I'm sure everything will be just fine.'

But for a long time everything was very far from fine. From the moment she took a seat next to Paul in the army car Diane felt the tension in the air. They sat in uneasy silence as Paul drove to the Étoile and into the glittering stretch of the Champs-Elysées. He had obviously chosen the restaurant to impress her, but she was instantly on the defensive among the crowded tables of American officers laughing raucously with their French girlfriends of the moment. By contrast, their conversation was stilted and subdued, related mostly to the menu and the surprising array of food that seemed to have been conjured out of thin air, or more likely, the *marché noir*. Diane

204

would have been far more at ease and comfortable in some tiny Left Bank bistro, but she had not the heart to say so.

After the main course he asked her if she would like to dance but she promptly declined and then felt rather badly about letting him down. She made an effort to ask about his work but then had to sit through an account of his time in Germany.

'I met this most amazing Frenchman while I was there. He had been a leading figure in the resistance before the Gestapo caught him and sent him to one of the camps. But he escaped, and one day he just came walking into our headquarters unit. He was in a bad way, but he still wanted to go on fighting, so we gave him a job interrogating German prisoners. He picked out more than one SS man masquerading as a simple POW. He was invaluable, a great guy. You might have heard of him? – his name is Alain Sagan.'

Diane shook her head. The name meant nothing to her. She said cynically, 'It astonishes me how many people you meet these days who say they were *résistants*. You would think no one at all had supported Pétain!'

To her dismay Paul then went on to talk about the awful conditions and harsh privations facing the German population in their bombed-out towns and cities.

'So you felt sorry for them?' Diane asked coolly.

'In the end, yes, I did. You know, Diane, it's pretty difficult to maintain hostility towards an entire nation. I don't believe they were all guilty.'

'No? Not even after all you've seen?'

Paul realized he had strayed into dangerous and contentious waters. 'I'm sorry. I have been going on, haven't I? I'm afraid you must be very bored. I

205

was going to suggest we go on to hear some music somewhere.'

Diane was going to plead a headache and ask to be taken home but she saw that Paul was genuinely contrite. He looked across at her with doleful brown eyes that reminded her of a labrador she had once had as a child in England.

The cellar club on the Rue St Benoît was Diane's idea. She was rather surprised to find it still existed, let alone that it was evidently one of the most popular venues for jazz in Paris. The casual atmosphere made quite a contrast after the stiff formality of the restaurant. Diane could feel herself gradually relaxing and feeling more and more at ease in Paul's company. Perhaps he was not so bad after all.

'Diane,' he said at last towards the end of their evening together, 'I hope you won't take offence, but I've been wanting to ask you about your daughter. Did you ever find her?'

Diane took a few moments to reply. She had quite forgotten that he even knew about Michelle. 'No,' she said softly, 'not yet.' She raised her eyes and he caught the threatening glint of unshed tears she tried hard to control. 'To tell the truth, Paul, I have almost given up hope. I've searched every register, every list of deportees and prisoners in Paris, but she just seems to have vanished without trace.'

'It just means that her name is not on the lists. Even the Nazis weren't one hundred per cent efficient.' He leant across their tiny table. 'I tell you, Diane, there are simply thousands of refugees all over Europe that aren't on anyone's register.'

'Even children?'

'Especially children. Germany is a country of lost kids trying to get home. Don't give up hope yet.'

'If I could just find one of the women who were with her when they sent me to Germany—'

206

'If there's anything I can do—' He stretched out a hand. 'The army has its resources. What were their names?'

'The one I remember was Sonia Dubois. She was in Fresnes for black marketeering, but her name isn't on the lists, I've already looked.'

'Leave it with me. I still have a few days and I'd really like to help, if you'll let me.'

Diane could not explain the resurgence of confidence that she suddenly felt, but her hope was rekindled and for that she was grateful to him.

True to his word Paul hunted down the elusive Sonia Dubois and succeeded in tracing her present whereabouts through some of his army colleagues with contacts in the black market. It seemed that Sonia, even after all her experiences in Fresnes, still dabbled occasionally in black market activities.

'And thank God for it,' Simone said to Diane as the two women set out to the address Paul had provided in St Mandé. It was a large imposing house on the edge of the green belt not far from a *lycée*, silent now for the long *vacances*. The door was opened by a maid and Diane and Simone exchanged glances as they were left to wait in the elegant salon overlooking the garden.

The lady of the house had hardly changed at all. As she came into the room all Diane's memories came flooding back and she took an instinctive step forward to meet her.

'Diane,' whispered Sonia, 'is it really you?'

Simone was deeply effected by their emotional reunion. The almost Chinese-looking woman was of indeterminate age but she was dressed to perfection and an array of diamonds graced her hands. It was hard to imagine that she had ever seen the inside of

207

a prison cell, let alone risked her life to help Diane and Michelle stay together.

As they sat on the Louis Seize sofa Sonia still held Diane's hand. She said, 'You want to know about Michelle.'

The story she had to tell was beyond anything they could have imagined. She spoke softly, carefully, picking her words, but her vivid dark eyes were constantly flicking between her two guests as if assessing the effect of her account.

'In the summer of 1942 after you had been taken from us, Diane, the *Boches* rounded up thousands of Paris Jews. They put them in the Vél d'Hiv until they could be sent on to Germany. But our own *flics*, ever eager to please their new masters, had also arrested thousands of children. After the adults had been transported, Laval discovered the *mioches* were left on his hands.'

'What happened?' demanded Diane breathlessly.

'Laval gave the order. The kids were deported to Germany. I mean, *all* of them, Diane. They cleared out all the jails.' She was squeezing Diane's hand. 'I'm so sorry, my dear. There was nothing we could do.'

'To Germany?' Diane repeated, dreadfully still.

'No one knows what happened to them after that,' Sonia added, looking towards Simone for some support. 'No one knows what became of all those little orphans.'

But Diane knew. She had seen for herself what happened to the smallest children as they came off the trains at the railhead. If they were not old enough or fit enough to work they were already past hope. The camp crematorium had always been busy the day the trains arrived.

19

It was Germany's *Stunde Null*, Zero Hour. The bitter winter closed over the crippled city of Berlin encasing the world in ice and snow. It was said to be the coldest winter in European history. The Silesian wind blew across the plain, mercilessly felling man and beast in its path. Wolves had been seen in the outer suburbs of the city wasteland.

In the shells of ruined houses where the snow invaded the rooms through black, gaping windows and cracked walls, many people simply froze to death in their sleep. There was not enough fuel, and food supplies were running out. Lydia had seen women crying in the street after being turned away without rations. The second winter of the peace was proving as disastrous as any of the war.

In their basement rooms on the Hohenzollerndamm Lydia and Renata had become obsessed with the need to keep their stove supplied. At night, with the temperature ten degrees below freezing and a blizzard hammering the door and windows, the ancient stove spluttered and threatened to die out completely. The next evening as dusk fell the two women, well-wrapped against the cold, were on the outskirts of the Grunewald at Teufelsberg with a sledge collecting firewood. Their breath steamed crystal in the dense shadows of the trees, but the physical exercise was invigorating. They took turns to wield the small chopper, stripping down branches and saplings and loading their booty on to the sledge.

They had to be on the alert. Allied patrols had been know to arrest the 'vandals' who were destroying the woodland piecemeal night after night merely to keep themselves alive. In the cold, brittle air the distant sounds of wood being chopped reached their ears. Renata had already pointed out two other evasive groups of foragers passing each other silently in the blue shadows.

Once, Lydia thought she heard the howl of a wolf. She clutched Renata by the arm and they froze knee-deep in snow among the silver birches, waiting to hear it once again. On the roads around the wood they had seen new signs which read, '*Achtung! Wolfen!*'

The cry came at last, a melancholy haunting wail that sent tremors down their spines. Lydia's hand tightened on her friend's sleeve and they stared at the running silver phantom that flitted between the dappled bark on padded paws. At the far side of the clearing the wolf hesitated and, for a fraction of a second, those alien yellow eyes turned in their direction, then she was gone.

The hardest part of the expedition was undoubtedly the return journey through the solemn streets. Both women held a rope over their shoulders, pulling the heavily laden sledge along the frozen and rutted paths between the rubble and snowdrifts. They were afraid of police and military patrols, afraid of being attacked by gangs ready to rob the women of their night's hard pickings. Finally, almost dropping from exhaustion, they stacked the twigs and branches securely in the living room beside the rapacious stove and wondered how many days they could make them last.

Even Jutta was aware of the crisis they were facing and set out to contribute her share. With other children she would watch and wait for the coal lorries as they left the army depots laden with their black nuggets, running in their tracks and collecting any stray pieces that fell off on the way. Then, at the end of the day, Jutta would bear her prizes home and display them to Lydia and Renata, beaming proudly.

She never spoke of the scraps and fist-fights she got into with rival gangs of boys and girls. She never troubled her mother with the stories of strange men who approached her with offers of chocolate bars and chewing gum. Rumours of cannibalism had even reached her ears. At almost seven years of age Jutta had learnt she must look out for herself.

Their train left the Gare de l'Est in circumstances very different from her last departure from Paris a few years previously. Travelling east among the rust-brown winter fields, Diane remembered, but oh, she did not want to remember that earlier fateful journey.

The thought that her small daughter, aged less than three years old, had followed the same road to Calvary was almost more than she could bear.

Simone watched her avidly, acutely aware of the traumatic thoughts that must have been going through her friend's mind. Simone had taken leave from her work to accompany her on this return to the heart of the enemy's territory to continue the search for Michelle. She could not let her go through this alone. The chances were that Michelle was still alive, somewhere in Germany, whatever Diane might have seen at Ravensbrück. But finding her – that was going to require nothing less than a miracle.

She knew that Diane would go on looking for years if necessary until it was proved to her that her child was beyond all trace, all hope. In many ways Simone thought it would even be better for her in the long term to discover that Michelle was actually dead. Then at least she could stop. Then at least she could put the past to rest and begin to think perhaps of the future.

211

But it was too early even to broach that thought. Diane was resolute in her determination to go to every Red Cross and refugee centre in Germany if necessary for news of her daughter. And for the moment Simone was content to go with her.

The journey, however, had its unanticipated revelations for her. The sight of the flattened cities of the Ruhr shocked Simone to the core. Nothing had really prepared her for the stark reality of block after block of skeletal buildings, of endless hills of rubble that had once had a thriving life all of their own. The scale of the destruction and the desperate poverty of the people moved Simone to tears, but as she turned to look at Diane she saw her face harden and in cold rebuke Diane said,

'Don't expect me to feel pity for them. They deserve it.'

UNRRA had taken over the awesome task of coordinating records for tracing displaced persons and had set up their headquarters in Arolsen-in-Waldeck near Kassel outside Hanover. The little town seemed overrun with archivists and legal experts, besides having become a mecca for the wretched relatives of missing persons from all over Europe.

As in Paris there was ample proof of the assiduous, almost manic attention to detail of the clerks employed by the SS. Their card indexes had been seized from every police station, prison and camp throughout the Reich and collected here, covering millions of lost souls. Here were thousands of different stories of individual courage and pain filed away for posterity, perhaps to be forgotten. A score of different nationalities, hundreds of ways of spelling the same names, thousands of unknown Jeans, Jans, Ivans, Maries, Marias and Marys. And what would a small child aged three years old have called herself?

Michelle Clements, Michelle Clément, or simply Michelle?

Again and again Diane and Simone returned to plague the overworked clerks at Arolsen with the same request. The UNRRA workers were for the most part sympathetic, but eventually even their patience was tested by a problem to which they could provide no satisfactory solution.

'I'm sorry, Madame Clément —'

'Haas, Madame Haas.'

'I'm sorry, Madame Haas, but you have to understand we have done our best to help you. This is not the only case that we are working on.'

'It's the only one of interest to me,' said Diane belligerently.

They were given a list of clinics and hospitals where children who had survived the camps were taken on liberation. One by one, they set out to cover them all. They went through thousands of registration and medical cards of astounding personal histories that appalled Simone by their cold-blooded callousness and brutality. She began to understand at last the true depths of horror to which the Nazis had dragged their nation.

The search was exhausting and heart-rending. Having failed with the hospitals there were still the children's homes and orphanages to visit. Many had been bombed and their records destroyed, leaving the terrible nagging doubt that Michelle might have been at that very place if only they could prove it. Looking for a blonde seven-year-old in Germany was like looking for a needle in a haystack. The weeks turned into months and Diane was becoming more and more obsessed by their impossible task. Simone trailed behind her with increasing despair and disillusion. The faceless bureaucrats, the hostility of the Germans, the cheap hotels were all draining her

213

strength and vitality. She was convinced that if Diane continued much longer it would not only be her physical health that would suffer.

They had come to a miserable bomb-wrecked town where the rain only added to the general air of seedy privation. Their hotel room was unheated but at least the place boasted a restaurant. As they took their seats at a table and waited for the standard dish of the day, Diane broke the uneasy silence.

'You had a letter. Was it anything important?'

Simone took a deep breath and prepared for the worst.

'I suppose I'd better tell you —'

'Tell me what?'

'I didn't mention it this morning because I knew that you would only be upset. The letter was from Paris, from the hospital. They're offering me a new post, as a consultant. It's quite important.'

When Diane said nothing, Simone added quickly, 'I'm thirty-two. This offer could not have come at a better time for me, Diane. I doubt I will ever get a chance like this again.'

'Then you must take it, of course,' Diane told her.

Simone thought she detected a certain coldness, even bitterness in her voice. 'It's only for two years,' she remarked defensively.

Diane stared down at her empty plate, afraid of the turmoil of emotions broiling just beneath the surface of their conversation. How selfish, she thought, how selfish of Simone to be planning for the next two years without a thought for her! She could scarcely think more than one day at a time, taking each new town, each chance of finding Michelle as it came. She was hurt that Simone could even think of leaving her to continue the search on her own. But she said,

'If you must go, then go. I can manage very well.'

214

'You mean that you will stay? You'll go on searching by yourself?'

'What did you expect me to do?'

'I don't know, I suppose I hoped that you would come back to Paris with me —'

'Without Michelle?'

Simone realized that Diane had been living on her nerves for weeks, that she was even in danger of a breakdown. She knew she had to tread carefully, for although they were such old and close friends, Diane was on a knife-edge of total collapse.

'I know she's not your daughter,' Diane was saying, her eyes suspiciously bright. 'It's not your search, after all. How could you understand what it means to me to find her? You've seen nothing but Paris, you understand nothing about the war and the camps —'

'That's hardly fair —'

'Why, even the Germans know more about suffering than you do —'

'Diane, I won't take that, even from you. Yes, you suffered. You suffered terribly, but you don't know what I went through, you don't know how I felt that afternoon I walked into the Rue de Rennes and found the flat turned upside down and the food rotting in the pan on the stove, and I realized they had taken you and the child. You don't know how I felt when I picked up those drawings of yours scattered all over the floor and I saw and understood – it was Pantin, it was Dieter – and now it might be you and Michelle, too!'

'Simone —'

'More than that, you don't know the guilt I felt when you had been taken, and then Patrice, and Gervais, Christian – and Lucien – everyone was taken except me, and I was left all on my own. I didn't suffer as you suffered but it was bad enough in its

215

own way. I didn't ask to be spared, it wasn't my fault —'

She was silenced abruptly by the arrival of the waiter with their meal. He placed the two dishes of anonymous stewed meat and potatoes down before them and gave them a look of open curiosity before retreating diplomatically.

'I'm leaving in the morning,' Diane said quickly, 'for Geneva.'

'Geneva?'

'There's some new United Nations organization there that is running an emergency children's fund. Perhaps they can help me.'

'Oh Diane, Diane!'

'Don't try and stop me. I'm leaving for Geneva in the morning, and if you won't come with me, then I'll go alone.'

It was the summer of 1947 when Karl Langen, alias Karl Ulrich, returned to Berlin a free man. On his release from the British prisoner-of-war camp he had been given identity papers. The British authorities had accepted without question his story of losing his papers in the fighting outside Berlin and the name he had taken from a trooper he knew had been lost somewhere in Ostland. He was not the only one to have played the same trick. In the camp he recognized other former comrades now living under false names.

Lydia was overcome with joy to have him home again, although the home was not their own and the cramped little rooms raised impossible problems of logistics. Renata was out and Jutta attending her shift at the recently re-established school. Lydia clung to her husband's arms and felt with surprise the wiry strength of his body that had been fed on good camp rations while she and Jutta had almost starved.

216

'You're looking so thin, *Liebchen,*' he murmured. 'And your poor hands, what have you done to them?' He turned them over in his brown fingers and examined the cuts and calluses.

When she told him the kind of work she had been doing in his absence she expected his pity or admiration, but he was quite furious.

'My wife a *Trümmerfrau?* Have you gone mad?'

'Karl, there was no other way to live. We had to have food —'

'It's unbelievable! And this place — I can't understand how you have lived here for so long.'

'We were lucky to get it. If it had not been for Renata —'

'And I suppose she's a *Trümmerfrau,* too?'

'She has friends, soldier friends. Perhaps you think I should have taken the easy way out, too?'

Karl stared at her in utter astonishment. 'Do you mean she has collaborated? She goes with enemy soldiers?' When Lydia did not answer, he began to stalk around the room in indignation. 'To think you have brought our daughter up with such a woman! Pack your things,' he said with resolution, 'we will leave the instant that Jutta returns. I'll not have any child of mine a moment longer under the same roof as a traitor and a whore!'

Nothing she could say could convince Karl that the world had moved on apace since he had given himself up for two years' internment. She had to remind herself that he knew nothing of the appalling struggle they had all had just to survive among the ruins in two terrible winters. He knew nothing of the sacrifices she had made, of Renata's tragic past, of the changes in a city controlled by gangsters and black marketeers, and rife with murder, rape and prostitution. He had lived for two years cocooned

217

from such reality. She could not bring herself to blame him.

She was packed and ready before Jutta returned to the garden flat. When she first saw her father in the doorway she failed to recognize him. They both stood looking at each other in a kind of stupor, and it was left to Lydia to say hastily, 'Jutta, Jutta, it's Papi, home at last!'

Karl took his daughter in his arms, astonished that she had grown so tall, yet appalled by her desperate thinness. He was bitter when he thought how much he had missed of her childhood, the precious years when she was growing up.

She was no longer the plump little baby with her serious face framed by neat golden plaits. She was taut as a whip, a skinny-faced little urchin with inquisitive eyes and dirty blonde hair scraped back into a pigtail. But she was, undeniably, Jutta, his beloved Jutta, and there were tears in his eyes as he kissed her and held her and promised her a bright new future and everything she ever wanted.

Lac Leman sparkled in the brilliant sunshine. The trees and surrounding snow-capped mountains were reflected in perfect symmetry in the tranquil waters. They had arranged to meet Dr Schoenlebe on the towpath at the head of the lake to hear the results of his search, but they were over-anxious and had arrived much too early.

For ten days since they had come to Geneva, Simone had seen the spirit flicker and die in her friend's heart. After their confrontation and the harsh words they had shared that last night in Germany, Simone knew she could not desert Diane when the end of their search was so near. The overwhelming guilt she felt at her own survival could scarcely be put into words. More and more she found

218

herself reliving those happy days long since gone by, the convivial evenings in the Café Bonaparte or Trois Mousquetaires when she and Diane had been surrounded by the fond arguments and laughter of friends, friends now dead and gone.

She could see them now, so full of plans for the future, a future they would not see. Christian, the handsome braggart, Gervais with his books and bumbling good nature – most of all Lucien, whose dear face would haunt her all the days of her life, her lonely life.

Paris would never be the same again. Her streets were too full of memories, her favourite cafés shadowed by phantoms. Why had she been so eager to return, to desert Diane when she needed her most? She and Diane now shared a bond greater than friendship, a bond of survivors struggling with their own grief and guilt in the cold world that was left behind. She had wired the hospital that she would be returning to Paris in a month, ample time to see the whole desperate gamble to its foregone conclusion.

Dr Adam Schoenlebe of UNICEF was a lawyer who had devoted himself to the cause of the lost children of Europe. There were, he assured them, half a million refugees still waiting helplessly in camps, a forgotten people. No country was eager to offer them a home, no one had an easy solution any more. If Michelle was somewhere among them then he would do his utmost to try and trace her, for just to help one child find her own family was a vindication of the everyday grind of relentless struggles with international bureaucracy and self-interested governments.

Simone looked at Diane and wondered how she would react if his news was bad. She was lethargic, drained. Simone wanted to take her back to Paris with her, to look after her and give her the chance to recuperate and rebuild her life once again.

'Ah, he's here.' She looked up and saw Adam Schoenlebe walking towards them along the towpath with his golden labrador puppy Lara.

'I hope I'm not late,' he apologized. 'Lara thought she had found a rabbit.'

He was a fine-looking man in his late thirties with a shock of dark hair already grey at the temples. He was very tall and walked with a slightly stooped back, as though his entire life had been spent bent over a desk wrestling with papers.

Although his face was composed, Simone knew instinctively that he had come to tell them the trail was cold.

They sat on a bench in the warm sunshine as he broke the news and Lara sniffed happily in the grass around their feet. Diane sat quietly, her hands twisted in her lap, but her eyes were old beyond her years, weighed down by sorrow and loss.

'We have exhausted every possible lead for the time being. But I promise you, Diane, I will contact you if I find the slightest news of your daughter. I will not give up.' His grave blue eyes met Simone's across Diane's back. 'I must advise you, for your own sake, Diane, go back to Paris. You have done all you can. You cannot go on wandering from country to country. The time has come for you to think of yourself for once.'

'He's right, Diane,' Simone said gently. 'Come back to Paris with me, *chérie*.'

'You are a young woman still, you have your whole life ahead of you. Look forward, my dear, not back.'

At last Diane raised her head and in a tiny voice she murmured, 'Perhaps I don't have so much courage.' She got stiffly to her feet. 'Adam, would

220

you mind if I borrow Lara for a walk? I'd like a moment or two to myself.'

Simone and Adam sat and watched her calling Lara to follow her down the path. The beautiful dog danced and ran after her, hoping she might throw a stick.

'Will she be all right?' asked Adam. 'What will she do, do you think? What was her profession?'

'She had none, not really.'

'She must find something. Something to give her new purpose.'

'She does drawings.'

'Ah, yes?'

'She is talented, I think. I don't suppose —'

'Why not? Art makes good therapy, they say. About her child – perhaps she is dead, perhaps she is living somewhere under a new name. There are still possibilities, but don't tell her that yet. Let me make further inquiries. I don't want her hopes raised.'

'I understand.'

'She is lucky to have such a friend.'

Down by the lakeside Diane stood throwing twigs for Lara to fetch back to her. She was fighting back fresh waves of grief and terror at the thought of going back to Paris without Michelle. The future seemed to stretch before her like one long black void, frightening and meaningless.

A breeze stirred in the mature trees by the lake. She stood listening to the harmonious sounds of the wind rustling the leaves and the serene lapping of the waters at her feet. She knew she had come to the end of her journey. Adam was right, it was now time to begin again, however pointless, however hard it seemed to her now. Life was a cycle of death and rebirth, and she was already a survivor.

PART THREE

20

The famous twin spires of the great Dom of Köln pierced the early spring sky that morning in 1954. The cathedral had miraculously survived a series of major air attacks in the last years of the war that had devastated the rest of the city. Now its proud facade stood witness to the dramatic reconstruction all around. As Dr Adam Schoenlebe walked from his hotel on the Hohe Strasse he saw ample evidence of the wave of building that was lifting the new city, phoenix-like, from the ashes.

His goal was the district between the Rathaus and the Rhine. On the edge of the Altstadt stood a block of flats, hastily erected in the years immediately after the war and already looking worn and rather dilapidated. Apparently the woman had a daughter who was the acting concierge of the building while her husband worked in the local fish market. According to his calculations the husband, Wendt, should be at his work all morning, but there was still the chance that Inge Wendt would be there to crowd his interview with her mother.

It had been a fortuitous accident that had led Adam Schoenlebe to the administrator of the children's home in Potsdam. Klara Anders had long since retired from her career in the social services. She was on record as having disappeared from Berlin at the end of the war, but reappeared there during the Airlift, having something to do with the evacuation of children suffering from tuberculosis. This much he had learned from one of her erstwhile colleagues at the children's home, a nurse who told him the details of the *Lebensborn* programme.

It was an interest of his. This *Lebensborn* programme that took children away from their rightful parents, gave them new names and attempted to turn them into good little Nazis. The nurse had witnessed scores of Aryan children passing through the home who were given – or sold – for adoption to 'vetted' parents. She remembered many individual cases, but she knew no names. She was probably paid for her silence. The home itself was destroyed by bombing early in 1945 and any records were lost. If it had not been for the nurse coming forward, Adam Schoenlebe would never have come to hear of Klara Anders at all.

He did not question her motives. When she answered his advertisement in the newspapers, she had made it very plain that she was less interested in his altruistic research than in any monetary rewards that might be forthcoming. Schoenlebe was sure that she also harboured some personal resentment against Klara Anders, and if there was even the faintest suggestion of retribution, she was only too willing to offer up Frau Anders for sacrifice.

His investigation was, of course, well outside the brief of his work for UNICEF. But it was not unconnected. He had been quietly appalled to discover the extent of ignorance about the Nazis' wholesale kidnapping of young children from their vassal subjects. A few ribald stories about SS stud-farms seemed almost the extent of public awareness of *Lebensborn*. Others might have heard what happened to the children of Lidice after the village was razed to the ground in reprisal for the death of Heydrich, but no one seemed aware that the brutal seizure of children from their parents was no isolated aberration.

226

The plight of Diane Clements had continued to haunt him. It was a case in point. A child taken from France in 1942 and transported to Germany. Blonde, blue-eyed, of German parentage on the father's side. Three years of age at adoption, four at most. If she was not already dead, Schoenlebe was convinced that she had been a candidate for *Lebensborn*. Somewhere along the production line from the railhead to the concentration camp crematorium, he was certain that little Michelle Clément had been singled out by some eager SS satrap for 'Germanization'. Perhaps she was even now walking around, going to the *Gymnasium* – for she would now be fourteen years of age – firmly convinced that she was really Bertha or Eva.

Michelle Clément was to be the test case. If he could only trace one of these children, who could say what can of worms would be opened up to view? All he needed was one name. The lawyer who had drawn up the adoption papers, a parent who knew. Anything that would advance his search one stage. Who knew how many children he would find in the end?

And so he had come looking for Klara Anders. She was the link in the whole sordid chain, his one firm clue. She was no longer a young woman, and if the apartment block was any indication, there was nothing left of her ill-gotten gains. He was certain that, given the time and opportunity, Klara Anders might be induced to divulge the name of her contact, the SS man who must have made a private fortune arranging adoptions for the *Lebensborn* children of Berlin.

The concierge's flat was in the basement. As Adam rang the doorbell he saw a net curtain tremble in the grimy window.

'Frau Anders?'

'Who is it? What do you want?' A tall spindly figure appeared in the crack of the open doorway. A pair

227

of wily eyes surveyed him suspiciously out of the dank gloom of the passage.

'Frau Anders, I believe that you may be able to help me with some information. Information for which I am willing to pay.'

The door opened a fraction wider. She was wearing a woollen skirt and a long shapeless cardigan in lovat green and mustard.

'What kind of information?'

'About Potsdam.'

He had expected a nervous reaction, some trace of fear. Instead he was pleasantly surprised to see that she was cautiously weighing him up, taking in his careful appearance, the camel-hair cavalry coat, the leather briefcase, the gold watch on his wrist, all his props. He realized she had been won over the moment he mentioned paying for the information.

'Perhaps I could come in and we could talk about it?'

It was the smell that struck him first. The over-powering odour of cat, the lingering fragrance of rotten fish, and something worse. As Schoenlebe eased his way into the passage behind her, several unseen furry bodies brushes around his legs and nearly tripped him up. He emerged into the living room accompanied by three cross-breeds, tails held high, who hissed and weaved a dance between his ankles and then leapt for the sagging sofa before he could sit down.

She did not offer him anything to drink, for which he was thankful. One look at the filthy room was enough to turn his stomach, but Klara Anders seemed oblivious to the squalor in which she lived. But at least his assumption about the state of her finances had been confirmed. He wondered how much money she would want for the name of her contact.

He began slowly, cautiously. He wanted her to trust him. He was a German after all. She could not guess his pedigree. With luck she might even take him for one of the old *Kameraden*.

'So you want to know about the programme? It was very successful. I had a great responsibility, of course. I was in charge of several hundred children at any one time.'

He got her to talk. He flattered and cajoled, learning how the children had been selected, how they had been brought to Potsdam, how the doctors measured and classified them.

'They were all true Aryans. The process was most thorough. Only the best were accepted, you understand.'

'And the adoptions? How were the parents chosen?'

'There were long waiting lists. Only the really reliable families were chosen.'

'And if they were not prepared to wait?'

She looked at him slyly. 'Why do you want to know?'

'Let us just say that an error was made. An error at a high level.' He leant forward confidentially. 'My superiors are willing to pay a handsome reward for information leading to the return of one child in particular. A girl of German parentage, aged three in 1943, who came out of Paris. I had thought that you might be able to help us, but if you can't —'

'Who said I can't?' Klara Anders retorted. 'No one knows more about the system than I do. In 1943, you say? You want to know how they jumped the queue? Of course, they did. They were willing to do anything, pay anything, some of them.'

'Did they approach you directly?'

'Do you think they were stupid? It was a business arrangement. Of course,' she added hastily, 'I never received anything for my part. The work itself was enough for me.'

He let the lie go. Now they were coming to the negotiations. He was about to ask her about her contact, the SS lawyer who held all the answers, when the cats evacuated the sofa and ran in mad excitement for the door. Klara Anders looked up sharply as a petulant voice was heard in the passageway and an irritable woman in her middle thirties pushed into the room.

Inge Wendt had all of her mother's grim-featured imperiousness and none of her charm. She took one look at Adam and was instantly suspicious, instantly on alert. She looked accusingly at her mother and Adam was astonished to see that Frau Anders lost all her self-confidence in the presence of the newcomer. If he had not known better, he would have said she was almost afraid of her daughter.

'I didn't know you were expecting visitors, Mother.'

Klara Anders pulled herself quickly to her feet. 'He's just leaving, aren't you, Herr —'

'Fischer. Yes, I have to go now,' Adam said promptly, sensible of the tension between the two women. He knew he would get no further with the mother while the daughter was present. He bent his head quickly over Frau Anders' hand. 'I urge you to consider what I have said.' He wanted her to know that the offer was still open and that he intended to come back.

What he did not add was his intention to come back with Diane Clements.

After the door had been closed upon him, Inge Wendt turned authoritatively on her mother and demanded, 'Who was that? I thought I told you never to let anyone into the house when I'm not here.'

230

Klara Anders slunk back to her armchair and the attentions of her cats. 'I wasn't doing any harm, Inge. We were just talking about the old days, that's all.'

'A man like that? What would he want with you?'

A trace of defiance glinted in her mother's eyes. 'There are things I know that people are willing to pay for.'

'What kind of things?'

'Ah yes, you're interested now. After you sent him away.'

Her daughter's lip turned down. 'How much?' she demanded.

'Enough for both of us, I daresay.'

Inge Wendt closed the door and took Adam's seat on the sofa. Her face was purposeful as she leant forward.

'I think you had better tell me everything, Mother, don't you?'

Diane took Schoenlebe's letter to read in the orchard. She knew it must be from him the moment she saw the Geneva postmark and her heart gave a tremor of anxious anticipation. It was cool in the dappled shade of the old apple trees and the light breeze welcomed her back with the familiar reassuring creak of the hammock.

It was more than a year since she had last heard from the lawyer. She had assumed that time that she would hear no more. He seemed apologetic, evasive. She couldn't really blame him, not really. It was more than five years, after all, since they had last seen each other that day down by the lake. Five years that seemed like a lifetime.

She tore open the envelope with a feeling of trepidation. It was a handwritten note; he had not sent it via his secretary at UNICEF. He wrote in a quick, bold hand, the words running across the page as

231

though trying to keep apace with his tumbling thoughts. He was excited, eager, and his optimism quickly conveyed itself to her.

He had found a woman in Cologne who might be able to help them to trace Michelle. He had paid her an initial visit and he was very hopeful that this might prove the breakthrough they had been waiting for. He thought she should come with him to Germany to see this woman for herself.

Diane let the letter drop into her lap. She lay back against the cushions and stared up at the brilliant summer sky through the rustling canopy of leaves overhead. She felt disturbed, uneasy. She found herself almost wishing that Adam had not written the letter at all.

Even two years before she would still have welcomed any suggestion or trace of a clue that would set her back on the trail for Michelle. It had taken a supreme effort of will to re-establish a new life for herself after their return from Geneva. For years she had nightmares, she could not put Michelle out of her mind so easily. She was constantly on the alert against the grief that threatened to overwhelm her, the desperate hope that never let go.

She no longer knew who she was, or what direction her life should take. After so many years without contact Diane had finally travelled to England to see her mother. Her father, it transpired, had died of a heart attack in the severe winter of 1941 and her mother, too, was now on her own. But England had nothing to offer Diane. She felt like a stranger in the new house to which her mother had moved, like an alien in the too-perfect cosiness of the little Home Counties market town. After a month away from Paris Diane knew where she felt she belonged. At Simone's suggestion she had taken up drawing again, plunging herself into the work with a sense of abandon that took her quite by surprise. She disco-vered painting with all the fervour of a child at nursery school. She began to produce stunning abstracts in which she untapped her own tortured memory and poured out all her despair and frus-trated longing for the phantoms of the past.

Each painting was a development of those earlier drawings of cubes, squares and stark, sharp angles. In black, white and shades of grey the paint captured all the manic horror of the sealed trains, the boxcars that had borne Dieter away, that had taken her to Ravensbrück and back again, that perhaps had taken Michelle to Germany as well.

The result was a remarkable series of searing can-vases that encapsulated the reality of war as seen through the eyes of the victims. Amidst all the her-oics, the war films and histrionic memoires, the work of 'D.H.', as she came to be known, was a startling revelation. Simone had called upon Daniel Dieu-donné, the gallery owner and entrepreneur, to view Diane's output, unknown to her. He was ecstatic. He waited for Diane to return to the cramped little flat in Neuilly, but it took him all evening finally to persuade her that his enthusiasm was not all an elaborate hoax.

Her first exhibition took the art world by storm. The critics, without exception, praised the debut of a great new talent. The press, intrigued by her desire for anonymity and reluctance for any kind of publicity, created public interest in her work and established a market that made the paintings of the elusive 'D.H.' highly sought after collectors' pieces almost overnight.

To Diane it was ironic that the images that had made her life a hell on earth should finally have made her life secure. She, who no longer attached any importance to possessions, now found herself with sufficient money to buy her own house with a studio in the countryside outside Paris and set herself up for the future.

Only Simone shared the irony of Diane's success. Even after Diane bought the cottage at Rambouillet, the two friends saw each other often. Simone had now established her own thriving practice as a consultant, dividing her time between the hospital and her private clinic. When she had a free weekend she would seize the opportunity to drive down to Rambouillet in her little Renault with a hamper of food and wine to supplement Diane's larder. They were entirely comfortable together, as relaxed and at ease as they had been in the early months in the Rue de Rennes.

Diane wished that Simone was with her now to discuss the letter from Schoenlebe.

She walked barefoot through the orchard to the farthest boundary of the wild garden. Gathering her skirts, she sat on the fence and gazed out across the summer field where the scarlet poppies rippled in the waving grass. The sun beat on her brown arms and caressed her bare neck. She reached up and pulled the pin from her leather barrette and her rich dark hair tumbled down her back.

She was so at peace, so free, she was loath to put all that at risk now for Adam's final gamble. She looked at her paint-stained fingers, aware of the familiar smell of linseed on her skin. At risk? Was she really so safe, so different from the broken woman who had come home from Switzerland that day in 1947? Hadn't she always known that one day she might have to lay the ghosts of the past by returning for the last time to Germany? In the back of her mind there had always been the knowledge that she would return. How could she ever really be at peace if she ran away from this last chance?

As she climbed down from the fence and returned through the garden towards the house, she knew she had to go to Cologne.

21

Berlin, the city of the ruins, was being reborn. Struggling out of the rubble, the glorious capital of the Greater German Reich that was to have lasted a thousand years, had suffered indignation and humiliation beyond measure caught between the Great Powers who had turned on one another. From the summer of 1948 the people of Berlin began a new struggle for their very survival. The introduction of a revalued German Mark triggered off the first major confrontation between the former wartime Allies when the Russian authorities in Berlin cut off all access to the city across that area of German territory under their control. The only corridor to Berlin was by air.

The Airlift began with a score of small twin-engined Dakotas flown by nostalgic pilots eager to relive the thrills of the war who, like mercenaries, were paid by the load. By August their numbers had increased dramatically until the skies over Berlin were filled with the familiar but no longer terrifying throbbing of aircraft by night and by day. Food, fuel, medical supplies were flown into the three airfields in the western sectors of the city to keep Berliners alive through the long winter months. By the spring the Russians had backed down, but the airlift continued right through until September. The west of Berlin was an isolated island in a landscape dominated by the Soviet authorities as prescribed by the Yalta Agreement signed by Roosevelt, Churchill and Stalin. It had just come through its first major test.

It might no longer be 'the world's capital' but it was still the heart of Germany.

With the reconstruction of Berlin Dr Horst Menzler felt safe enough to return in the spring of 1951. He'd had enough of the sleepy little Bavarian town where he and his family had lived in exile since the end of the war. The Airlift had proved beyond all doubt that the Americans and the British were willing to back the German nation against the Russians in the astonishing volte-face occasioned by the Cold War atmosphere. In May 1948 the Western Allies had granted an amnesty to all members of the SS who were not wanted for major war crimes. The tide had turned. Horst Menzler was reassured in his belief that he still had a future in Germany. He moved his family into an expensively renovated apartment block in Dahlem and set up his new law practice not far from his old offices on the Ku-damm.

It was to this office that Inge Wendt came one summer's morning in 1954. She had made the appointment by telephone and travelled directly to Berlin. Her name meant nothing to Menzler but her obvious eagerness to talk to him was intriguing. He greeted her formally and offered her a seat in his elegant book-lined room, taking in her unsophisticated appearance with ever-growing curiosity.

'And how might I help you, Fraulein Wendt?'

'Frau Wendt,' she said hastily, sitting uneasily on the edge of her chair. She wore no make-up and was seen to gnaw anxiously at her lower lip, her hands playing with the straps of her cheap navy-blue handbag. 'I believe you knew my mother – Klara Anders.'

Menzler raised an eyebrow. 'Is she dead then?' he asked rather too eagerly.

'No, no.' She looked startled. 'No, she's very much alive.' He thought he detected a clear note of regret. 'In fact she has sent me here to ask —'

'Yes?'

'To ask your advice. You see, *Herr Doktor*, my mother has been offered a considerable sum of money for certain information about her work at the children's home in Potsdam during the war.'

After a long moment, Menzler demanded, 'Who is it?'

'He calls himself Fischer. A very smart gentleman, of military bearing. We thought —'

Menzler raised a hand to silence her. He knew very well what they thought. They were making a clumsy attempt to blackmail him. Whatever this Fischer, whoever he was, had offered them for information, they were expecting more from him to pay for their silence.

The lawyer leant forward over his empty desk. 'Frau Wendt, you must listen very carefully to what I am about to say, for I do not intend to repeat myself. You came to me for advice, and this is the best that I can offer you. Go home directly to your mother. Tell her that I remember her very well, and that I am pleased to hear she is still in good health – in Köln, isn't it? – and I pray that her good health, and yours, dear Frau Wendt, will continue.' He sat back in his leather armchair, his strong white fingers closing in a cage. 'That is my advice to you and your mother, *gnädige Frau*. And now, I'm afraid, I must bid you good day.'

In appalled silence, Inge Wendt stumbled to her feet, realizing that she had just been dismissed.

Adam had been waiting for Diane on the station platform in Liège as her train from Paris drew in. He had a car waiting outside and loaded her single suitcase into the boot, talking light-heartedly about her journey and the sudden change in the weather.

As they drove out towards the German border he was thinking how much she had changed from the weary, wasted young woman he had last seen in Geneva. Now she dressed with elegance while yet retaining a certain unorthodox individualism. He knew, of course, of her changed circumstances and privately had been quite taken aback by his first sight of her work. The paintings held him riveted, reawakening thoughts and feelings he had long since suppressed, if not quite forgotten. He felt drawn to their creator, deeply impressed by her compelling talent to express all that he, for years, had imagined no one else could really understand.

All this and more he wanted to share with her, but it was scarcely the right time. She was very tense. She sat in the passenger seat passing polite comments on the scenery and the weather, and skirting the real reason for their journey together.

Diane stared at the aquamarine tints of the woodland and neat black and white villages, thinking how strange it was that so much was untouched by the scars of war. She felt suddenly old, like a survivor from a bygone age, uncertain any longer whether she had made the right decision in coming with Adam on what would probably turn out to be a wild-goose chase.

That evening they checked into a hotel in Köln and, after a quiet dinner together in the hotel's restaurant, said goodnight and went each to their separate beds. Diane had trouble sleeping, not because of the strange room and the noise of the traffic on the busy street below, but because of what tomorrow might bring.

She was up even before her early morning call, and took her time to dress carefully, choosing the

239

deceptively simple Chanel suit that she wore only for business meetings.

In the taxi they passed a kindergarten where tiny children screamed and shrieked with enthusiasm as they chased one another in the playground. Diane watched the fair-haired girls, and dangerous thoughts threatened to invade her mind in spite of the censor inside her own head. Years ago she had set out for Germany in search of a small child. Eight years further on she had to accept that the child no longer existed. If Michelle was still alive, she was now a young woman, fourteen years of age, who for a decade or more of her life had been brought up in the belief that she was German through and through.

The apartment was hardly the kind of place she had been expecting. As Adam helped her from the taxi, she hesitated a moment before following him to the door. As if he sensed her uncertainty, he gave her a reassuring smile. They waited together as they heard the shuffling footsteps approaching the door.

'Frau Anders, it's Herr Fischer, you remember me?'

The woman in the passageway stared at them with watery eyes that filled with alarm. She raised a liver-spotted hand to her trembling mouth and looked anxiously back over her shoulder.

'I can't talk to you. I've nothing to say.'

'But, Frau Anders, I've brought one of the children's mothers to see you. Her husband was German, her daughter is half-German. A terrible error was made in this case. The girl must be found and only you can help us.'

Klara Anders stared at Diane as Adam added, 'We are willing to pay a great deal for the name of the lawyer or the family who took the child. You said you would help us.'

For a moment Adam saw the woman hesitate, but in that fraction of a second he heard the sound of urgent footsteps in the passage and Inge Wendt appeared behind her.

'Mother! What do you think you're doing?'

She was greatly changed. Adam saw at once that she was terrified that her mother would talk to them.

'You have to go away,' Inge Wendt hissed at the couple on her doorstep. 'We don't want you here, do you understand? My mother was wrong. She told you about the wrong person. She's an old woman, she gets mixed up.'

'What's wrong?' asked Adam. 'Who has been talking to you?'

'Go away!' screeched Inge Wendt, thrusting her mother aside. 'Go away or I will call the police!' And with dreadful panic on her face she abruptly slammed the door on the unwelcome visitors.

'Diane, I have to apologize to you. To have brought you here and all for nothing —'

'Please, Adam, let's walk.' She slipped an arm through his, trembling slightly. 'She was clearly terrified. What do you think had happened?'

'Someone has warned them not to talk to us. Someone is afraid we will learn too much.'

'Yes, but who?'

'Her contact, perhaps, the lawyer whose name I need to know.'

'He must be an important man.'

'Unfortunately, yes, I fear so.'

They were walking in the shadow of the great cathedral. A bevy of pigeons ascended before them with slapping wings and a warm current of air.

'Adam, do you truly believe that Michelle is still somewhere in Germany?'

241

He stopped walking and looked down into her grave face.

'You know I do.'

They found a bench in a rectangle of sunshine outside the main door of the Dom.

'The main market for the children of *Lebensborn* was undoubtedly Berlin. The home where Klara Anders was the administrator was in Potsdam, just a short drive out of the city. The chances are that the lawyer who arranged the adoptions had his practice in Berlin, and that the new parents were contacts or friends of his.'

'And Michelle?'

'If she left France in 1942, she might not have been adopted until 1943 or even 1944. They almost certainly changed her name. I doubt whether her new family would even have known her true origins.'

'How can that be? Surely anyone would want to know how the child came to be in the orphanage?'

'Not necessarily. Not if the arrangement was not entirely legal.'

'You mean they bought Michelle?'

'It seems very likely. Klara Anders suggested as much. And no doubt the lawyer, whoever he is, made a very decent profit from the business.'

'So Michelle has been brought up all these years in a family of ardent Nazi supporters?'

'That was the entire aim of the *Lebensborn* programme, Diane, but personally I believe that profit became more important than ideology. They might not have been Nazi at all. There were some Germans, after all, who opposed Hitler.'

Diane said quietly, 'I hadn't forgotten. But like my husband, most of them were in concentration camps.'

Schoenlebe frowned. 'You think I don't understand? I was one of them.'

'You?'

242

'Oh yes. I was in a camp, too. Dachau.'

Diane looked stricken. 'Adam, I never realized—'

'No, I don't choose to talk about it. Nine years from 1936 to 1945, it was long enough without letting it destroy the rest of my life.' His intense blue eyes held hers. 'Oh, don't misunderstand me. I have forgiven nothing, forgotten nothing. I hated them, I loathed and detested the vermin who had crippled and contaminated my country and trampled its name and heritage into the mud. I wanted revenge. I wanted to see every petty politician and sadistic camp guard made to pay for the shame they had brought down upon us.' He drew a long breath, staring at the ground. 'But it couldn't go on like that.'

'Why? What changed you?'

'The realization, finally, that only the really important names would ever have to answer for the crimes of an entire régime. The initial horror at the discovery of the camps could not be sustained. I had foolishly expected the Allies to hunt down all Nazi suspects, all those responsible, as the Russians did in their zone. But besides a few show trials like Nuremberg I realized they wanted to be done with everything as quickly as possible. Germany could not run without its civil service, its judges and police and teachers. There were over fifteen million Nazis, Diane. How could the new Germany survive without them?'

Diane placed her hand over his.

'You know, Diane, as well as I that every survivor must pay a price for survival. My redemption is my work for UNICEF.'

'And what about me? What price must I pay?'

'You, Diane? You have paid in full already. You know that Michelle is somewhere out there and yet you cannot go to her.' He squeezed her hand. 'Go back to Paris, go home and try and forgive me for raising old ghosts.'

'I don't blame you, Adam. It was my own choice. I had to come while there was hope.'

'Diane, you are one of the most remarkable women it has ever been my honour to have met.'

'Adam, I —'

'No, Diane, please allow me to give you a final word of advice. Go back to Paris, my dear. Allow yourself to have a new life, even a new family, while there is still time. I have seen too many people destroyed by the past. You do not deserve to be one of them.'

Not so far across the city of Berlin from the new apartment owned by Horst Menzler in Dahlem stood a large removal van waiting to be loaded. The tenant of the flat that was being so rapidly vacated, a successful architect, stood on the upper landing with his well-dressed wife and watched the furniture being taken outside.

'What has got into the child? I've never seen her so rebellious.'

'She's upset,' explained Lydia. 'She doesn't want to leave all her friends.'

'She will soon make others.' Karl Langen shrugged his shoulders. With so much on his mind, Jutta's tantrums were irritating in the extreme. 'It's not my fault, Lydia. Try and make her understand, will you? We must go away, there is no other choice. We'll go to Bonn where they've never heard of us. We'll build a new life where we will all be safe.'

'I hope it's the right thing.'

'Of course it is. It's for Jutta's sake, isn't it?' With a quick kiss, he added, 'Have a word with her, for heaven's sake. I've got to see to the men.'

Lydia watched him briskly giving orders down by the removal van and turned away in resignation. Bonn was not her idea. They had only just started to make a life worth living in Berlin. They had a good flat, Karl was making money again and Jutta was a success at school.

'Why do we have to go?' Jutta had asked her, and Lydia was alarmed to see there were tears in her eyes. 'Everyone is always being taken away from me.' She had done her best to comfort her, but in her heart Lydia realized she was right. All her life the poor child had been uprooted. But how could she explain to a girl of fourteen that her father was afraid, that he was more afraid than she had seen him since the day they fled Berlin before in 1945?

This time he said they would be safe, this time they would begin again. Lydia just prayed that this time he would be right.

22

'I'm afraid I am a little early for my appointment.'

The smartly dressed young woman in the inner office merely smiled at him. 'I'm sure Dr Menzler won't be very long. Do take a seat. Perhaps I can get you a coffee?'

'Thank you.'

Adam Schoenlebe looked around him at the elegant and well-furnished suite of offices. The very walls spelt out money. As his eyes travelled over the prints and the array of law certificates he felt tense with expectation, waiting for his first sight of the man he had hunted for so long.

Had he known in 1947 that it would take him all of thirteen years to trace Horst Menzler he would surely have abandoned the search. Even after tracking down the uncommunicative Frau Anders – now dead, as he heard – it had been another five years before he came across a likely candidate in the figure of Horst Otto Menzler, respected *Doktor-Advokat* at law. If it had not been for his highly publicized suit for the former Nazi industrialist Manfred Panzinger, he might not have come to Adam's attention at all. It seemed that in 1960 the old *Kameraden* network was still very much in evidence.

'Here's your coffee, *Herr Doktor*.' Menzler's young assistant offered him cream and sugar.

'A welcome change after the ersatz coffee they serve on the plane.' He saw her glance at him and added by way of explanation, 'I just flew in from Geneva this morning. I work for UNICEF.'

'That must be very interesting. I expect you travel a lot.'

'Quite a bit, yes. But I haven't been to Berlin in years.'

'It's great, isn't it?' the girl said brightly. 'I just love the city. I'm hoping that Dr Menzler will offer me something permanent when I pass my final Bar exams next year.'

Adam looked at her in a new light. 'Ah, so you are a *Lehrling*? I'm sure you will do very well.'

Just then the outer door to the office opened and Dr Horst Menzler could be heard bidding good day to the secretaries in the outer room.

'Ah, Dr Schoenlebe? I'm sorry to have kept you waiting.' The effusive lawyer swept into the office and off-loaded his coat and hat to his young apprentice. He was a portly man approaching sixty with a full, fleshy face and heavy jowls. He had a good tan, either the legacy of a summer spent in warmer climes or the result of a sunray lamp. His alert grey eyes flicked from the student as she prepared to leave them and focused upon Adam with the full force of his intense curiosity.

As Jutta Langen hung up Menzler's coat and hat in the outer office she could hear the low murmur of their voices under the clatter of the secretaries' typewriters. She wondered why she had not been asked to sit in on the consultation to take notes. That was the part of her work she enjoyed the most, observing the great lawyer's tactics and approach to his clients. He was a smooth operator, always straight to the point, but cunning as a fox. Sometimes she had to remind herself that Menzler and her father were old friends, they were so very different in temperament, in approach and, surely, in background. It was hard to imagine that they had ever had anything in common, and yet she knew very well

247

that it was because her father was Menzler's friend that she was given her chance to work for him.

As she settled to the stack of files at her desk the voices in the adjoining room grew progressively louder. She looked up, catching the eye of one of the secretaries. Obviously the interview was proving contentious. She heard Menzler's voice take on the tenor and volume he normally reserved for the court-room when he was cross-examining a particularly difficult witness.

The secretaries stopped typing and in the sudden silence Jutta heard Dr Schoenlebe say quite plainly, 'It's *Lebensborn* I'm talking about, as you know very well!'

The word meant nothing to Jutta but Menzler was clearly incensed. His voice rose to a new pitch that reverberated through the walls so that the women in the outer office exchanged embarrassed glances. A moment later the door swung open and Menzler himself appeared, red in the face, eyes glinting, as he demanded in an inflexible command, 'Jutta, kindly see Dr Schoenlebe out. My business with him is finished.'

As Jutta complied with his instructions she noticed that the man from Geneva was equally perturbed. His handsome face was rigid in anger, his mouth tightened into a compressed narrow line. At the outer door he barely gave her a glance, just a nod of his grey head, and then stalked off quickly down the corridor towards the elevator.

Jutta Langen at twenty years of age was a remarkably independent-minded young woman. This was her third year back in the city where she had grown up as a child, a city that had drawn her like a magnet from the oppressive comfort and unexciting mon-otony of family life in provincial Bonn.

248

Since her parents had taken it into their heads to move to Bonn when she was fourteen years of age, Jutta's one desire had been to break free. At the first opportunity she had announced her intention of returning to Berlin to attend law school and surprised her family by coming out top of her class, thus guaranteeing her free choice of university places. At eighteen she travelled back to the city of her childhood, the city she had known and loved all through its terrible past: the air raids, the panic-stricken flight from the Russians and the postwar years of the street gangs and the Airlift. All her earliest memories were of her beloved Berlin.

Nearly three years further on Jutta looked back on the naive, feisty little schoolgirl she had been with a curious mixture of embarrassment and affection. She felt she had grown up beyond all measure, finding her feet in the brash, modern city, getting a flat, managing her own money – meeting Harro.

Harro Grasse was her one secret. Her parents would have died if they had known that she and Harro were living together. They were impossibly old-fashioned and strait-laced in their attitudes. They still thought of her as a child, although Jutta could not remember a time when she had not had to fight and struggle to look after herself. Perhaps one day she would take Harro to Bonn to meet them, perhaps even at Christmas if she could inveigle him into agreeing.

That evening she had said she would meet Harro at the Boden. He was going straight from the university, but she wanted to change first of all from the rather formal dark skirt and white blouse that were obligatory in Menzler's office. She always felt something of a fraud in her 'lawyer's uniform', as she called it. She supposed that at heart she was still very much a tomboy.

Jutta was tall and rather too slim for fashion. Her metabolism was like quicksilver. She could eat anything and everything in sight – and frequently did – and yet she never seemed to put on weight. Her friend Christa Schaeffer, who was seemingly on a permanent diet, constantly chafed against this injustice. But Jutta could still remember very clearly the years when she and her mother had both gone hungry, years that were ingrained in her memory and would always be part of her.

In her faded jeans and loose white shirt, Jutta looked no different from the rest of Berlin's population of students. A little avant-garde, a little rebellious, but at heart still very much bound by convention. Her healthy bob of bright gold hair was cut in the new geometric style, her eyes outlined with a kohl pencil. She was aware of her looks but did not actively exploit them. Rather, she took them for granted, much as she took her other natural gifts of intelligence and self-preservation. She felt she knew herself, knew where she was going and what she wanted from life.

She was very soon to learn how wrong she was.

The Boden under the S-Bahn arches was a popular meeting place for students. A noisy buzz of conversation welcomed Jutta as she squeezed between tables where friends and classmates drank beer, smoked too much and compared lecture notes. She found Harro in his favourite corner happily arguing with Christa over glasses of Berlin Weiss, the local pale draught with an added shot of raspberry syrup.

Harro Grasse was twenty-three, a postgraduate economics student hoping to complete his thesis in this new academic year and impress one of the major multinational companies with his theories for the redevelopment of German industry. He was an ambitious young man who was planning to go right to the top. He was also extremely attractive and popular, especially with the female students of the university.

By contrast, Jutta's friend Christa was something of a loner. She was also a law student, working part-time as a *Lehrling* for her father's firm, Schaeffer's, specialists in criminal and social cases. One day, Jutta was sure that Christa would be made a partner in the firm and become one of Berlin's leading advocates. She was an earnest young woman with shoulder-length dark hair worn normally in a practical plait that only emphasized the roundness of her face. She had known Jutta for two years and Jutta was a frequent visitor to the Schaeffer home near Strand-bad.

As Harro stood up to kiss Jutta on the cheek, Christa said from her seat, 'We were just talking about the news. Have you heard the latest about Eichmann?'

Since May the world had been agog with the story of the kidnapping of Adolf Eichmann from his hideaway in Buenos Aires by the Israeli Secret Service. Eichmann, claimed the Israelis, was responsible for the death of over five million Jews during the war and now he was to stand trial in Jerusalem for his war crimes.

For Jutta and her friends, the generation of war babies whose only memories were of defeat, destruction and the austerity of the postwar years, the Eichmann affair was a subject of enduring fascination. The spate of magazine and newspaper articles that followed in the wake of his kidnapping were a revelation, opening doors that had been firmly closed for more than two decades.

That Eichmann, a simple electrician from Vienna, could have risen to become a section head in one of the highest bureaus of the SS, wielding the power of life and death over millions of Jews, the so-called 'architect' of Hitler's Final Solution, had been released at the end of the war by the Americans was a scandal. That he had then lived incognito until 1950 in Germany was a scandal. That some kind of association of ex-SS members existed and operated and had arranged for Eichmann to emigrate to South America was also a scandal, raising many important questions about the new German state and those who ran it.

The questions raised by the press and taken up with enthusiasm by the younger generation did not readily find answers. Parents and teachers alike showed a curious reluctance to open up what could prove to be a Pandora's box. Only Christa's family, who were regarded as 'intellectuals' and lifetime socialists, seemed at all prepared to discuss the past with any degree of openness. But then, as Christa was fond of reminding them, her father and mother had suffered persecution at the hands of the Nazis, having been forced into exile in Sweden where Christa had been born.

Christa had been brought up on stories of Nazi crimes and atrocities. Her parents wanted her to realize the depths of depravity and sheer evil that human beings were capable of. The whole ghastly weight of guilt borne by the German nation had been explained and analysed – the six million Jews, two million gypsies, twenty million Russian dead, horror upon horror. The Schaeffers believed that the memory must be kept alive, the lessons learned.

'They must be crazy,' Harro remarked bluntly. 'What's the good in dragging all that dirt out into the open? It's over and done with. It's got nothing to do with us.'

252

'Didn't your parents tell you anything about it?' Christa asked in astonishment.

'Not a thing. I don't even know what my father did in the war, and I don't really want to know. It was all so long ago. What difference does it make?'

'What do you mean what difference does it make? Would you let Eichmann go free? After everything he's done?'

'Alleged to have done,' Jutta put in fastidiously.

'He's an old man now,' said Harro. 'How long can you go on raking up the past?'

'What, live and let live? That's easily said,' Christa retorted. 'What about his victims?'

'Putting Eichmann on trial isn't going to help them now. I don't see that any of it matters any more. I don't know why people are getting so worked up. After all, it's got nothing to do with us, has it? The future is what counts.'

Jutta had kept quiet, listening to the argument. She felt ashamed at the extent of her ignorance for, like Harro, she knew so very little about the war and her own family's part in it.

Of course she had seen articles in the newspapers about the concentration camps, she had seen the appalling pictures of the charnel houses with their gas chambers and limp piles of human corpses. But pictures were just that, pictures. They bore no relation to her own experience, her own memories. She had never met anyone who had survived a camp, she had never known anyone who admitted belonging to the Nazi Party, for that matter. She did not know what her father had done in the war besides be an architect.

All the talk about Eichmann made her realize that her parents had never talked to her about the war or their attitude to the whole Nazi period. She thought perhaps she should ask them. She was going to Bonn for Christmas, after all. How could they object? She was old enough now surely for an adult discussion of the past. She thought they might even welcome it.

In the end Jutta travelled alone to Bonn for the Christmas holiday. Harro had opted out of her invitation with bad grace, crying off at the last moment. Although she was angry with him, Jutta was not really surprised. Harro was something of a coward when it came to committing himself. The thought of a meeting with her parents smacked ominously to him of wedding bells and settling down, everything that threatened to curtail his plans for the future.

'It's not that I don't love you,' he told her plaintively, 'you know that I do. It's just that – well, we're still too young to be tied down. We both have our careers to think about.'

'Don't be so defensive,' she had retorted. 'Marriage is the last thing on my mind, I assure you. And anyway, what makes you think I plan to marry you?' She had enjoyed the look of shock on his face. That will give him something to think about while I'm away, she thought. He's not the only fish in the sea.

The train ran across the plain of Berlin as the first snow fell from a bruised sky. Isolated in the train, Jutta's breath clouded the frost-starred window and she rubbed at the glass with her woollen mitten to watch the brilliant green pines clustered along the track. The snowflakes melted and trickled down the panes from East into West Germany.

Bonn was everything that she hated and despised. It was claustrophobic, conservative, a city manufactured by and for the bureaucrats. As the train crept down between the hills of Königswinter, where Siegfried bathed in dragon's blood on the Drachenfels, mist and sleet closed in around her. By the time she had found a taxi it was already growing dark and the Rhine was a glassy black void.

She had mixed feelings about coming back here. The house, a neat nineteenth-century villa standing in its own patch of garden, had never really been home to her, although she had lived there from the age of fourteen. She seemed to lose something of her identity when she crossed the threshold of her parents' house. She felt her independence was under threat, she felt the warm clinging love of her father and mother close about her.

They were waiting by the door as her taxi drew up and her father came out to greet her. She hastily kissed his cheek, thinking how frail he seemed in his loose-fitting cardigan, noticing his knotty blue hand as he took her case. By contrast her mother still looked youthful and full of energy, her plump face with its trace of make-up, her dark blonde hair neatly waved.

But it was good to be back. She felt safe and loved, and Christmas came quickly with its round of drinks parties and old friends dropping in to see 'the budding lawyer'. Amidst the goose and sauerkraut, potato pancakes and Glühwein, Jutta missed Harro and secretly counted the days until her return to Berlin.

On her last evening in Bonn she remembered her plan to ask her parents about the war. They were gathered around the log fire with coffee and cakes when she raised the subject. Instantly the whole atmosphere in the room changed from relaxed security to an uneasy and embarrassing silence.

'Why do you ask such a thing? It's not the kind of question you come up with out of the blue.'

'It's this Eichmann business. Everyone in Berlin is discussing the war now.'

She caught a look exchanged between her parents, and then her father said gruffly, 'I can't imagine why. It's over and done with, surely.'

Jutta said defensively, 'I just realized how little I actually know. I mean, I don't remember ever talking with you about the war. I don't even know what you did yourself, isn't that odd?'

'Your father served two years in a British prisoner-of-war camp. Surely you remember that?' Lydia rebuked her.

It was an answer and yet answered nothing. If she had been sensible Jutta supposed she should have given up then, but now she had broached the topic she was determined to press on.

'What about the concentration camps? Didn't you ever suspect what was going on?'

After a long silence her father acknowledged quietly, 'I was amazed by the way it was done.'

Jutta wondered if that meant he knew all along what was going on. He seemed upset by the whole subject.

'Why do you have to bring up a thing like that? Why do you have to spoil everything?'

Karl went over and put an arm around Lydia, looking back at Jutta with scarcely concealed anger. 'What's got into you, Jutta? I don't understand your generation, always running down their own country. Where's your pride? Where's your sense of loyalty? I don't understand you, I don't understand what you can be thinking of.'

Disappointment was written all over his face. Jutta knew somehow that she had let him down, but for the life of her she could not imagine how.

23

The gaudy strings of Christmas baubles still garlanded the Paris boulevards that first week of 1961.
Electric blues, reds and molten gold reflected in the
rain puddles, churned to neon frenzy by the wheels
of the cars and taxis as they pulled up outside the
gallery. Their passengers alighted two by two, with
hasty umbrellas sprouting for the seconds it took to
run for cover into the building.

All the glitterati of the art world had gathered at
Daniel Dieudonné's invitation for the long-awaited
exhibition of work by the celebrated D.H. Even the
monotonous rain could not dampen the enthusiasm
of admirers and critics eager for their first view of
paintings Dieudonné was calling 'an entirely new-
wave approach by one of France's greatest living
artists'. It was even rumoured that D.H. herself
would be there, although she was rarely seen at
public functions and always refused photographs and
interviews to the press.

She stood at the top of the stairs with Dieudonné
as he greeted his guests. At forty-two, Diane had
come into her own. She was vital, vibrant, with a
magnetic aura of self-awareness and serenity that
drew the attention of everyone in the room. In
contrast to the lavish haute couture gowns of the
other women, her dress was disarmingly modest, an
eggshell blue silk sheath in the 1920s style, with
delicate silver beading complemented by long silver
earrings of Mexican design.

Amidst the white-walled austerity of the gallery's main salon on the first floor, Diane's new paintings made an immediate and dramatic impact.

For so long she had been locked into a world dominated by sombre dreams and haunted memories. She had been absorbed by the stark precision of ivory, jet and oyster-grey. But now everything had changed. A new decade had superseded the old, erasing, or at least diminishing, the obsessive hold of the past.

Her first canvases in the exhibition showed a daring breakthrough in the use of colour, a single flash of canary yellow or coral among the opal and translucent mother-of-pearl. The next encompassed a freer use of bold brushwork in russets, copper and alexandrite. As the series progressed even the forms lost their classical severity, until the last and most startling pieces were stunning examples of free form at its most radical and breathtaking. Suddenly she had broken free of all restraints. Jade and malachite, ruby and claret, sulphur-yellow and sapphire, the jewel-like colours were a feast for the senses.

With her glass of champagne untouched in her hand, Diane nervously watched the guests for their reactions. The new exhibition meant a lot to her, not only to reaffirm her professional reputation, but to bolster her confidence in this new approach. For the first time in more than twenty years she felt free to pursue her own instinctive way forward, to create the conditions for a truly hopeful future at last.

She was pleased to see one face in particular among the guests. As Simone divested herself of her raincoat and streaming umbrella at the bottom of the stairs, she raised a reassuring hand. It was amazing how little Simone had really changed over the years. Her blonde hair had grown a shade or two darker it was true, and perhaps she had put on a little weight now that she had more control over her time, but Diane thought that at forty-five she had never seen her looking better. The black and white Jacquard gown was very modern and bold, indicative of a new adventurous spirit that had been apparent in Simone over the past year.

Marc Brunel, her escort, had a lot to do with that. After a succession of short-lived affairs with men of her own generation, usually already encumbered by wives of long standing, Simone had made the acquaintance of Brunel, editor of the dynamic and often outrageous news magazine, *Le Weekend.* Extremely tall, wiry, with famous craggy features, Brunel was an imposing figure in any company. At first there seemed little in common between the successful consultant and the investigative journalist who at the age of thirty-seven had taken over *Le Weekend* and turned it into the best-selling paper on the Paris bookstalls. But perhaps it was their very differences that made their relationship endure all the sly rumour and innuendo when they moved into an apartment near the Étoile together.

'Well, you have certainly pulled in a crowd,' Marc greeted Diane, kissing her on both cheeks.

'It's going to be a great success,' Dieudonné remarked, looking at the crowd.

'I wish you would let me run a feature, Diane.'

'On my work or on me?'

'Both, of course.'

'I'm afraid your readers would be horribly bored by anything about me, and if they are really interested in my work then they should come along to the gallery and see it for themselves.'

'I can see that you are determined to be a recluse.'

'She's not a recluse, Marc,' said Simone, slipping her arm through his, 'she just likes her privacy.' She took a glass of champagne from a passing waiter. 'Come on, Diane, be our guide to the exhibition.'

They had only progressed to the third in the series of paintings when they were approached by a woman of about fifty wearing an elegant wine-red velvet gown liberally adorned with a diamond and ruby collar.

'You don't remember me.'

Diane stared at her, aware of something vaguely familiar about the fine bones of her face and the way she held her head. But it was Simone who caught her breath and said in an astonished whisper,

'Suzanne! It is Suzanne, isn't it?'

Diane looked again at her and thought, Suzanne Drouot! It was twenty years since they last met, the third year of the war, when Paris was still reeling from defeat and the resistance was in its infancy.

'My God, Suzanne,' she said, 'you don't look any different!'

A little ironic smile touched Suzanne's lips and she exchanged a look with Simone, as if to say, surely I look different to you from that time in Montmartre in August 1944 when they shaved my head and denounced me as a Nazi whore?

'I would have known you anywhere,' declared Simone, leaning forward to bestow a kiss on either cheek. 'You look wonderful, Suzanne. Life has obviously treated you very well.'

'Well enough.' She held up a hand and amidst the heavily encrusted precious stones shone a simple gold band. 'That's my husband over there.'

'Albert Moreau, the industrialist.' Marc Brunel recognized him at once.

Simone looked across at the elderly millionaire who stood in conversation with Daniel Dieudonné's wife Thérèse and she could not help but think, how typical of Suzanne!

'We've all come a long way, so it seems. I must congratulate you on your success, Diane. I won't say I understand your work but Albert is more of a connoisseur. We have two of your paintings hanging at home. He says they are sure to double in value over the next few years.'

'I'm sure Diane is very gratified to hear it,' Marc commented drily. 'If you will excuse me, ladies, I want a few words with Daniel.'

The three women were left alone, a little awkward with each other over the missing years. So much had to be left unsaid, so much taken for granted.

Meeting Suzanne again after so long, Simone was reminded of the tangle of deceit and betrayal that had wiped out the resistance group and for which Suzanne had erroneously been blamed. Diane had returned from Ravensbrück and against all the odds had made herself a new life. Patrice Lamartine had come out of the camps a sick and broken man, who died of tuberculosis within eighteen months of his reunion with his wife Juliette. Lucien had faced the firing squad, but of the others, of Christian and Gervais, there had been not a word, not a trace in all these years.

As the reception broke up and the guests began to leave in search of dinner, Suzanne took Simone to one side.

'I made many mistakes in the past, you know, but now I'm paying for them. I have a tumour, Simone. They tell me I have a year, eighteen months at the most if I'm lucky.' She gave a self-deprecating and wistful smile. 'I'll end my days in Villejuif at the Cancer Institute. Ironic, isn't it?'

Simone watched her leave on her husband's arm and felt saddened and shocked. The taint of betrayal still hung over Suzanne's life and would probably never be erased.

261

On 12 April 1961 the world entered a new era when the Soviet Union fired the first man into space. But if Yuri Gagarin made history of one kind, in August that year history of another kind was in the making. At dawn on the 14th German police vehicles noticed unusual security on the border of the British and Soviet sectors in Berlin. The S-Bahn line into the Russian zone was abruptly interrupted and rumours began to fly round the city that another blockade was in preparation.

Crowds began to gather down by Checkpoint Charlie and the Brandenburg Gate. There was plenty to watch by mid-morning as East German troops began to roll out barbed wire and lay concrete posts.

'What is it? What's going on?' Soon the whole of Berlin, the whole world wanted to know.

'It's a wall, a damned wall!' Horst Menzler exploded, putting down the telephone and looking at the troubled faces of his employees.

By the time the office closed that evening his inside information had been confirmed. It seemed that the eastern sector was indeed about to be segregated from the west by a formidable wall running the entire length of the boundaries. The staff were all eager to return to their homes and families. Only Jutta Langen opted to stay on, making the excuse that she had some urgent work that had to be finished. She even offered to lock up behind her, but when the others had gone she sat alone in the outer office and brought out a file she had hidden away earlier in the day.

The buff cover bore a label marked 'Confidential'. The file was one of a batch of several hundred that were years old and scheduled for incineration. Probably Jutta would have taken no notice had the address on the cover not caught her eye. The name read 'Ulrich', the address an apartment in Charlottenburg.

She remembered her mother once talking about the house where they had lived on Zellerstrasse in Charlottenburg. She was far too young to remember, of course. Her first memory was of two rooms in a basement that they shared with Renata, her mother's friend, when she always seemed to be hungry and the days were so cold she ran after coal lorries to try and keep their stove alight.

But as she read the details written in brown ink in old-fashioned script on the front page, her interest had been caught and held. It was not only the reference to Zellerstrasse that alerted her. The details of the family seemed oddly familiar, far more than coincidental. Karl Ulrich, profession architect. His wife Lydia, married 1932, no children.

No children. She read it again. The date of the file was the December of 1943.

In the dark office by the light of the Anglepoise lamp, Jutta read the application for adoption of a child under the *Lebensborn* procedure. The form did not mention whether the child was a boy or a girl, but the adoptive father's signature appeared on a document inside, just under that of *Doktor-Advokat* Horst Menzler.

'Interesting reading?'

She looked up in guilty and startled alarm to find Menzler himself in the doorway.

'In all the excitement I forgot my briefcase. Perhaps it was just as well.' He rapidly crossed the room and plucked the file out of her hands. 'I can't imagine how you came across this, young lady. I thought it had been destroyed.'

Jutta sat back in her chair and looked up at his half-shadowed face.

'Is it true?' she demanded. 'Are these my adoption papers?'

Menzler pulled one of the typists' chairs to face her on the opposite side of the desk. The file lay under his hand on the tabletop between them.

'Permit me to give you a word of advice. From an old friend of your parents. Forget you ever saw this.'

'Then it's true?'

He neither confirmed nor denied it.

'If you won't tell me, then I'll have to ask my father.'

'No,' said Menzler sharply. 'No, don't think of doing that.' He frowned, watching her closely. Jutta knew that closed lawyer's face so well. She had observed the same expression of anticipation and speculation time after time as he assessed the truth or reliability of a client's statement.

For his part Menzler looked at Jutta and debated how much of the truth she could take without losing her head. She was a normally sensible, intelligent girl, probably the best *Lehrling* he'd had working with him in years. He would almost certainly offer her a permanent position with the company after her Finals in a few months' time, and yet he could see she was upset. Women could be ridiculously emotional and irrational over this kind of thing.

In his most reasonable voice he said calmly, 'Let's proceed as though your assumptions were correct. What difference does it make? Adopted or not, you have had a good home and decent parents.'

Jutta's head tilted defiantly. 'It makes all the difference to me.' She was surprised by the evident hurt in her own voice. 'Why didn't they tell me?'

'They have their reasons.'

'What reasons could there possibly be? I'm not a child. I should have been told the truth.'

264

'Things were different then. You were not adopted under any statute that would be recognized in law today. You were barely four years of age, as I remember. It was 1943 or 1944. We were in the middle of a war.' His eyes glinted like steel chips in the narrow stream of light. 'It was a different time, an age of promise. Berlin was the capital of the world. You were being given a golden opportunity, the chance of a lifetime. It was a marvellous time to be alive.'

The first seed of doubt showed in her eyes as she looked across at him. 'Unless you happened to be in one of the concentration camps.'

'That was all just propaganda! Communist propaganda!'

'I've read the books, seen photographs —'

'Books! Your generation understand nothing.'

'The gas chambers —'

'Never existed!' He was laughing at her. 'They were invented to sow dissent in the minds of the credulous, to blacken the name of the German nation.' He leant forward, his elbow on the file now, and said in a sombre, melancholy voice, 'I'm disappointed in you, Jutta. I thought you had more sense.'

There was something almost hypnotic in the force of his grey eyes. Jutta shifted uncomfortably and pushed back her chair. 'If you won't tell me about the adoption then I will go to Bonn and ask my – my adopted parents who the hell I really am!'

Menzler's fleshy mouth turned down sharply at the corners. 'It won't do you any good going round asking questions. You will just upset your family.'

'Upset them? They have lied to me all these years!'

'Why stir up more problems for yourself? It's over now, over and done with.'

'For you, perhaps.'

'For you, too.' There was a cutting edge apparent in his voice now. 'Your father will hardly thank you for stirring up a hornets' nest.'

Jutta halted in her tracks to the door. 'What are you saying? That my – father – that he has something to hide? It's a lie. He's just an architect. He always has been.'

'That's what he told you, of course. But there were architects and architects.' He saw that he had her complete attention. He recognized fear when he saw it. 'Be a sensible girl, Jutta. Let the past stay buried. It's in your own interests, I assure you.' He smiled at her. 'We are all Germans, after all.'

24

'But I have to talk to them about it, can't you see that?' Jutta pleaded, her face white and strained.

Harro thought she was on the verge of tears, and grew exasperated. 'No, I can't see that,' he snapped irritably. 'If Menzler told you to drop it, you should do just that. He's been a good friend to your family. Why won't you listen?'

'Because I can't just go on with my life as though nothing has happened.' She stalked round the apartment, her arms folded over the breast of her towelling robe. 'I don't understand why they should have kept it from me for so long. They never told me anything.'

'Perhaps because there is nothing to tell.'

'Oh yes, there's certainly something underhand about the whole business. You should have seen Menzler's face. He was virtually warning me off. I wish I had brought the file home with me.' She ran a hand over her dry lips. 'There was some word they used, some procedure or statute that Menzler said would never hold up in court today. I can't remember. It was *Lebens* – something.'

'Christ, Jutta, does it matter? You're just making yourself unhappy.'

Jutta turned on him furiously. 'Yes, it damn well does matter! I find out I'm adopted. I have no idea who I am, or who my real parents were.' Her face was taut and her eyes were suspiciously bright. 'I'm going to Bonn. I'm going to get at the truth. I don't care what problems I cause for my so-called family.

For years they lied and deceived me. It's high time they were open and honest with me.'

In the harsh morning light the Berlin Wall made an alien intrusion into the familiar landscape of the city she knew so well. They were sinking concrete piles and laying firm foundations. This was to be no overnight phenomenon. Nothing remained constant and unchanging, least of all her beloved Berlin.

Jutta sat on the train heading south through the no-man's-land between East and West, feeling lost and vulnerable. She should have known better than to expect Harro's support. He was above all a realist, always looking ahead, never back. What was past was unimportant, he had said, the future was all that counted.

'And if you persist with this crazy scheme and go down to Bonn, you'll only alienate Menzler. He's bound to hear about it.'

'I don't care if he does.'

'Don't be a fool, Jutta! Do you think he's going to offer you a permanent post if you go against him in this? He's not a man to cross. He's got influence.'

'So I find a place in another law company.'

'I'm glad you think it's so easy. It's your whole future I'm talking about. You could be throwing your career away.'

Perhaps he was right, but Jutta would not give him the satisfaction of letting him see she was worried. The future would have to take care of itself. She knew she would not even be able to concentrate on her final exams until she had uncovered the truth about the adoption. If any part of it was true then in Bonn she would come face to face with her past.

Even in the summer there was an autumnal quality about the new German capital. The barges on the Rhine were swallowed up by mist filming the sluggish

268

waters. A lonely fog-horn echoed mournfully up river, offering a sad greeting.

She should have known that Menzler would have warned them she was coming. They stood on the doorstep as her taxi came to a halt, their anxious faces already full of recriminations. Jutta had deliberately to set her mind to the task ahead, willing herself to remain unmoved by the hurt and disappointment she saw in the eyes of the two people she had loved best in the world.

'So he called you, did he?' she greeted Karl and Lydia, putting her small overnight bag in the hallway. 'He shouldn't have interfered.'

They sat down very formally in the lounge, Karl and Lydia electing to sit together on the chesterfield, offering a united front. Jutta felt that she was being put on the defensive.

'Just answer one question, that's all I ask. Just tell me if I am adopted.' She saw the quick look shared between them and added bitterly, 'I'm twenty-one years old. Don't you think I deserve to know the truth at last?'

'It's not so simple — ' Karl began.

'Am I adopted?'

'Yes, yes!'

'Oh God! All these years and you never said a word to me!'

'There didn't seem any reason to tell you.'

'No reason? Don't you think I need to know who I am, where I came from?'

'You're our daughter, Jutta,' Lydia cried pitifully.

Karl gripped Lydia's hand. 'You were only four years old when you came to us. We had tried for a child for years without success. We were overjoyed to take you, Jutta. No one could have loved you more.'

'Except perhaps my real parents. Who were they?'

269

'We don't know. We never knew.'

'Then who does? Menzler?'

It was fear she saw in their eyes.

'Leave well alone,' Karl warned her.

'Why is she doing this?' Lydia demanded, tears starting to roll down her cheeks. 'Why does she want to hurt us?'

'Don't cry, Lydia. Look what you've done now,' he told Jutta, his eyes full of accusation. 'Your mother is deeply hurt. Come on, Lydia, come and lie down.' He helped his wife to her feet, adding brusquely over his shoulder, 'I'll be down to talk to you in a moment, young lady.'

Jutta waited impatiently for the scene she knew was coming. She had not meant to hurt her mother – her adopted mother – but didn't they see that she was hurting too? Why couldn't they understand that she felt betrayed and lost?

'I hope you're satisfied,' Karl announced, coming back into the lounge. 'Your mother's upstairs lying down. Did you see the look on her face? She's not well.'

'I wish you would stop calling her my mother.'

'She's always been a devoted and loving mother to you. I hope you will never have to suffer what she's been through. She supported you all alone for years. She starved herself and worked on building sites just to give you a chance in life — '

'I know, I know. Don't you think I remember? I was there, you weren't.'

'What's got into you, Jutta? You've changed. I don't know you any more.'

'We have all been living a lie. You know more than you have told me. I want to know about my real parents, my real mother. What happened to her? What made her give up her baby?'

'It was wartime. Anything could have happened.'

270

'I asked you before about the war, but you're so damned secretive. What's the matter? Why does all this scare you so much?' She looked directly at him. 'What is *Lebensborn*? What does it mean?'

Karl got to his feet and went to stand at the window. When he finally spoke, his voice was under control.

'You said we should have known what was going on. You said we should have done something, but what could we have done? Throw our lives away? That was the price, that was the penalty for resistance.'

'But the Nazis were evil — '

'There was no other choice. We had to make the best of things as they were.' He turned wearily to face her. 'Young people today have it all so easy. You have no idea what it was like to be unemployed, to have to struggle. In 1933 Hitler seemed like a godsend. In a few years he had Germany back on its feet, we were respected again.'

'At what price?'

Karl's eyes narrowed. 'Who are you to judge us? What do you know? Are you blaming us for beginning the war – or for losing it?'

Jutta stared back at him, seeing him for the first time in a completely different light. He was no longer her father, and her vision had cleared. She saw him now as a sad figure, a man no longer young, and full of bitterness. Life had dealt him blow after blow, but he had persevered for the sake of his family, vainly defending the undefendable.

'I'm sorry I came,' she said slowly. 'I'm sorry you can't understand why this is important to me.' She turned on her heel and rang for a cab from the telephone in the hall. She glanced up the stairs and reluctantly went up to stand outside her mother's door.

271

She knew she ought to knock. She had never before just walked out of the house without saying goodbye. He said she was ill, and she had certainly been very shaken. She could never remember a time when her mother – adopted mother – had not been calm and strong. Why, even her earliest memories were of the *Trümmerfrau*, optimistic, indomitable, the loving mother sharing out the rations and fiercely defending her only child.

Jutta bit back her tears, unable to bring herself to knock. What could she say? I love you, even though you lied to me, even though you're not my mother at all? I'm grateful to you for all you've done for me throughout the years, but now I want my real family, my real mother?

She retreated to the bathroom and rinsed her hot face with cold water. In the mirror she saw the disturbed vision of a girl, blonde, blue-eyed, a girl without even a name to call her own.

She would go back to Berlin, that was where it all began, that was where she would find the answers. But as she came to the top of the stairs she heard Karl's voice in the hallway below, and realized that he was speaking on the telephone. It took only a moment for Jutta to realize he was ringing Horst Menzler.

'Yes, she's adamant. She can be very stubborn when she makes up her mind to something.'

Jutta froze at the top of the stairs, an unwilling eavesdropper. She could almost imagine Menzler's distinctive voice at the other end of the line. But then Karl said quickly.

'No, no, we've made our lives here. How can we start all over again? It's too late for that. We can't run for ever.'

He fell silent again and his face looked old and fragile as parchment. At length he said quietly, humbly, 'Yes, very well, I understand. Thank you, *Kamerad*, thank you.'

As he hung up and turned abruptly he caught sight of Jutta standing on the stairs.

Without a word she came down into the hall, picked up her overnight bag, and walked out of the house to wait for her taxi.

She had a long wait at the station and sat miserably in the buffet drinking endless cups of black coffee. It started to rain just as the express pulled out and Jutta tucked herself into a corner seat, staring aimlessly at the mountains through the steamy windows, feeling as though she was passing through a foreign country.

She knew she had made an irreparable mistake. She had plunged wildly into something far greater than she, in her naivety, could hope to understand. Menzler was tied to her family in a way that was far stronger than friendship. Her father was afraid of him. She had discovered that much for herself. He took his orders from Menzler, perhaps he always had.

She remembered the way her father had suddenly made up his mind to move away from Berlin when she was fourteen. A fresh start, he said, a new beginning. No one had bothered to explain the real reasons for the move. She had been bitterly unhappy, her mother had been worried, and her father behaved quite out of character. What had they been running from? Had Menzler warned them to get out of Berlin?

Her resolution to return to Berlin and demand the whole truth from Menzler began to falter. As the train ate up the miles, she convinced herself that Menzler would tell her nothing willingly. Whom could she turn to? Who knew about the war and was prepared to talk about it?

273

If she could piece together the information perhaps she would come to understand the secret of her past. She would start with *Lebensborn*, the word she had seen written in Menzler's file. It had a faintly familiar ring and yet she could not remember where she had come across it before.

Suddenly she thought of Christa Schaeffer and the way she had talked about Eichmann. Her parents had openly discussed war crimes and talked about the Nazis in a most enlightened way. Perhaps they would talk to her. Perhaps she could even confide in them, ask their advice. She had to have someone to talk to, someone she could trust.

'So you want to know about *Lebensborn?*' Reiner Schaeffer sat in the armchair opposite her, his glass of wine cradled in his large-knuckled hands.

'I want the truth,' Jutta insisted, looking from the lawyer to his wife Selina sitting next to Christa on the sofa.

'The truth? It's subjective. It depends who is writing the history books.'

'I don't know about Christa, but my school text-book had just ten lines on the whole Nazi era.'

'Ostriches. They buried their heads in the sand,' said Selina bluntly. 'Perhaps we have all grown too complacent.'

'*Lebensborn*, my dear Jutta,' began Reiner, 'was a typically euphemistic expression for a particularly loathsome Nazi practice. Namely, the criminal seizure of other people's children to increase the racial stock of the nation.'

Jutta stared at him.

'Reiner, explain it properly to the poor girl. Can't you see she's worried out of her mind? It's quite simple,' Selina declared. 'The Nazis developed a pseudo-scientific basis to justify their own superiority

274

and claim to power. The so-called Aryans were the Master Race, blond, blue-eyed, the Nordic descendants of the Gods of Valhalla. The rest were *Untermensch*, sub-humans, fit only to be slaves.'

'And every child that seemed to fit the bill was examined and classified as Aryan, while the others — '

' — the others were sent to concentration camps with their parents.'

Jutta sat forward in her chair. 'Wait a minute, you mean that the Nazis took these children out of the camps?'

'Usually before they even got there,' Reiner answered promptly.

'Or from round-ups, raids on resistance families. From any available source.'

'And then,' continued the lawyer eagerly, 'once the children had passed all the tests and were classified as suitably Aryan, they were given new names. German names.'

'They lost their true identities.'

'They were given away to loyal Nazi families, to childless couples — '

' — who could be counted upon to bring up the children according to the Nazi creed.'

'Stop, stop!' cried Christa, leaping up and going across to Jutta. 'Can't you see what you're saying? Jutta was adopted, and now she thinks that you must be talking about her.'

'She asked for the truth,' Selina said defensively.

'Can it be true?' asked Jutta in a low whisper. 'Can that really be the answer?'

'My dear Jutta,' said Reiner Schaeffer, 'just look in the mirror. I don't think I've ever seen such a prime candidate for Aryanization.' He glanced ironically at his own daughter. 'Poor Christa wouldn't have stood a chance.'

275

'But how am I ever going to discover the rest of it? I don't know who I am or where I come from. I was four years old when I was adopted. There must be a record somewhere — '

'In 1945 there were thousands of displaced children trying to find their real parents. The United Nations set up special agencies to try and help them.'

'Do you mean UNICEF?' Christa asked her mother. 'They are in Geneva, aren't they?'

'Geneva?' Jutta suddenly stood up. 'I know where I heard about *Lebensborn* for the first time. It was in Menzler's office some time last year. He was arguing with a client, no, a visitor. He practically threw him out, in the end. The visitor worked for UNICEF in Geneva and he was asking Menzler about *Lebensborn*.'

'It sounds as if you've found your man.'

For the first time in days Jutta smiled. 'Yes,' she said, 'yes, it does, doesn't it?'

Harro had been asleep but she must have disturbed him. He came to the bedroom door, shrugging into his dressing gown and running a hand through his ruffled hair.

'Your parents rang,' he announced between yawns. 'They were pretty upset. They want you to ring them back.'

'Aren't you worried what they'll think, hearing you answer the phone? Do you want a coffee? I'm just making some.'

'Have you been travelling all this time? They said you left hours ago.' When she did not answer, he added knowingly, 'I told you it wouldn't do any good charging off down there. You've upset your parents and antagonized Menzler — '

'Did he ring, too? For God's sake, Harro, I wish you would stop fussing! And don't call them my parents. I'm adopted. I'm probably not even

276

German, do you know that? No, why should you? You don't understand anything.'

'I understand you've been filling your head with all kinds of nonsense when you should have been studying. Your Finals are just weeks away!'

But she did not seem to have heard him. 'Harro, I've found out that the Nazis had this scheme called *Lebensborn* and they stole babies and young children — '

'Are you crazy, Jutta? What the hell have the Nazis got to do with you?'

'Everything, so it seems. And not only me. There's this lawyer in Geneva, Harro, and I'm going to see him.'

'What, in Geneva?'

'Harro, won't you come with me?'

He stared at her aghast, and she knew his answer before he could even open his mouth. She brusquely pushed past him into the bedroom and began to repack a suitcase.

'Jutta, what do you think you are doing?' He put an arm round her but she shook him off. 'I love you, Jutta, but I can't bear to see you like this. You're throwing away your whole future, your career, everything, for nothing.'

Jutta slammed the case shut and picked up her raincoat.

'You're not really going?' he called out after her.

She stopped at the front door of the flat and gave him a last desperate look. 'Oh Harro, why can't you understand?' His tormented face filled her with a mixture of pity and exasperation. She pulled open the door. 'Remember me sometimes,' she called over her shoulder and ran down the stairs and out into the street.

25

No one observing the carefree crowds at the Sunday race meeting at Auteuil would have imagined that Paris was in the throes of a deadly terrorist bombing campaign. It was less than a week since the right-wing OAS had attempted to assassinate de Gaulle at Pont-sur-Seine. The colonial war in Algeria had reached new heights of violence as peace talks seemed inevitable. But none of this seemed to disturb the fashionable patrons in the Bois that afternoon in September 1961.

It had taken a good deal of persuasion to get Diane to agree to accompany Paul Rafelson to the races. She had insisted on Simone joining them, confessing privately to her friend that Paul was becoming a good deal too persistent in his attentions.

'I don't want to offend him, God knows. He's a good friend, Simone, but that's all he is. I've tried my best to let him down gently but he's so stubborn. He just won't take no for an answer.'

'He's in love with you, Diane. I think he always has been.'

Diane grimaced. 'Why can't he understand that marriage is the last thing on my mind? I'm happy as I am. I've got my home and my work. I don't need any complications.' She saw the look on Simone's face and grew impatient. 'Oh, don't you start, too! You're so starry eyed over Marc that you think everyone else should settle down too. I like Paul, I like him a lot, but I've no intention of marrying anyone, least of all an American who wants to take me away from Paris at the first opportunity.'

So Simone gave in with bad grace and acted as chaperone at Auteuil although she was aware of Paul's chagrin. Racing was not her preference any more than it was Diane's, but Paul wanted to introduce them to an old friend of his who owned a couple of runners at the day's meeting.

'Alain Sagan. You remember I told you all about him. He's come a long way over the years.' In fact, said Paul, Sagan had become extremely wealthy thanks to some judicious investments. He kept a string of fine racehorses and apparently flew to meetings all over Europe to see them run.

'He was in the resistance here during the war,' Paul added for Simone's benefit.

'I don't recognize the name.'

'Well, he was caught by the Gestapo and ended up in Germany. That's where we met. He was invaluable to us. He's a fine man, very modest. You'll like him.'

'Does he know we're coming?' asked Diane.

'No, I thought I'd give him a surprise. Come on, I expect he'll be down in the paddock.'

The runners for the next race were parading in the ring for their owners and the aficionados. A number of elegantly turned-out horses preened in front of equally smart men and women who looked as if they had stepped straight out of the society pages of Marc Brunel's *Le Weekend*. Diane and Simone exchanged a glance, judging that they were both sorely underdressed for the occasion.

'We should at least have worn a hat,' Diane whispered in a quick aside.

'Hey, there he is!' Paul exclaimed, catching sight of his old friend among the crowd at the ringside.

Diane and Simone followed obediently in his wake as he enthusiastically advanced among the cluster of large picture hats obscuring their view. It was only as they emerged from the crush that they had their first sight of Paul's resistance hero, Alain Sagan.

He was quite tall, with a fine head of curling hair now a dusty grey in colour. He had really changed very little considering that more than twenty years had passed since Diane had last seen him. Although he now wore an expensively tailored suit and discreet gold at his wrists, Diane had no doubt it was the same man who had once called himself her friend, who had come to dinner bringing his own rations, who had crawled on the floor to play with Michelle, her baby.

'Ah, *mon Dieu!*'

Simone had recognized him, too, seizing hold of Diane's arm and coming to an abrupt halt.

She was remembering the night before the abortive raid at Pantin when the members of Lucien's group argued whether it was safe to continue with the operation. Patrice Lamartine had been betrayed, arrested. Simone wanted it all called off, it was too dangerous, she told them. But she had been outvoted. The operation had gone ahead, with disastrous consequences. The Nazis had been waiting for them.

For years they had thought him dead, a victim like Lucien, like Patrice Lamartine. But now he stood here large as life, laughing and talking animatedly with Paul, showing off his thoroughbred horse with not a qualm of conscience to disturb his wellbeing.

Could this really be the man who now called himself Alain Sagan? The resistance 'hero' who had allegedly suffered at the hands of the Gestapo and yet miraculously escaped from a concentration camp?

'Alain,' said Paul, turning round to introduce the women, 'meet some very good friends of mine, Diane Clements and Dr Simone Blanchard.'

Alain Sagan opened his washed-out blue eyes and blinked at the all too familiar faces staring back at him.

'Hello, Gervais. So you survived after all.'

Gervais Rousseau's face went through a metamorphosis of raw emotions, from shock to guilt, and from guilt to panic. As Paul raised questioning eyes towards Diane, his friend took a step towards Simone in spontaneous fury. For a moment she thought he was going to hit her, but he suddenly seemed to remember where they were and regained control of himself.

'Do you know each other?' Paul asked in astonishment.

'I think you must have made a mistake,' Gervais said quickly, but his voice was unsteady.

'No, no mistake,' Simone challenged him. 'I would know you anywhere.'

'What's the matter, Gervais? What are you trying to hide?'

Paul looked at Diane and then back to the man he had only known as Sagan.

'I think you have some explaining to do,' he said quickly, aware of the curious glances of the crowd around them.

'It's quite simple, Paul,' Simone declared, her voice carrying. 'This man is not Alain Sagan but Gervais Rousseau who disappeared after betraying his friends and comrades to the Gestapo. How you fooled us, Gervais! We blamed Suzanne, Christian, everyone but you.'

Gervais stared around the circle of appalled faces.

'She must be insane! I've never seen this woman before in my life.'

'How many did you sell over the years, Gervais? Did it begin with Diane, sent to Fresnes with her two-year-old child? She survived Ravensbrück, as you

281

can see. That wasn't part of your plan, was it? Or was her husband your first victim? Was it you who betrayed Dieter to the *flics*? For what – money? They must have paid you well for Lucien – he faced the firing squad at Mont Valérien – and for Patrice and for Christian —'

'Shut up, shut up!' Gervais' face contorted in a frenzy of rage and he lashed out at Simone, screaming, 'How did you manage to slip the trap, you bitch!'

He raised his hand to strike her down, but Paul had foreseen the attack and was there before him. In the ring of horrified faces, with the horse shying away from the sudden movement and raised voices, Paul seized hold of him, wresting him away as the crowd broke apart.

'And we stood there, holding one another up so we wouldn't faint with shock, and eventually the *flics* arrived to take him away.' Simone sat back in her chair and watched Suzanne for a reaction. 'Now he'll have a taste of his own medicine. He's in a top security jail.'

'I knew it couldn't be Christian, whatever anyone else believed.'

'And I knew it couldn't be you,' said Simone, grasping the hand that lay so limp and still upon the bedcovers. The weak smile on Suzanne's transparently thin face made her heart turn over. In spite of the crêpe-de-chine nightgown, the private room, the flowers and cards from her well-wishers, Suzanne was unmistakably dying.

'Why did he do it, did he say?'

'For money in the beginning. He had no grant, no job, and his mother was very ill. I should have known something was wrong. His mother was transferred from hospital to a private nursing home, but I didn't follow it up. But in the end I think he enjoyed the sense of power it gave him. He played out his role that night at Pantin, driving that damned truck into the trap *he* had set for them! He even pretended to be arrested. Perhaps he was hoping to continue the game, but it must have become too hot for him. Paul found out that his contact in the Gestapo arranged for a new identity. Gervais Rousseau became Alain Sagan.'

'And Germany? How did he come to be in Germany?'

'His Gestapo friend got out of France just in time after D-Day. He took Gervais with him.'

'And the concentration camp?'

'It was just a fiction, a story he spun to the Americans in an attempt to save his own skin. And he got away with it. They thought he was a hero.'

Suzanne lay back wearily against the pillows. Simone saw that the news had exhausted her. The hospital room was suddenly full of ghosts from a time when they were all young and optimistic about the future.

'Thank you, Simone, thank you for thinking of me.'

Simone was touched. 'I'll go now and let you get some rest.'

Simone left the Cancer Institute at Villejuif and sat for a long time in her car, knowing that Suzanne would never leave the hospital alive.

Gervais' guilt had freed Suzanne of the stigma that had hung over her since 1943. Now she could rest, now she could die at peace with the world and with herself. There was a French adage, 'To understand everything is to forgive everything.' Simone thought, Yes, perhaps in the end we can even forgive Gervais for all that he did. But we can never forget.

The lake was in one of its still moods, mirror-silver, reflecting the overcast sky. There was snow on the fringe of mountains that ringed the valley and the taint of autumn bit the air. Jutta paced the towpath at the appointed spot to keep warm and to calm her nerves. She knew she was too early and too anxious.

The previous morning she had arrived at the Palais des Nations, the former League of Nations complex on Lac Leman, in search of Dr Adam Schoenlebe. Full of bravado on the surface, but really stricken with fear and apprehension, she stood in Adam's office and reminded him of his visit the previous year to see Menzler in Berlin. His intense blue eyes stared at her with fresh appraisal as she went on to tell him about the discovery of her adoption papers.

'What did you say your name was, young lady?'

'Langen. Although it says Ulrich on the papers.'

'No, no. Your first name.'

'Jutta.'

His face took on a pinched expression as if he was suddenly in pain. He immediately pulled his appointments diary across and began checking his commitments.

'Can you meet me again? Tomorrow at eleven, shall we say?'

She felt that he was trying to get rid of her but, as if he had read her thoughts, he added hastily, 'I may be able to help you, although I'm not promising anything, you understand?' And he got to his feet and gave her directions on where they should meet the next day.

Jutta spent a long solitary afternoon in the damp streets of the city, her thoughts clouded by pessimism. She hardly slept at all that night in the cheap pension, wondering if Harro had been right after all and she was throwing away her career and her future all for nothing. Her Finals were now just a week away and she had not even sat down to her revision. Even if she decided to return to Berlin at once she doubted if she could do more than just scrape through the exams.

No, she had gambled everything on this trip to Geneva, and if Schoenlebe could not help her then she had not really burned her boats. There was still next year, she told herself. But she remained unconvinced. Her mind refused to be reassured and she tossed and turned in the strange bed, finally falling asleep only as dawn turned the mountains a luminescent pink.

Down by the lakeside she waited for Schoenlebe with growing disquiet. What would he say to her? What news would he bring, if any? He had not seemed very hopeful yesterday, almost chasing her out of the office. He had looked at her obliquely, giving no indication what he thought of her story. Today she was determined to ask him more about *Lebensborn*, if nothing else.

At the appointed time she caught sight of his tall distinctive figure in the distance and walked to meet him. His pace was slow, not because of his own age, because after all he could only be in his early fifties, but for the benefit of the dog at his side.

'What a beautiful labrador,' Jutta greeted them.

'I'm a little late. I'm afraid these days I have to adjust my walks to Lara's pace. She's over thirteen, you see. That's more than ninety by human years.'

Jutta stroked the dog's golden coat that felt like silk under her hand and missed the nostalgic smile that appeared on Adam's face.

'Let's walk a little, shall we?' he suggested. 'Yesterday you told me about your adoption and how Menzler arranged it for your adopted parents. You were four, you say?'

'That's right. It was December of 1943.'

'How do you know you were four? Had you some document or means of identification?'

Jutta looked puzzled. 'No, nothing.'

'I'm interested, you see, in your early memories. What, if anything, you may remember from the time before you were adopted. For example, when is your birthday?'

'December, December 1st.'

'Yes, but *is* it?'

'Oh, I see what you mean. You think in the orphanage they just picked any date, as they gave the *Lebensborn* children new names?'

'You don't remember ever being called anything but Jutta? You don't remember speaking anything other than German? What languages do you speak now?'

'English, we did that at school – we were in the American sector, you see. And French.'

'Good French?'

'Well, not bad, I suppose, but why?'

Adam called Lara to catch up and suggested they all sit down. They sat on a bench and Lara settled down thankfully at their feet.

'Let me show you something.' Adam produced a small book from the pocket of his raincoat. 'This has been in my possession only a few months.' He handed her Klara Anders' tattered diary that he had taken from a security box at his bank only that morning. He remembered how astonished and excited he had been when Inge Wendt offered to sell it to him. Her mother had recently died, from pneumonia she said, and she had discovered the wartime diary which she had not even guessed had existed.

'Turn to the entry on 12 August 1943.'

Jutta obediently turned the pages blotted and stained with damp.

286

Adam had had to pay a considerable amount to Inge Wendt for the diary to prevent her offering it to Menzler. Her mother had been a very much shrewder woman than any of them had suspected. The diary was her insurance policy, her private record of transactions at the children's home in Potsdam.

'It's just a list of names.' Jutta sounded sorely disappointed.

'That was the day the administrator of the orphanage gave her new charges their new names. This column here, they are the original names, while this one shows the new Germanized identities chosen for them.'

'Jutta! One of them is Jutta!'

'And the original name at its side?'

'Michelle. It says Michelle.' She looked up at Adam, her blue eyes dancing. 'Is it me? Is it my real name?'

'The dates fit.'

'But that's wonderful! Does that mean we can find out where I came from? Or – do you already know?' She seized Adam by the arm, her face animated and full of hope. 'Oh, please, if you know anything at all you must tell me! My parents – my adopted parents – would tell me nothing.'

Adam tried to calm her, hoping that she was ready to be told the truth, this twenty-one-year-old girl, so like and yet unlike her mother.

'In Paris in 1942 a member of the resistance was separated in prison from her two-year-old daughter, Michelle. The mother was sent to Ravensbrück concentration camp. The child stayed in Paris until she, too, was sent to Germany by the French government later that year. There she disappeared.'

'But how do you know —'

287

'She was three years of age when she arrived in Germany. She was blonde and blue-eyed and, more important than that, she was of German heritage. I believe that the *Lebensborn* selectors sent her to the children's home in Potsdam after she successfully passed every test and was classified as Aryan. And there, on 12 August, Klara Anders changed her name from Michelle to Jutta.' He nodded his head, his sincere eyes compelling hers. 'Yes, Jutta, I believe that child was you.'

'And my real parents?' she asked breathlessly. 'You mentioned German heritage.'

'Your father was German. He was an anti-Fascist journalist who fled to France to escape Nazi persecution. But when Paris fell he was sent back to Germany, to one of the camps.'

'What – what was his name?'

'Dieter Haas.'

Jutta sat very quietly, her hands coiled in her lap. After what seemed like a long time she said, 'And my mother was French?'

'Half-French, half-English.'

'What was her name?'

'Diane.'

Jutta's lip trembled. 'And she was in the French resistance? And she died in Ravensbrück concentration camp?'

Adam was shocked. He grasped her hand and said sharply, 'Died? No, no, Jutta, Diane is not dead! She's still very much alive!'

He saw she was taken completely by surprise, as though she had long resigned herself to the thought that her real parents were dead and lost for ever.

'Oh God, oh God!' whispered Jutta, tears surging into her eyes. A mother alive whom she did not know even existed! I'm falling apart, she thought desperately.

'Your mother and I have kept in touch all these years,' Adam told her. 'When she was released from Ravensbrück at the end of the war she set out to try and find you. She searched everywhere, in the displaced persons' camps, in Red Cross centres in France and Germany. Finally she came here, to Geneva. We sat and talked in this very spot. She had come to the end of the line and I had to persuade her to go home, to return to Paris and try and make a new life for herself. She took my dog for a walk, I remember. Lara was just a young puppy then, weren't you, girl?' He stooped to pat Lara's head.

Jutta rubbed her hands across her cheeks, impatiently brushing away the tears. 'I want to know everything about her. Where is she?' she demanded. 'Where can I find my mother?'

Adam grinned suddenly, the years falling away as he recognized Diane in her daughter.

'In Paris,' he told her delightedly. 'You'll find Diane Haas in Paris.'

26

The art gallery was strangely deserted. There was no one sitting at the reception desk downstairs and so Jutta went straight up to the main salon. The first thing that caught her eye was a brilliant abstract that occupied the far wall. She felt drawn towards it, entranced by the rich texture of the painted circles that reminded her of a spinning catherine wheel in hypnotic shades of gold and green.

'Do you like it?'

Jutta turned abruptly and found a well-dressed middle-aged woman at her side. She looked like a typical Parisian, dark and well-groomed, wearing a smart woollen coat and fashionable boots.

'It's wonderful,' she replied in her unaccustomed French. 'I don't know anything about art,' she added rather defensively, 'but it looks like the sun, like dawn breaking.'

The woman gave her an indulgent smile.

'What about this one?'

They moved on to stand in front of a smaller canvas, a more solemn painting of subtle steely greys and shades of black and white. Jutta shivered involuntarily.

'It frightens me.'

'It's one of the early pieces.'

'By the same artist? That's quite a change of style. I think I prefer the other one.'

'So do I.' The woman heard a door opening behind them and turned abruptly away. 'Ah, there you are!' she exclaimed as a rather dashing looking man came out into the salon followed by a young woman carrying a notebook.

'I'm sorry to have kept you waiting,' he said in a flurry of rapid French, kissing the woman affectionately on both cheeks.

Jutta watched as they left the gallery together arm in arm.

'Who was that?' Jutta asked the gallery receptionist as they came to the top of the stairs.

The girl looked at her with a quality of arch superiority and answered nonchalantly. 'That? That was Daniel Dieudonné, the gallery owner, and D.H., the famous artist.'

Jutta was left on the stairs feeling extremely foolish. She had just been talking to her mother about her own work and she did not even know it!

It was the following afternoon, in time allotted to work on her new painting, that Diane was disturbed by a persistent ringing at the front doorbell. She had few callers at the cottage in Rambouillet and that was the way she wanted it. The cottage was her retreat from the garish pressures of Paris, the one place where she found enough peace to work.

It was therefore with a degree of annoyance that she laid down her palette knife and, still wiping her paint-daubed hands, pulled open the door and demanded somewhat ungraciously, 'Yes?'

The girl who stood on the doorstep seemed nonplussed by her greeting. There was something oddly familiar about her with her tall, slim figure in the casual student jeans and denim jacket, and the precise bob of blonde hair. Then Diane realized with a sinking heart that it was the girl she had talked to briefly at the gallery only the day before.

Oh Lord, she thought, she must have coaxed my address out of someone and has followed me down here.

'Can I help you?' she added, rather more brusquely than she had really intended.

A mixture of curious emotions played across the girl's features. She appeared at first stunned, then confused, then alarmingly hurt by the welcome she had received. She stared back at Diane and seemed to take her courage in both hands, as if steeling herself to say something at last.

She deliberately set down the blue barrel-shaped holdall at her feet and with wide frightened eyes, she said simply, 'I am Michelle.'

For a moment Diane just stared at her, unable even to digest this bald statement of fact. Michelle? What was she talking about? Michelle? Was this some kind of black joke?

She put out a hand and supported herself against the lintel of the low cottage doorway.

'I – I don't understand —'

The stranger likewise seemed on the verge of panic.

'I've come from Geneva,' she insisted. 'Adam Schoenlebe sent me.'

Diane swayed and almost fell, but the girl's reactions were good and she caught and supported her just in time.

'Oh God, oh my God,' whispered Diane in English as she looked into Jutta's face so close to her own.

She reached up and touched her short blonde hair, searching the wide blue eyes for the truth, for some trace of her missing baby. But in the adult contours of her captivating and beautiful face she found nothing of the child whose image had haunted her dreams for so many fruitless years. That child had long gone, only to be replaced by the uncanny resurrection of the strong brave features of her father, Dieter Haas.

'Michelle? Is it really you?'

Tears sprang at once to Jutta's eyes.

'I hope so, oh I really hope so!'

Diane wrapped her arms around the girl's taut shoulders in wonder. The tears of both women mingled as they hugged each other as though afraid to let one another go.

'I've so much to tell you,' sobbed Jutta. 'I've been looking for you everywhere.'

Diane erased the tears on her own face with the back of her hand, forgetting the paint stains.

'*You* have been looking for *me*?'

'Oh yes,' Jutta told her with a sudden trace of laughter in her voice, taking the rag from her mother's hand and gently wiping the paint off her cheeks. 'Ever since I found out that I was adopted.'

Diane shook her head in amazement.

'I think we had better go and sit down,' she said, realizing that the front door was still wide open.

Jutta retrieved her bag and shut the door on the fields and forest beyond. The calm and peace of the cottage closed about her as she followed Diane into the one long main room that ran the length of the ground floor. It was sparsely furnished but comfortable, with a sofa and two hoop-backed country chairs either side of the hearth. A profusion of richly patterned Indian rugs and cushions gave the room warmth and colour. A number of prints and drawings hung on one wall, and there was an earthenware jug full of fresh flowers standing on a small wooden chest. On an easel near the French windows at the far end stood Diane's work in progress next to a trestle table laden with paints and brushes in jars.

'So this is where you paint,' Jutta remarked, awkwardly standing in the middle of the room still holding her bag.

'Why don't you put that down? You look so uncomfortable standing there.' Diane produced a bottle of red wine and two glasses. 'How did you get here?'

'I hitched. It didn't take long.'

'Is that safe?'

'I do it all the time back home.' She stopped abruptly. 'In Germany, I mean,' she hastily corrected herself.

Diane sat on the sofa and patted the seat beside her.

'I want to hear everything. I want to know all about you.'

Jutta sat down with her long legs tucked under her. 'Would you mind very much if we talked in English?' she asked, switching languages. 'I'm a bit rusty with my French.'

Diane looked startled for a moment but quickly recovered. 'We have so much to find out about each other.'

Jutta seemed to relax, taking the glass of wine and tasting it. Suddenly she smiled. 'Why, you don't even know my name – I mean, the name they gave me in the orphanage. It's Jutta.'

'Jutta?'

'They changed our names. Adam showed me the record of the woman who ran the children's home. He said you knew about *Lebensborn* and how they gave children for adoption. I was given to a childless couple called Ulrich, Karl and Lydia Ulrich.' She looked uncertain. 'Do you want to hear all about this?'

'I want to hear everything.'

As Jutta talked about Karl and Lydia and her childhood years in Berlin she lost her reserve and seemed more at ease in her mother's company. She found that she could talk about them without rancour now, as though time and distance had healed some of the open wounds and imposed a certain detachment with which she could view the past.

'It's ironic,' Diane commented. 'I was in Germany at the very time you are talking about.'

'Looking for me?'

'In every bombed-out city. Life couldn't have been easy for your mother.'

'My *adopted* mother,' said Jutta swiftly. 'No, it wasn't easy. She was very good to me. She loved me as if I was really her own child.'

'Is she still in Berlin?'

'Oh no. When I was fourteen we moved to Bonn. I hated Bonn. I'm a bit of a rebel, I suppose,' she added sheepishly.

Diane smiled at her. 'I would be disappointed if you were not.'

'I returned to Berlin to university. I have been studying law.'

'Law? You have done well. You obviously inherited your father's brains.'

Jutta sat forward, setting down her empty glass.

'I want to know all about my real father.'

'There's time enough for that,' said Diane kindly. She abruptly got to her feet, announcing, 'It's turned cold in here.'

The light had declined with the rapid approach of night. Diane drew the heavy curtains and switched on a table lamp.

'You must be hungry. Look, why don't you put a match to the fire while I make us something to eat?'

Jutta readily agreed, enjoying the sense of informality and eager to make herself useful. By the time the fire was roaring in the grate, Diane had an omelette sizzling in the pan on the stove in the tiny adjoining kitchen and garlic bread on the hot plate keeping warm. Jutta offered to toss the salad and opened a second bottle of wine. The two women were companionable and relaxed, no longer strangers but friends.

'I was very young when we first met,' Diane began after they finished eating. 'It was in a bookshop in Paris. I was younger than you are now. Dieter bought me a copy of Hemingway's *A Farewell to Arms*.' She smiled at the memory. 'Dieter was older, clever, more worldly. He knew so much. He was a journalist, you know. But the articles he wrote against the Nazis made him enemies. He had to get out of Germany. He was living illegally in France without identity papers. It was very dangerous for him.'

'Did you love him very much?'

'Oh yes. He was a marvellous person to be with. So bright and full of life. He was a great talker, he had a great sense of humour. I remember —'

Diane's face was vibrant and alight with heightened emotion as she talked about Dieter for the first time in many years. She related fondly that day when he had waited for her in the rain in the Luxembourg Gardens, reliving the romance and pleasure of that distant reunion. Her long silver earrings caught the firelight as she turned her head, and she pushed her long hair back off her shoulder. Jutta realized that her mother was still a very beautiful woman, full of inner warmth and magnetism. The ravages and harsh experiences of life had only enhanced her humane and tender spirit. It made Jutta proud beyond measure to realize that this woman was connected to her by more than mere friendship.

'My one regret is that you never knew your father.'

'Adam told me they sent him back to Germany.'

Diane's face grew shadowed with remembered grief.

'A friend brought us word. We went to the rail-yards at Pantin in the hope of getting news of him, perhaps even catching sight of him —'

Jutta could scarcely restrain herself. 'And did you?'

'We saw the trains. We were standing next to the line of boxcars – padlocked, sealed boxcars. And we never knew, we never realized, we could not guess that inside –' She hesitated and Jutta leant forward, 'Yes?'

'The boxcars were full of prisoners.'

'Oh God.'

'It was hard, it was very hard for us to understand in those days,' Diane whispered in the firelight. 'Later, of course, we understood only too well. Well,' she added, her voice seeming to falter, 'in time one can grow used to anything.'

She turned her head and looked at her daughter, seeing for the first time the tears coursing down her cheeks.

'Oh no, please don't.' She pulled the girl towards her. 'He wouldn't want you to cry. He'd be so pleased, so happy to know that we've found one another at last. Look,' she said, trying to inject some gaiety into her voice that was on the verge of tears, 'you see that picture? It's a drawing I did of you as a small baby. I sold most of them at the university, but Simone saved this one.'

'Simone?'

'You mean I haven't mentioned Simone? But she's my greatest, my oldest friend! She's a doctor here in Paris. We shared a flat for years. Oh, how thrilled she will be to hear about you! We searched for you together. She'll want to meet you!'

Jutta stood in front of her portrait in the leaping firelight. 'And I want to meet her, too.'

They talked through the night, refuelling the fire and refilling their glasses. For the first time in her life Jutta felt really close to someone, able to talk about the past and unravel its secrets. Diane had carried her lonely burden for so long. Jutta's heart went out to her and she felt a bond so strong that it was almost mystical.

'For years I kept remembering how they tore you from my arms that morning in the prison at Fresnes. They were sending me to Germany, but you were to stay behind.' Diane's eyes shone with unshed tears. 'My last sight of you was in the arms of a Nazi wardress.'

Jutta stretched out and took her mother's hand. 'What you must have gone through, all those years on your own.'

'There are things I still find it impossible to talk about. Even to you.'

Jutta sat quietly, knowing that they had touched on an open nerve.

'One day, perhaps,' Diane added uncertainly, wondering if her daughter was offended to be denied the whole truth, however raw and painful. 'I hope you can understand. I've tried to put all of that behind me.'

'Adam tried to explain it to me,' Jutta told her. 'He said he was in Dachau for nine years.'

'He's a wonderful man.'

'Yes, he is, isn't he? We talked for a long time down by the lake.' She was recalling the way Adam had spoken about her mother's time in Ravensbrück, the way he had cautioned her to be careful, not to press too far. His great respect and affection for Diane had shone through every word he spoke about her.

'In many ways,' Diane was saying, 'he reminds me of your father.'

'You know, he's doing so much at UNICEF. He says there are still so many children in need all over the world. I don't think I ever realized before the kind of work they do for them.'

'You sound interested.'

'Perhaps I am.'

'We haven't really talked about you, about your future, have we? What are your plans now?'

'All this has happened so quickly,' Jutta began evasively. 'I'm afraid I've rather burnt my bridges. My going to Geneva, then coming on here – well, I've missed my Finals, my bar exams.'

'Can you take them again?'

'I suppose so. If I wanted to.'

'But you don't want to?'

'I'm not sure that I do. At least, not in Berlin.'

Diane shook her head. 'I hope you haven't turned completely against your friends and your family back there in Germany. I wouldn't want you to do that.'

'No, I know you wouldn't.'

'Were you thinking of staying here? You're twenty – twenty-one. It's your decision. I suppose it would be possible to sit the exams in Paris —'

'No, I hadn't really thought about that either. You see, Adam and I were talking and he made the suggestion that –'

'Yes?'

'That if I chose I could serve a year as a *Lehrling* with him at UNICEF. I could qualify next year. In Geneva.'

'And is that what you want?'

Jutta's face lit up. 'Yes, oh yes, I really think it is. You see, I feel that I've been so lucky. I've had two families, two mothers who love me. I can't help thinking of the other children – those who were not selected for *Lebensborn*. I know it's too late to help them now, but there are other children, thousands

299

of them, who do need help. You do understand, don't you?'

'Of course I do.'

'I'll be in Geneva, but I'll see you often.'

'I should hope so. I'll come down to see you, and Adam.'

'Now I've found you, I'll not let you go.'

'It's never too late to begin again,' said Diane, stroking her daughter's hair. 'That's one lesson I've had to learn.'

'There's something else I wanted to say,' Jutta announced. 'I've been thinking so much about who I am and what I should call myself. I don't see why I should keep the name given to me by Klara Anders at the orphanage.'

'What do you mean?'

'I can't accept being known as Jutta Langen any longer, even less Jutta Ulrich. No, now that I know the truth, I want to revert to my real name. I want to be called Michelle Haas.'

Diane's face crumpled and fresh tears sparkled in her eyes. She held out her arms and hugged her daughter for a long time, whispering again and again, 'Oh, Michelle!'

Finally they drew apart and both women wiped away their tears.

'Do you know how late it is? It will soon be dawn.' Diane got up and drew back the curtains.

The stars had already begun to pale into the soft blue recesses of the night. Beyond the trees in the orchard the sky was a glowing vermilion band. Framed in the window Diane put an arm around her daughter and said, 'Oh, look, the start of a new day. Morning is breaking.'